Hero *of* Blackpool

A Joe Parrott Mystery

BY ALYSSA HALL

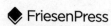 FriesenPress

One Printers Way
Altona, MB R0G 0B0
Canada

www.friesenpress.com

ISBN
978-1-03-917032-2 (Hardcover)
978-1-03-917031-5 (Paperback)
978-1-03-917033-9 (eBook)

1. FICTION, MYSTERY & DETECTIVE, PRIVATE INVESTIGATORS

Distributed to the trade by The Ingram Book Company

Also by Alyssa Hall

Trusting Claire

Wanting Aidan (featuring Joe Parrott)

Romero Pools

Show me a hero and I'll write you a tragedy.

F. Scott Fitzgerald

PROLOGUE

He stood up slowly, wincing in pain. He wasn't sure how long he had been here under the pier. When he had climbed into his hiding place behind the steel girders, the tide had still been out and the sun had not yet set. He had fallen asleep and now it was dark. A swift moving cloud unveiled the moon, which was now casting its glow on the sea. The shimmering moon-lit waters swirled dangerously close to him. It looked to be a high tide.

The cramp in his leg had worsened, as the space was not high enough for him to fully stand, and the pain seemed worse when he sat or lay down. But she would be out of harm's way by now, and for that, he was grateful.

For himself, he knew he was safe for the time being but had no way of knowing if watching eyes had seen him as he walked off the sandy beach and up the slope towards the footings beneath the pier. Only time would tell, for he would need to make his way out of here once the water began to recede.

He sat leaning against the steel girders and closed his eyes. He was hungry and thirsty, having given her the last of the food and water. Perhaps he could sleep a bit longer. He hummed the tune to himself, which seemed to ease his discomfort. The gulls were crying. He knew they had a vocabulary of their own, and it seemed now that they had picked up his melody and had begun to sing along, as if knowing he was there.

He was still thinking of her when next he opened his eyes. The wind had died down. Yes—he was sure the water had begun to recede. In another hour or so, he would be able to leave this hiding spot, whether or not it was safe to do so. Although going back to his flat was not an option, neither was staying here any longer.

It was starting to get light outside, much to his relief. The mocking cries of the seagulls increased, and the sound had now turned into a choking yelp. He could now make out the odd glimpse of the white of their wings as they swooped low against the tide, which seemed to be receding at a more rapid rate. Soon he would be able to make his way down the rocks to the safety of the sandy beach and the way out.

When he thought the sea had receded sufficiently, he took a deep breath, wiped his grimy hands down the front of his jeans, and squirmed through the narrow opening between the broken and protruding steel reinforcing bars, emerging from the area that had granted him safe haven. Carefully, he took a few steps forward, testing his footing on the slippery rocks. These rocks had been concreted in place, to prevent erosion and to provide stability to the pier footings. The rocks themselves were extremely slippery, while the mortar between was a safer bet to stand on.

Feeling a new sense of urgency, he took another deep

breath and prepared to make his descent. The wind had died down and the waters were calm. Hurrying now, he started down the wet rocks despite the still high water level. As he took the first steps down, he suddenly froze in his tracks. He realized now that the gulls had been warning him, not serenading him. For right there, not far from where he knelt, stood the men. And they were staring right at him.

Chapter 1

Sally stepped off the curb in an obvious hurry, head down, seemingly focused on something else. The sound of screeching tires snapped her back to the present, and she abruptly stepped back, visibly rattled. The driver of the car hollered at her as he drove by, his words deadened by his closed window. He hollered nonetheless, his mouth opening and closing, his words unheard. Her brows knitted as she frowned slightly, and she looked the other way in the pretense of having not seen him. Her actions were of someone unaccustomed to navigating her way around the busy streets of Sheffield, yet she was not a stranger to the city, having lived here all her life. Looking around quickly, she made her way to the crosswalk.

Today, this area looked cheerless and unfamiliar to her due to the roadwork and building overhaul happening at present. It was hot and humid, and the construction dust clung to the storefronts and windows of the shops, giving the area the appearance of run-down dreariness. The sight of overhead cranes and the sound of jackhammers messed with her judgment, making her uncertain as to which direction she should be headed, but as she crossed, she knew in an instant where she needed to be. Although it was warm, she wrapped her yellow cardigan tightly around herself in an unconfident manner. While not unkempt, the young lady certainly appeared dishevelled. Turning left, she hurried down the street. It was hard to tell if she was running towards or away from something.

Private Investigator Barry Dyck sat at his desk behind the counter in the front office of ARD Investigations, engrossed in the paperwork in front of him, his head down. It had been a curiously uneventful morning in the office, which was usually bustling. To an onlooker, it may have been difficult to determine whether the man was working or had nodded off.

The room was quiet until the front door was opened with such force that it swung hard and hit the table that stood just close enough to catch the edge of it. The sounds coming from outside jolted Barry from his reverie. His hand quickly slammed down on a pile of papers that were about to take flight from the rush of air. As he looked towards the door, in walked a young woman in a yellow sweater.

"Oh, sorry, it must have been the wind," she said with a nervous smile. "It pulled the door right out of my hand." She quickly closed the door, checking to make sure it had clicked tightly. Turning, she took a step towards the counter, brushing the hair from her eyes.

"Excuse me, but is Joe here?" Sally managed just the slightest of smiles.

Barry studied her for a minute. "Joe's not here, love."

Looking at her now with a fragment of recognition, he added, "You're family, aren't you?" He appeared to be struggling to place her.

The girl smiled. "I'm Sally. Sally Booth. My parents live out at the Parrott farm. My dad, George, helps out with the sheep, with Joe's dad."

Barry chuckled. "Of course, that's what it is. You were in here once, quite a while ago now, with some information on that girl that was murdered."

"Yes, I do remember you," she answered curtly, clearly not wanting to have a conversation about that right now. "Anyway, where's Joe?" Sally turned her head around, panning the small blue-and-white waiting room, finally resting her eyes on the door to Joe's office as if expecting him to appear.

"Like I said, Joe's not here. He's in Luxembourg with his lady friend, Miss Hunt. Some concert they are attending."

Sally screwed up her face. "Do you know when he'll be back?"

"Not for another three days, Miss Booth. Maybe I can do something for you," he asked gently. Barry surveyed her face, noting how tense she looked. He tried a different approach. "Are you all right, Sally?" he asked.

"No, it's okay, thank you. I mean, yes, I'm all right. I can come back another time. I suppose I can call him as well. Perhaps I should have tried that first. Sorry to trouble you," Sally muttered as she turned to leave.

"Are you sure I can't help you with something?"

She hesitated as though to say something else.

Changing her mind, she merely shook her head. Walking back towards the door, she opened it carefully, so as not to let the wind grab hold of it again.

"Call if you change your mind," Barry shouted after her.

Without answering, Sally stepped outside and looked around, contemplating her next move. She had counted on Joe being available and hadn't considered needing an alternate plan. It was perhaps a little foolhardy to think he would be here. In truth, she hadn't seen Joe since her twenty-second birthday, more than a year ago, when she had moved from her parents' home and into her own flat with her friend Hanna. Sighing heavily, the absurdity of assuming he would be readily available to her was now crystal clear. With a sense of hopelessness, Sally slowly began walking back in the direction from which she had come, some of the panic having abated. She was no longer in a rush yet no less distressed. Taking her phone out of her handbag, she tried the number again. It went straight to voicemail like it had done for the past three days, but she had to keep trying.

"Pick up the phone, will you!" Sally was not the crying type, yet she wanted to scream in frustration. Taking a deep breath, she slowly started walking, careful not to step on the cracks, making some of her steps longer, others shorter. Before long she quickened her pace with aplomb, now determined to walk all the way home.

Sally lived on the other side of Sheffield, in Hillsborough. It would take her nearly an hour to get there, but she thought the exercise might do her good.

She had been on early shift and had taken a bus to see Joe immediately after. But now Sally felt the walk might calm her nerves and allow her some time to think.

She gradually made her way along the streets and away from the noise. Her breaths were steadier, and she had settled into an easy, rhythmic pace. Now walking along St. Phillips Road, she sighed heavily. No, this plan was not going well at all. Be damned that she would wait three more days to see Joe. She would need to go back and see the man in that office tomorrow. If that didn't work, she would try to call Joe in wherever that place was.

The trek home took longer than usual, and by the time Sally arrived at her front door, her feet ached from walking on concrete in her very inappropriate shoes. Entering the flat, she walked past Hanna's room without looking inside. Hanna's door was open, and everything in the room was as she had left it before getting on the train headed for the coast four days ago. Sally tensed at the quiet that met her. She went straight to her room and lay on her bed, feeling the warm breeze wafting in through her open window. She took her cell out of her bag and tried the number again. The call went straight to voicemail. Sally was so very tired from the past few sleepless nights. She lay on her side, her knees curled up in a semi-fetal position. With her eyes closed, her throat dry, and her feet aching, she soon drifted off to sleep, her hand still clutching the phone.

She woke with a start and couldn't believe it was already

after seven in the morning. Sliding out of bed, she stumbled to the loo, still feeling groggy from having slept so long. All her muscles ached, likely because she had lay clenched up all night. She immediately began getting ready for the day, with the intent of first going back to Joe's office before her work shift. With her morning ablutions concluded and a piece of toast in her hand, she soon headed out the door.

Once seated on the bus, she again became aware of the stiffness in her shoulders and sighed. She hadn't relaxed since yesterday, and it was beginning to annoy her. Sally was steadfast in her intention to speak to Joe today, whatever it took. Every now and then she would take her phone from her purse and dial the number, and each time she stamped her foot in frustration as the call went to voicemail. By the time she exited the bus at her stop, she was quite on edge. Knowing precisely in which direction she needed to be heading, Sally quickly made her way through the now familiar construction zone and went straight to Joe's office.

She arrived only to find the door locked. She sat on the front step, at last feeling defeated. Had she the energy, she would have kicked at the door. She checked the time and tried to think of a reason why no one would be here. Sally's determination wavered as she debated whether to stay. With an audible groan, she decided to stand up and wander down the street, perhaps a walk around the block to kill some time. With any luck, someone would show up by the time she returned.

While looking around, trying to decide in which

direction to walk, she noticed a familiar-looking man in the distance, walking in her direction. She knew him, she was certain of it. But who was he? He was tall and lean, standing a good head above everyone else on the street. His hair was pale blonde and wispy, and something about his demeanour made him stand out. He wore a loose-fitting white cotton shirt and sported a closely shorn beard, barely detectable from this distance. The man walked with ease, a gentle sway to his gait, and an almost incredible amount of confidence. As he drew nearer, his face lit up in a smile of recognition and his hand came up in a wave.

"Sally, isn't it?" he asked, stopping directly in front of her. "Fancy running into you here. I've not seen you for a long time."

By now Sally was standing, and she looked at him, slightly bewildered. "I know you, don't I? Yet, I can't remember from where." His eyes, she noticed, were very intense yet friendly.

"I'm Stefan Nowak. Joe's friend, remember?"

"Yes, of course! How are you?" Then her voice lowered as she added, "You're Rita's brother, aren't you? Wasn't it Joe that investigated her murder? I was so sorry to hear about your sister, Stefan."

"Thanks, Sally, that's kind of you. It's been easier lately, all these years later. But I learned that I can't dwell on the past. I had actually lost her years before that, you know. But enough about that, what brings you here? Why are you standing outside?"

"I wanted to see Joe, but the door is locked. You're still

Joe's friend, are you?"

Stefan nodded assuredly. "Yes, I'm still very much Joe's friend. Well, actually, soon enough I'll be Joe's partner."

Sally hesitated before speaking. She was stuck on Stefan's last word. Joe's partner, he had said. "Are you really Joe's partner?"

"Well, I will be soon enough. I've become a PI, and we plan on working together."

"Well, then maybe you can help me. I wanted to speak to Joe today, 'cause it's really important, but he's away for a few days. And I don't know why there isn't anyone here." Sally took a step closer to Stefan to allow a woman to pass by her on the narrow walkway. She spoke with a lowered voice. "It's my friend Hanna. She's gone missing."

Chapter 2

Stefan looked at Sally curiously. "What do you mean, she's gone missing?" he asked her.

"Can we go inside and talk? I really don't want to stand here on the street."

Stefan shook his head. "I'm sorry, I don't have a key—and I wouldn't know why there's nobody here." Looking around, he touched her shoulder gently. "Want to go somewhere for a coffee or something?" he offered.

Sally nodded, not raising her head to look at him. Taking her by the elbow, Stefan directed her towards the intersection. He had spotted a small coffee shop on the corner, and she looked like she could use something to calm her nerves. They walked at a hurried pace, both seeming eager to get off the street so they could sit down and talk. Walking into the almost empty café, Stefan motioned for Sally to find a table. "What can I get you?"

"Just tea, please," replied Sally as she headed for the nearest booth. She needed to sit down, feeling unsteady on her legs. Stefan headed to the counter to speak with the hostess.

Once seated across from Sally, Stefan quickly asked, "So, for starters, why do you think she's missing?"

"Well, 'cause she ain't here, see?" Sally answered, although the sarcasm was unintended. Her edginess was showing.

"Okay, perhaps a somewhat foolish question," muttered Stefan under his breath. Trying again, he asked instead, "When did she go missing? I mean, when is the last time you saw your friend?"

"She was supposed to come home Sunday. Today is Wednesday. I've been trying to call her, but it just goes to voicemail."

"Where did she go? Is she with someone?" asked Stefan, certain that these questions were better than his first.

"Well, last I saw her, she was headed to Blackpool on the train to see some bloke she met online, on a dating site. She was going to visit him for a few days."

Stefan sat upright, his back hitting the wooden backrest of the booth. He hadn't intended to bolt up with such momentum, and the creak of the old wooden bench made a bit more noise than one would expect. "That maybe wasn't very smart, to go to Blackpool alone to meet a stranger. Is this something that was out of character for her? I mean—had she done it before?"

This time, Sally's eyes met Stefan's. "This is out of character, yes. Well, sort of, but not entirely. She's met blokes on the Internet before, but there's something different about this one. I tried to tell her she shouldn't go. This is her second time going there, and he's been here to see her once before. She said he's very nice, that they'd gotten on well and had a good time. But each of those visits was only for an afternoon, you know? Now she's been gone for four days. I had told her that it might not be wise, and I asked if she was planning on staying with him in his flat. I mean—so soon after knowing him?" Sally was shaking her head in displeasure. "He looked a creepy sort. She went anyway, on the train as planned, and stupid me—I went with her to the station to see her off. I should have stopped her; that's what I should have done. Not sent her off with a kiss and a wave."

Stefan rubbed his chin, wondering what Joe would have said next. "Have you heard from her at all since she left?"

Sally nodded affirmatively. "I think it was on Saturday morning, she sent some pics and messages and stuff, but I haven't heard anything since that. I called Sunday morning to ask how her evening was and to see if everything was still a go for me to meet her at the station. She didn't answer, but I didn't really think much of it. Then Sunday evening, when I went to meet her, she wasn't on the train. I waited for hours, thinking she might have missed it and maybe caught a later one. I've been calling her ever since."

"So, could she still be with this bloke?"

"I suppose so, but why won't she answer her phone?"

Stefan nodded in agreement, then added, "Did you call police?"

"No, I have nothing really to report. She's a grown woman who's gone on a holiday. What would the cops say to me if I said my roommate is with a man and has not come home? It's not like I know something bad happened; something that I could report. They might laugh at me, is all."

"That's a good point," was Stefan's fast response. "I should have thought of that myself." Then, almost as quickly, he added, "Well, maybe it's true then. Maybe she's not missing and just decided to stay on holiday."

"I have thought about all of it, but still, I know her. She would have called me. If for no other reason than to keep me from freaking out—like I am doing."

Stefan nodded as he played with his spoon. He didn't look up.

"Well, another reason I didn't call the cops is that I don't want her parents to find out she's missing. They would be really upset if they knew what she's been doing. I was hoping to find her before they call around looking for her. If they've been trying to reach her as well, they will be really upset."

Sally was getting up to refill her teapot when Stefan asked, "You said she sent you some pictures. Can you show them to me?"

With shaking hands, Sally retrieved her phone out of her bag and handed it to Stefan.

"May I?" he asked. Sally nodded and walked away. Stefan scrolled slowly through the photos while Sally fetched her water. The photos were of various shots of whom he assumed was Hanna and her fellow, smiling and making gestures with their hands. In one shot, the man was holding a beer and he had his tongue hanging out in a mock thirsty pose.

Once Sally had returned and sat down, Stefan leaned

forward with the phone and pointed at an image. "So, I assume this is the guy she went to see?" He was looking at a picture of the man sitting on a bench, shirtless. He was darkly tanned, black hair shaved to within a few inches of his scalp. He was wearing sunglasses, so it would be difficult to know exactly who he was. Frankly, he looked like anybody.

Trying to be helpful, Sally leaned forward and pointed at the phone. "It looks like him. There are a few of the two of them where it's easier to see his face. See? It looks like they took selfies. And these other few I suppose are of the sights. I can't remember exactly how many pictures she sent, but you can see there aren't more than a handful."

Stefan was studying another photo. "Look at the big sign overhead and the paintings of animals. Looks like they were at the zoo."

"Yes!" cried Sally. "I remember! Hanna said he worked at the zoo."

"Good!" cried Stefan. "That's something, isn't it? Do you remember his name? Did Hanna tell you the guy's name?"

Grabbing the phone back from Stefan, she frantically began scrolling. "Yes, I have it here in other messages. Here it is. His name is Ian. Ian what, I don't know, but I know it's Ian."

"So, it's Ian who works at a zoo. I imagine the zoo is in Blackpool," said Stefan, wanting to be sure of the details. Sally returned the phone, and he continued scrolling through the photos. He paused. Something else had caught his eye. "But did you see, Sally, in most of these pictures there's another guy? This one here, do you see?" Stefan leaned over to Sally again as she turned to look closely at the photos. Stefan pointed to the figure in the background. "He's in almost every shot."

Sally used two fingers to zoom in on the other man. He appeared unkempt, was unshaven, and looked to be around fortyish. His chin was too small and his ears too big. It was hard to tell if he had a lazy eye or if the camera lens was revealing an unphotogenic side of him. His bushy hair seemed to need washing, as did his clothes. It was difficult to establish height, but he wasn't a man of girth. In one photo, he was standing a distance behind Ian, looking in the other direction. The photo revealed a black boot with a full foot lift, likely a result of having a leg-length discrepancy.

"I dunno who that is. Is he with them, or is he just someone standing nearby to have a look? He'd be a nosy bugger if he didn't know them!"

Stefan thought for a moment before asking Sally, "Did Hanna say anything about some other guy? Maybe a good friend of Ian's?"

Sally was trembling uncontrollably. "No. But I'm really scared. I have to go to work and I need to be focused. But I can't stop thinking of where she might be."

Not convinced that there was something sinister going on, Stefan turned to Sally and softened his voice. "Maybe she's just not ready to come home. I mean, she's an adult, and to me it looks like she's having fun. I don't know if three days is enough to call someone missing."

"You'd not say that if you knew her, so you couldn't

possibly understand. She wouldn't do this. There's her work, and her mum. You don't know her mum! And the biggest thing is that we had tickets to go to a show last night. She would have called if she meant to stay away— she bought the bloody tickets! She was really looking forward to this show."

Stefan took the phone back from Sally. "Can I send some of these pictures to myself, Sally? I will see what I can find out." She nodded consent, and choosing all of them, he forwarded them to his phone.

"Did you mean it when you said you'd look into it?" She was looking right at him now.

"Oh, absolutely! Joe may not be here, but I can look into it while he is away."

Having nothing left to ask at this point, Stefan stood to leave. "We should go now. I don't want to make you late. I'll call you later tomorrow, Sally. In the meantime, keep trying her. And call me if you hear anything, okay?" he instructed. "But wait—before I give you your phone, I'll put down my number and then you can send me yours. You can call me later if you like. Oh—and remember, keep trying her."

Sally stood also, smiling at Stefan as he handed back her phone. She touched his arm lightly as he held the door for her. Walking back outside into the fresh air, she was suddenly aware of how stuffy it had been in the café. She breathed in deeply and relaxed as she exhaled. "Thank you. I can't thank you enough." Sally's eyes lingered for a moment before she looked away. She had not remembered Stefan to be so strikingly handsome.

Chapter 3

While Stefan wasn't entirely sure what he was going to do to help Sally, he did know that Joe would have gone to Blackpool. So this was his plan. He would try to figure out the rest when he got there. Questions remained, such as what would he do if he actually found this Ian? What would he say to him? He headed home to conduct some preliminary searches to familiarize himself with Blackpool and the zoo in particular. He could feel the electricity surge through his body with anticipation. There was little doubt that he was eager for this adventure, to try out his new skills. With his newly acquired PI licence, he felt more than ready to give it a go. His hope was to impress Joe enough to reintroduce the idea of going into business together.

It was relatively easy to become a PI in England. While the licencing wasn't necessary, it would, however, be difficult to put in the required one hundred hours of practical education. Equally challenging was putting in the hours without being hired, and to be hired without the hours. But Stefan chose the education, as he wanted to know what he was doing, what could be expected, and he wanted to be good at it. He wanted to be trained and ready, and to have some semblance of the skills required in the legal, privacy, and practical sides of the craft before committing. The chance encounter with Sally had caught him off guard and left him feeling both enthusiastic and awkward at her request for help. Although he had doubts as to whether he was up to the task of going alone, his ambitious curiosity had gotten the better of him—curiosity that outweighed any reluctance.

Once back at home, he searched the area on his laptop. Stefan figured it would take him about two hours to drive to Blackpool. Checking the time, he decided he would not go at this late hour but would leave first thing in the morning. With cautious optimism, he began to prepare mentally for the journey to the coast.

The night brought little sleep, and so, rising before dawn, he headed out the door. His first stop was to fill the car up with petrol. As the tank was filling, so was his head, with random thoughts and vague expectations of the day ahead of him. Once he left the petrol station, he set his GPS to take him directly to the Blackpool Zoo. He turned on the radio and headed towards the motorway.

Stefan arrived in Blackpool in just under two hours. But rather than heading straight to the zoo, he wanted to see the seaside, his curiosity getting the better of him. He had rolled down his window in anticipation, ready to inhale the sea air. It was his first time ever by the water, and he found the excitement exhilarating. He had started the drive at Bond Street, and after turning right by the Colwyn Hotel, he had found himself on Promenade. Stefan was amazed at what he was seeing. His head turned in rapid succession from left to right, trying to take it all in. By now, he had rolled down all the windows. Even over the sound of the traffic, Stefan could clearly hear the crash of the waves and the screaming, almost laughing of the seagulls. Blackpool at first glance was nothing like he had imagined. He had initially thought he'd be indulging in some sort of guilty pleasure, driving to a tranquil scene of beach and the ocean. Instead, he was met with a cyclonic blast of slow-moving traffic, honking horns, and an outpouring of pedestrians strolling across the road, often into the path of moving cars. Even at this early hour, the street was rife with activity, with some type of sound coming from every direction. Along the Promenade, the shops were slowly opening—he caught glimpses of brightly coloured signs peddling everything from candyfloss to fortune-telling services. So this was what summer on the coast looked like!

Despite not having nearly seen enough, once Stefan had driven as far as Central Pier, he turned right on Chapel Street to make his way to the zoo's entrance. Parking his car in the virtually empty car lot, he walked to the entrance and sighed deeply when he came face-to-face with a large red *CLOSED* sign. Checking the time, Stefan noted the zoo would not open for another hour.

Looking around, unsure what to do in the meantime, he wandered along a winding path, where he noticed a steady stream of people entering the building at the side. Clad in uniforms, he deduced these were employees arriving for their shifts. Stefan strolled over towards the activity, panning the faces for a glimpse of recognition.

But none looked like Ian. After making eye contact with one of them, Stefan hurriedly approached the man, who seemed to be about Ian's age. He needed to ask him if he knew Ian.

"Yeah, mate, I know Ian, but he's not been in for at least two days. Not sure why—I didn't ask. Don't really care. It could be that today is his day off, so in that case, he's not likely to show up. You can usually find him hanging around down by the water. There's a cocktail bar at the end of the north beach pier, where they usually hang out. Although I doubt he'll be there this early."

Stefan thanked the man and walked back to the car park. Leaving the property, Stefan realized his first mistake had been coming so early in the morning. His second was assuming he'd easily find Ian. Despite that, he drove in the direction of the pier, hoping at least to make some use of the journey here. Arriving roughly in the area of the north beach, he noted all businesses were closed. Most of these probably wouldn't be open until later in the afternoon. The North Pier itself was gated and chained closed.

Feeling defeated, Stefan turned back on to the main road to head home. He was no wiser than when he arrived. For starters, he was overwhelmed with the size and sprawl of Blackpool. Hanna could be anywhere. This might not be as easy as it seemed.

While driving back to Sheffield, Stefan went over his moves. He knew what he should have done differently. More research. He had been too hasty arriving in Blackpool so early. He laughed at himself. The least he could have done was check the hours of the zoo. He might have adjusted his times had he done a bit of investigating rather than come straight away without ample information. This was to be his big day one on the job, and he had failed badly.

Arriving back at his home, Stefan's first instinct was to call Joe. It seemed a good way to calm his mind, and he was very eager to share his experience. Finding the number, he dialled and was relieved when Joe answered on the first ring.

"How is your holiday, Joe? Sorry to interrupt," he began.

"We are coming home, Stefan. We will be back tomorrow morning. Aisha is needed back in Sheffield. I'm sorry but I can't talk right now."

"Can I swing by and see you, Joe? I can come early tomorrow afternoon if that's okay. There's something I'd like to speak to you about. It's regarding Sally—don't know her surname—but you know her, right? She's been over to see you, and it seems she has a bit of a problem."

"I really have to go, Stefan, but is she all right? Is it about her parents?"

"It's about her roommate. I will tell you tomorrow. See you then." He disconnected and put the phone on the side table.

Feeling quite purposeless, Stefan retreated to the kitchen to wash his dishes. When his phone rang, he quickly wiped the soap from his hands and ran to the other room to pick it up. He heard a soft voice begin to speak—a voice he immediately recognized as Sally's.

"Hi there, I've been waiting for you to call me." She spoke slowly and deliberately, yet there was an edge to her voice, as if she could explode any second.

"It didn't quite go as I had expected," Stefan admitted. There was a quiver to his voice as he sat down and timidly told Sally about his trip to Blackpool. He closed with, "I am sorry I didn't find anything there." As he finished his sentence, he was glad they weren't seated face-to-face. He felt like an idiot, having told her emphatically how he could help. He really didn't have a clue what he was doing.

"But I spoke with Joe, and he will be in tomorrow. We can talk to him then."

Whatever Sally said came out as a mumble as she hung up the phone.

He listened to the dead line for a moment before he too hung up the phone. Stefan was very much looking forward to seeing Joe. He sat back, losing himself in reflective thought about his and Joe's beginnings.

Stefan Nowak was the brother of Rita, a young runaway girl who had been found murdered outside of Joe Parrott's home nearly two years ago. Stefan, then barely in his twenties, had his first encounter with Joe when he was summoned to identify the body of his sister, whom he had not seen for many years. As a young girl, Rita had left her home to escape a life of abuse at the hands of her father. She unfortunately could not escape other abuses.

By the end of the disturbing investigation, Joe's mate was behind bars, Stefan discovered he had a nephew, and

Joe and Stefan had formed a strong bond—a meeting of the minds. A bond held firmly together, in part due to the outcome of Rita's murder investigation, which had greatly impacted them both, albeit in different ways. Stefan himself had endured his share of struggles, trying to make a life for himself from a young age, when he too had left the family home. His and Joe's friendship was based on a mutual moral support and a shared admiration for one another.

Stefan's life had changed drastically in the nearly two years since Rita had been murdered. His life in Leicester had been satisfactory, but it was only after he had a sample of life in Sheffield that he realized he really had no life at all. For years he had lived in a two-room flat above the ironworks shop that he ran with his employer and mentor, who had later become his partner. But Joe had opened his eyes to a whole new world—one where "friend'" and "family" were not just words. Stefan had been heartened by people's kindness and caring; Joe had treated him like a son, and Joe's daughter, Susan, had treated him like a brother. After discovering he had a nephew, Aidan, in Cottingham, Stefan had even more reason to want to live closer.

Now twenty-six, Stefan's recent move to Sheffield had come on the heels of the passing of his mother, who had at last succumbed to the cancer that had been plaguing her for some time. Having newly relocated to a small apartment on Greystone's Close, he was eager for this new life, and for his first real adventure. He hadn't been in the city for more than a few months before being called

away to London. Now back, he was very eager to reconnect with his friend Joe.

Over the years, Joe had been a major source of
support for him. He had tirelessly answered all of Stefan's
questions and offered advice where he could. Joe had
been more than helpful this past year, generously assist-
ing Stefan in finding the right location to live, tirelessly
helping him set up home. Susan had come over to add
some finishing touches to the place, to make it look
cheerful and inviting.

Stefan had never known what it was like to have his
own flat. What joy it was to have a kitchen and a proper
bedroom. He could never find the words to describe to
anyone how he felt inside. And he would never use the
word "lucky." He had worked hard to be where he was.
Stefan had been keen to follow in Joe's footsteps ever
since meeting him, and he was now ready to pursue his
dream of being a private investigator.

Chapter 4

Stefan arrived at Joe's early in the afternoon. He entered the lobby, only to see a sombre-looking man standing in the doorway to Joe's office. He looked over at Barry, who mouthed something quietly, but Stefan could not make out what he said. He nonetheless nodded at Barry and stood quietly. The man was speaking inaudibly in a hushed tone. Stefan made his way towards a chair in the waiting area, knowing he needed to wait until the meeting was over.

But seeing Stefan, Joe motioned him over and introduced him to Ray Lawson, father of Sally's roommate. Leaning against the wall, the man looked at Stefan and managed a nod of acknowledgement. Mr. Lawson reiterated that he had been calling Hanna for days and said it was unlike her to not be picking up. He had also been trying to reach her roommate, but Sally was not answering either. Then when his attempts to reach her at work had been unsuccessful, he began to panic.

"Not knowing what else to do, I had driven to your dad's farm, in the hopes of running into Sally or at least speaking to her father, George." Mr. Lawson was clutching his cap and looking at Joe pleadingly. "While I was there, your dad, Ivan, had come out of his house; I suppose he heard my voice carry in through the windows."

Stefan moved quietly to the far wall and sat in the red padded chair. He struggled internally, not quite knowing what to do. Sally had expressly voiced her concern about this man not discovering Hanna's whereabouts. He decided to wait for Mr. Lawson to leave before telling Joe what he knew. So he kept his eyes on Joe and listened as he calmed Mr. Lawson. Stefan was in awe with the way Joe spoke to the man—with such clarity and proficiency. He had just the right body language, and he knew just what to ask and what tone to use while asking. And he never promised he would find Hanna. Are these skills he could ever develop one day?

After the men had finished speaking, Joe again invited him to sit down. The man approached Joe's desk but remained standing. Joe continued, "So, now that you are here, what is it that you hope I can do for you, Mr. Lawson? Do you have reason to believe your daughter is in danger? And if so, have you called the police?"

Mr. Lawson, who seemed somewhat calmed by Joe's demeanour, explained that yes, he had first called the police. "They didn't seem bothered. All they did was listen to me, then the man said they would log the call. '*There is no reason for concern,*' the policeman told me." Mr. Lawson raised his voice to mimic the man he had spoken to. "Hanna is an adult, and there has been no indication at this point to suspect foul play. So, until more time has passed, or until something happens, all they could do was note my concern." His voice was full of angst and frustration. "Log the call! That's all they gave me. But I know something's wrong. The Lord told me that things aren't right. It was your father who gave me one of your business cards. '*Ring up my son Joe*,' your dad said to me. '*He knows Sally, he's like an uncle to her. Maybe there's something he can do.*' So here I am."

Ray was a handsome but tired-looking man. He was of average build and had a healthy head of sandy-brown hair and nearly perfect facial features but for the taut, rigid expression. He carried himself well and spoke eloquently. He reminded Stefan of a minister, and he could sense by the way he spoke that this was, without doubt, a man of religion. He said that God had spoken to him and told him his daughter was in trouble. Leaning in very close to Joe, Ray Lawson then said he knew Joe could help him find his daughter.

Joe had to take a small step back to create some space between them, as with each sentence Ray Lawson inched forward. He spoke slowly. "Yes, Mr. Lawson, the police would need to log it. But there is an enormous database of missing persons, as you may have been made aware. And I can tell you, I know that searches are seldom conducted without cause. There just isn't the manpower."

"Could you at least look into it, Mr. Parrott? I'd not know where to start. This is not like her, to go off like this. She could be in trouble or be hurt." And with that comment, Joe knew he would have a hard time saying no.

Joe kept glancing at Stefan curiously, as the lad had said he spoke to Sally and they both needed to see him. Yet he sat quietly and said nothing. He didn't push, feeling there must be a good reason why Stefan wasn't speaking, particularly if it somehow involved Sally. At this point, all Stefan would offer was a wink and a shake of his head, indicating now was not the time.

Turning to Ray, Joe announced, "Yes, Mr. Lawson, I will get your details and see what I can find out. But I have to say, if Hanna is staying away by choice, there's not much I can do. Then again, hopefully I can at least find out where she is. Either way, you were right to call."

At that point, Ray immediately sat down, the relief on his face seeming instant. After briefly discussing the terms, Ray stood to leave. Joe asked Ray to please see Barry at the front counter to arrange the necessary paperwork.

"Thank you. I will arrange for immediate transfer of the retainer, Mr. Parrott. I want nothing to hold this up."

Stefan waited patiently until Mr. Lawson left. He had a lot to tell Joe, frustrated that he had missed the opportunity to speak with him before Mr. Lawson had arrived.

He cleared his throat before beginning. "I do have information about this," he announced to Joe.

"I thought as much. Can we go for a walk and do this somewhere else? I've hardly had a chance to catch my breath since walking in the door," Joe remarked while wondering how Stefan might have knowledge and sensing the news might not be favourable. "My day has started with a bang, and something tells me I'll need a beer."

"You'll definitely need one after I tell you what I know," answered Stefan as he held the door for Joe.

Joe Parrott was born in Seattle, Washington. At the time of his birth, his American father, Ivan, was working as a policeman, and his mother, Emma, had been a British exchange student when the two met and quickly married. His parents then took him to live in Britain when he was just a lad, which had been quite a traumatic event for him at that young age. He felt lost without his home, his friends and cousins, and his grandparents. He struggled with suddenly being the son of a sheep farmer. During the awkward years that followed, Joe certainly had his highs and lows while growing up. He struggled through puberty, school, and had felt lost after graduating. It seemed that Joe had become the kind of person he didn't want to be.

But after marrying Janet and quitting his job as a security guard, his life slowly improved. Starting his career as a PI brought him real satisfaction and had grounded him, so to speak. Then years later, after a distressing but amicable divorce, he and his best mate, Simon, had a spell of partying and alcohol misuse before again rediscovering himself.

Presently, he was living one of his highest highs. He could now boast an improved career here at ARD Investigations, good relationships with his ex-wife and her new husband, his lovely daughter, Susan, her husband, Nigel, and their new baby. And of course, there was Aisha, his loving companion, whom he met while investigating the brutal murder of Stefan's sister, Rita.

Sally Booth was much like family to him. Her parents, George and Olivia, had come to work on Ivan's sheep farm when Joe was a teen. He had come to view them like an aunt and uncle. When Sally was born, Joe was by then married and had just become a father as well, and thus Sally became somewhat like a niece. As she grew older, she would follow him around the farm, helping to feed the animals and reading her assignments to him while he tended to chores, and quite often she would come out to watch during lambing. He had thought she lived too sheltered a life and was always happy to spend the time with her.

Stefan, on the other hand, was a relatively new acquaintance. Joe had been introduced to him when he had come to identify Rita's body. He had liked Stefan within minutes, after only a few sentences. Stefan's idealism and hopefulness had caught him off guard. Throughout the course of the investigation, the two had formed an unlikely friendship; Joe found Stefan to be a refreshing change to the people around him. He actually attributed much of the positive changes in himself to the good will and honest optimism of Stefan.

Later, Joe had been surprised to hear of Stefan's desire to move to Sheffield and had done all he could to help him settle in. It seemed like Stefan's move had not happened that long ago, and then he had vanished to London for the past month, so right now, he found it odd that somehow these two worlds collided and that both Stefan and Sally had now become involved in this girl's mysterious disappearance. It went without saying that Joe was extremely curious to hear what Stefan had to tell him. With ready anticipation, he moved through the door that Stefan held open for him.

Chapter 5

Joe's eyes watered as he squinted against the sunlight, regretting not bringing his sunglasses with him. The two men walked down the street to a pub very near the place where Stefan had taken Sally just two days previously. When entering, Joe blinked away the brightness, having to adjust to the dark indoors. Did it always take this long for his eyes to make the switch, or was he getting old? Once seated with their pints of lager, Stefan began telling Joe of his conversation with Sally.

"I hoped I would have had a chance to speak with you before that man, Mr. Lawson, showed up. You see, speaking with Sally, it seems she knows where Hanna went and whom she was seeing there. It was a few days back. I was on my way to see you and I ran into Sally outside your office, and then we went for tea because she was very upset. It seems Sally knew exactly when Hanna left and had even told her that she shouldn't be going."

Joe put down his glass. "Do I need to ask you about it, or will you eventually tell me?"

"I wanted to tell you sooner, but never mind that." Stefan exhaled as he explained. "Hanna has gone to Blackpool. I'd say about four or five days ago. She met a bloke a while back on a dating site and had gone to visit him. Sally says she never came back."

Joe lowered his glass and moaned, "Bloody hell, I wasn't planning on running back and forth to Blackpool. Are you sure she's still there?" He was loosening his tie as he spoke.

"Sally doesn't know, Joe. She's been trying to call her. Then I thought I could help." Stefan then explained how he had gone to Blackpool the previous day to have a preliminary look around the zoo. He had asked after Ian but had no luck.

"Although one bloke did say that Ian was due to be at work and he hadn't shown up. So perhaps he and Hanna went somewhere else? She could be having a good time and is just not ready to come home, and likely knows if she calls Sally, she'll be talked into coming back."

Joe smiled. "So perhaps we have a case of a smitten young lady wanting to extend a visit with a desirable young man. Okay, first thing is, I need to speak with Sally. Did you say she was coming in to see me?"

"Yes, she said she'd see you this afternoon. I was surprised she hadn't come earlier, but I expect she will be around shortly."

"We best be on our way, then, and see what she has to say," replied Joe as he raised his glass to Stefan.

Finishing up their beers, the men quickly made their way back to the office. As expected, they found Sally in Joe's office, pacing. She froze as they entered the office, her fierce blue eyes glaring at Stefan.

"What's this then, you telling me you are Joe's partner?

Were you making fun of me, pretending you could help?"

Joe looked at Stefan, who had turned a sickly shade of white, and asked, "What does Sally mean?" Seeing that Stefan was incapable of speech at that moment, Joe looked back at Sally. "What do you mean, Sal?"

Sally, now appearing livid, replied indignantly, "I just asked the man out front if Joe or Stefan were here. The man asks me, *'Who is Stefan?'* I said Joe's partner, and the man says, *'Not at this company. Joe has no partner here.'*" As Sally said this, she lowered her voice a few octaves and made a face, as if to mimic the man out front.

In a split second, both Joe and Sally were scowling at Stefan, who was looking at Joe pleadingly asking for a chance to speak. "I can explain, Joe."

Joe shut his eyes for a moment, not wanting to get between two people whom he cared a great deal about. He figured he had about twenty seconds to turn this around, and he was exhausted already. "Okay, this isn't getting us anywhere, and we have work to do. Sally, love, please go wait out in the lobby, just for a bit, so I can talk to Stefan."

Sally smiled feebly at Joe as she obediently headed to the door but was sure to glare at Stefan again before brushing past him on her way to the waiting room. The fury had not left her eyes. "You tosser, I should punch you. You lied to me," she snapped.

Closing the door, Joe looked at Stefan and shook his head. "It's always nice to see you, you know that. But what did you tell her? That we're partners?" Joe himself was out of humour at the news.

Stefan was wearing a flimsy grin. "I might have said that. But that's what I wanted to talk to you about. It's why I had come to see you in the first place. Then when I came, Sally was here. I really did want to help her. It just slipped out, Joe. She may not have told me her problem otherwise."

"But why was her problem suddenly your problem, Stefan? Don't you think you were overstepping?"

"It just happened, and it seemed like an opportunity to put in some hours of training. Besides, she looked upset, and beyond question, I really did want to help. I remembered her from back then, when she mentioned she had once worked with Rita." He looked at Joe apologetically. "And then I wanted to tell you right away, but when I came today to speak with you, that Ray bloke was already here. This issue with Hanna seemed important, and I'd not had the chance to say anything to you."

Stefan headed towards the chair by the window and heavily plopped himself down, prompting Joe to sit as well. Suddenly, Joe felt all of his forty-seven years.

Stefan continued, "As you know, I've finished my training. I know you've been pleased about my results and that I had done so well. I've not talked to you for a few months now, not since I've come back to the city. The money I received from mine and Rita's fund really helped me get on my feet, as you know, and I was just starting to think about what I might do now, with work and all. Then I had news from lawyers in London. That's where I've been, Joe. I had to go to London. It seems I have an inheritance, from my mum and, believe it or not—also from my dad."

Joe was still confused. "What kind of inheritance, and how does that affect what you said to Sally?"

"Well, it turns out my dad had gone back to Poland, and after a few years he had secretly started paying for Mum's house. She was too sick to know, but he had spoken to my aunt, who had taken care of everything. My mum never thought about the bills anymore. Then my dad moved overseas, without another word. When Mum died, I was her sole heir. Eventually it cleared probate and came to me. So I sold it," Stefan said with a proud smile.

"I still don't know how this affects what's happening here."

"Joe, I want us to start our own practice. Together. It'll be good for both of us. Working with you last time, for Rita, it was brilliant! It's all I've thought about, the way you help people. So I might have told Sally that we were planning to be partners. I never said we actually were."

"Not so fast, Stefan. Remember, I already have a job. Here, in this office."

"Yes, but just think, Joe—this will be us! You can be your own boss, decide who, what, and when. And you'll have me!" Stefan's grin was absurdly close to levitating him.

Noticing Joe was not sharing in his exuberance, he softened his voice. "It was why I wanted to help Sally. I thought if I could go to Blackpool and find something out, you would be impressed enough to take me seriously."

"We have to talk about this later, Stefan. Sally's waiting for us."

In two long strides, Joe was at the door. He opened it and smiled as he motioned for Sally to return. She walked quickly past the desk clerk, avoiding his stare, and came into the room. Directing her to the chair by his desk, Joe asked her to go easy on Stefan. "It seems that what he said wasn't entirely untrue. It was premature, perhaps, but not untrue. It is something the two of us will need to deal with later. But right now, we have a job to do."

She eyed Stefan suspiciously as she slowly sat down where directed.

"Sally, Hanna's father was just here, and he's very upset. He's not fooled by your evasive behaviour, and he knows something is wrong. So please start at the beginning and tell me everything you know."

Leaning forward on her elbows, she began speaking in semi-coherent blather. "Hanna has been meeting blokes online, and somehow, she's got hooked on this one. I told her to stay home, but she wouldn't listen. She was selfish to go off like that, knowing what it would do to her parents if they found out. And what if something bad did happen? She was selfish again to leave me here to explain. And how am I supposed to explain when I haven't a clue either? She never seemed interested in boys around here, so why is she suddenly so keen about this bloke she met on the Internet? It doesn't make any sense to me."

The anger was building on Sally's face when her phone rang, causing her to jump. "Maybe it's Hanna!" she cried, pulling the phone from her purse. Checking her call display, she looked at Joe and mouthed the word "Mum" as she answered the phone.

The volume was loud enough that Joe could hear her mother speaking: *"Sally, what's this about Hanna disappearing?"* There was concern in her voice, but she spoke kindly and evenly.

"She's with someone, Mum. She's gone away on a bit of a holiday. She doesn't really want her dad to know. We are trying to find out more news. I'm at Joe's right now. Yes, okay, I'll say hello. I gotta go, Mum, bye." And she quickly hung up, her eyes glued on Joe as if waiting for a solution.

"I will look into it, Sally. But you need to talk to me and not leave anything out. So, please start again—at the beginning. Firstly, who exactly is this Hanna?"

Chapter 6

The flat that Sally shared with Hanna was in a brick terraced house on a small dead-end street that backed onto Hillsborough Primary School. The flat took up the main floor of the house, which had been recently renovated. The entrance led to a bright and cheery front room, aided by the tall windows that had been installed last year. The walls had been brightened up with a coat of pale-yellow paint, and while it was not Sally's favourite colour, Hanna had done a wonderful job of accessorizing with wall hangings and such in order to minimize the yellowish glow about the place. Their yard was small, with high brick walls on all sides, and this was about the only time of year the garden had a decent amount of sunshine. There were many days that Sally came home from work and retreated directly to the back garden.

All the streets in this neighbourhood were lined with identical red-brick terraced houses; originally all had small iron fences bordering the properties. Little remained of the iron fencing, as most had been cut down to help the war efforts in the forties, although oddly, the railings in front of their flat were intact. There had been much debate about this, with complaints in regard to the amounts of iron being removed. The railings were to be smelted by the local steel industries to make weapons and ammunition to help the troops. Many believed the railings removed never actually made it to the factories to be smelted. Later, it was revealed there was a major cover-up, and much of the scrap iron and ornamental railings had actually been loaded onto barges and dumped into the Thames. One journalist wrote that Britain had failed in its attempts to turn the scrap into weapons of war. And so, all these years later, the bits that were left on the street walls remained, and the bulk that had been taken away was never replaced.

Sally worked at the nearby Tesco. She could get to work in about twelve minutes on the blue line tram. She preferred this location to the Co-Op she had previously worked at, on Ecclesall Road. Here, the store was bigger, busier, and her co-workers were all very kind. She had never regretted the move here. Having been raised on a sheep farm in Ringinglow, a western borough of Sheffield, she grew to dislike the smells of hay and feed and, most of all, the manure. Aside from the smells, she had often wished that just once, the sheep would cease their incessant bleating. As a child, she had loved helping with the sheep, bottle-feeding the lambs, herding them out to the fields, but as she grew older, she'd had enough of that life.

Here, she loved the concrete and the sound of cars and honking horns. She loved hearing the sounds of life around her. Sally had met Hanna just over a year ago, shopping on the Moor. Before long, Sally had asked her new friend if she would consider sharing a flat, as she desperately wanted to move into the city. She had immediately agreed, saying she too had long wanted the same thing, but never had anyone who was willing to make the move. Now she and Hanna were quite content with their independent style of living. They loved having access to so much within walking distance and enjoyed getting to know one another.

Sally's flatmate, Hanna Lawson, worked in the parcel collection department for Royal Mail, at the North Delivery Office, as a parcel sorter. Hanna was a bit of an anomaly in that she was never one for excitement yet seemed to always be looking for it. She was extremely sociable yet preferred to spend most of her time alone. Sally thought that Hanna's life had been terribly boring, but Hanna never seemed to mind. Hanna had been raised in a religious household and had always been sheltered, meaning all her time as a child was accounted for and monitored. She had been taught that friends were unnecessary, and that sex was for married people for the purpose of procreation and was otherwise disgusting. As Hanna grew older, she grew curious about the world around her and, over the years, had decided that the main purpose of the Bible was for it to be used as a scare tactic.

By the time Sally met Hanna, she had developed this new surreptitious side to her, which her family knew nothing about. She wanted to learn things and often went to places others wouldn't venture. She had told Sally that, out of curiosity, she would wander through strange areas of the city and would sometimes peek into alleyways and seedy bars, just to have a look. She even admitted to taking walks along the Don near the Victorian warehouses at Neepsend late at night, watching for hookers. Most of all, Hanna loved to go to the cinema to watch questionable indie movies, many of them bizarre and twisted, but she felt they all had something to say. Aside from those infrequent outings, Hanna maintained her usual boring life and, oddly enough, often had to be coaxed to a night at the pub with Sally and their mates.

Sally was exhausted following her conversation with Joe. Arriving home after a dreary bus ride, she turned the key and walked into their flat. Of late, she dreaded coming home, as it felt quite eerie being here alone. The schoolyard was empty, as it was late in the day, and today Sally missed the sounds of children, their screams and laughter. The silence sounded like Hanna screaming for help.

For days, Sally had passed Hanna's room barely daring to look inside. But today, try as she might, she couldn't stop herself from entering the room. She walked in stealthily, on her toes, as if afraid of being seen or heard. Uncertain of what she was looking for, she went over to the far end of the room and opened the creaky wooden closet doors. She knew she was breaking their roommate code by being in here, but she would explain to Hanna later that this fell under the category of a bloody emergency.

She stared at Hanna's clothes, hung neatly, blouses and sweaters on one side, skirts and trousers on the other. There were a few boxes on the upper shelf that

Sally would not look into, but she did rummage through a few bags that were on the floor. Nothing really of interest, just some old CD's, a huge vanity case full of makeup, and about a dozen pairs of socks. Sally stood up, her eyes panning the room for any glimpse of something that looked out of place. With a sigh, she left the room. If Hanna wasn't home in the next day or two, it might embolden her to start going through her drawers with more ferocity and might even prompt her to look at the computer, which stood silent on her nightstand.

Sally went into her own room and began stripping down to have a shower, but not before going back to make sure she had engaged the deadbolt on the front door. She had never used it before, but now was grateful it was there. Returning to the bathroom, she carefully placed her clothes on the small wicker stool that she and Hanna had purchased at a flea market. She stepped into the hot spray, sat on the floor, and began to cry uncontrollably.

Feeling better, Sally shut the water off and stepped out of the shower. She put on her robe and walked into the kitchen. Although she had no appetite, Sally knew she best eat something. Opening the fridge, she quickly settled on a frozen burrito. Popping it into the microwave, she looked up at the clock. The time was passing too quickly. She would need to leave soon for her shift. She ate her burrito standing over the sink, feeling disgusted at her lack of decorum. Then after changing into her uniform, which consisted of blue smock and trousers, Sally headed into the bathroom to tie up her hair, suddenly full of enthusiasm. She was looking forward to getting out of the flat. Understandably, work had suddenly become her safe place.

The grocery store was unusually busy, and Sally enjoyed the presence of cheerful co-workers. The time flew by, and following her regular shift, she stayed late to help stock some shelves, grateful to be avoiding her return home. Sally actually enjoyed this task, and performing it now took her back to the days of teaching Rita Nowak how to stock shelves. She felt bad for having been so short tempered with the impassive girl. Of course, she knew nothing at the time of the pressure that Rita had been under. Recalling what had eventually happened to Rita sent her blood running cold. She tried not to think that the same fate might befall her friend.

Although days had gone by, to Sally it felt like one nightmarishly long day. She had arrived home quite late and, after a terribly restless night, had slept well into the morning. Now seated on the sofa, waking up with a cup of tea, she stared blankly out the window. Sighing deeply, she picked up the remote and turned on the telly to break the deafening silence. She felt lost, totally immobilized and no less in a state of shock. As she stood to clear away her dishes, her cell rang. She rushed over to the counter and grabbed the phone. "Please be Hanna," she prayed. But it was just another damn telecommunication service trying to sell her something. She held back the temptation to throw the phone against the wall as she wandered back to the kitchen. "This is crazy," she muttered to herself.

Feeling the need to be out, Sally quickly changed into a T-shirt and a pair of capris and set about thinking up a destination for herself. Wishing there was more she could do to help Hanna, Sally suddenly remembered the postal uniform that was hanging in Hanna's wardrobe. Her job! Hanna would lose her job for not showing up for work! Returning to Hanna's room, she began searching through her friend's things for a pay stub, or something with the phone number of her employer. She would need to call and make an excuse for Hanna, perhaps even lie and pretend she was Hanna's mum calling to say her daughter had taken ill. She let out a tiny squeal of delight when she came across a drawer with a large white envelope, which was filled with Hanna's tax documents, of which contained her employment information. Hurrying to the phone, she cleared her throat and tried hard to sound like Mary Lawson, although she hadn't the faintest idea what Mary Lawson might sound like. Hanna had been ill, Sally explained. She had no idea that her daughter had not called in. She would call back in a day or two with an update. Yes, yes, she would make sure that Hanna had a doctor's note when she returned. She was smiling proudly when she hung up the phone.

Assuming the call was successful, Sally let out a big sigh; it was with satisfaction that she left the flat, destined for the bus stop. On her way out, she hesitated and caught her breath before closing the door to Hanna's room. She hoped she wouldn't need to go in there again until Hanna herself came home and opened the door.

Walking to the corner, Sally breathed in the air,

grateful for being outside. She got on the yellow line tram towards West Street, where she planned on walking to the Moor to wander the shops. After walking aimlessly down the pedestrian thoroughfare, she realized she was not much in the mood for shopping. She had nothing but time, and it felt good to be outside, but she found herself wanting solitude, not crowds, so she decided to walk to Crookes Valley Park to feed the ducks. She had walked over halfway there and was on the university campus when her phone rang again. This time, seeing the call display, Sally welcomed the call.

But it wasn't Hanna calling from the station asking to be picked up. The woman on the line identified herself simply as a clerk from the luggage department at the train station. They were, it seemed, in possession of an unclaimed suitcase that had arrived on the train from Blackpool. The woman described it as a dark blue canvas suitcase with a matching tag bearing this number.

"Are you Sally Booth?"

Sally froze in her tracks. She had lent Hanna the bag for her trip, and she must have not bothered to change the name and phone number on the tag. Behind her was the wail of a siren. Someone across the street was laughing.

The woman waited for Sally to say something. When she didn't, she continued speaking. "You best come pick up the bag as soon as you can. Like I said, it came in on the Sunday train, and we've been holding it, thinking someone would come for it. Am I correct in assuming this is your bag?"

"Yes, yes, I'm sorry. I'll come and get the case, thank

you, thank you so much," she said. "You say it came on the train by itself?"

"No, I'm saying it's here now. I don't know whether someone brought it here then forgot to collect it when they arrived, or whether someone missed the train at the origin. Was it not you travelling with your bag? Either way, it's here now and has not been claimed." Sally's head was spinning. The woman's voice sounded like it was coming from an echo chamber as she gave Sally directions to the lost baggage department.

Sally hardly heard the instructions as she again thanked the woman. She quickly hung up the phone and looked around for something to lean on, if only for a moment. As she was not far from Joe's office, she slowly got her bearings and looked around for a bus stop while typing a message to send to him. "I'm coming to your office, Joe. It's about Hanna—the train station has her bag!"

When she arrived, Stefan was there speaking with Joe. Without looking at him, she turned her direction to Joe. "I hope you got my message. So, why is there a suitcase and no Hanna?"

"Sit down, Sally, and stop shouting. Take a breath."

"I want you to come with me to get the case," she said, doing her best to sound calm, although her voice trembled. "I don't think I can go alone." She leaned against the filing cabinet by the door but didn't sit down.

"Would you like me to take you?" Stefan was looking at her somewhat cautiously, with an apologetic look on his face.

She looked at Stefan and returned a similar careful smile, but there was no apology there. "Well, if you're working with Joe, maybe you could come with us. I don't want to wait any longer to find out what's going on. I need to get that case." Sally looked at Joe. "So? Is he working with you?"

Without answering the question, Joe looked at Sally and said, "Is it okay if Stefan takes you? You can bring the suitcase back here if you like. I have some things that require my immediate attention. I normally wouldn't be here at this time, but I was held up leaving."

Sally nodded but not before rolling her eyes. As she turned towards the door, Stefan grabbed the handle before she could reach it and held the door open for her. Their gazes brushed each other's as she walked past, being careful not to get too close to him. Both were very quiet. Stefan glanced over at Joe with a "help me" look as he left the room close behind Sally.

Watching the two leave his office, Joe shook his head and sighed. Why did he feel like he was babysitting? The coming days would not be easy, he feared, now that Stefan was back on the scene.

Chapter 7

Stefan was delighted to be driving Sally to the train station. He badly wished he could do something to end the tension between them. He kicked himself for causing her to be annoyed with him in the first place. Once in the car, Sally didn't say a word about what had passed between them, for which he was grateful. Before long, she began nervously chatting about Hanna.

"It's not like Hanna. She's smart, you know? A lot more street-smart than most people I know, believe it or not, regardless of how sheltered she was raised. She can usually spot an unsavory type from a mile away. Maybe it was going places she knew she shouldn't go that made her street smart. And she has a good mind. She remembers everything. She knows every punch line, every character in every movie she's seen, never forgets a song or a person's name. Perhaps lately, she's just been bored. I think she wanted an adventure. But she wouldn't be careless and lose her bag, and she'd never go this long without calling."

"I don't know, Sally. Maybe she's not as smart as you think she is." Stefan rubbed his chin. "Maybe she's not even as smart as she thought she was."

The train station was not far away; Stefan estimated twenty minutes there and back, depending on traffic, which right now was good. This was not always the case on Hanover Way, and so they made good time. Before long, they were on St. Mary's Road. Sally had sat silent for this part of the drive, her fingers clutched together. In her lap lay written instructions as to where she needed to go to find the lost property department. Stefan opted to wait in the car, as parking may have proven more difficult.

"I'll circle the block, Sally, so when you come out, wait right here, in this same spot and I'll pick you up when I come round again." She got out and nodded before running to the curb. Stefan pulled out into traffic and only needed to do one loop around. As he approached the curb, Sally had already returned—she stood there waiting with her blue suitcase. A small gust of wind caused her hair to flutter around her face. Stefan flashed his lights and she quickly came over to where he had stopped the car. With hazard lights flashing, he jumped out to open the boot and Sally unceremoniously tossed the suitcase into the hold. Both quickly got back into the car.

Sally seemed much calmer as she brushed the hair from her eyes. "The lady inside was very nice. She said I was very lucky that there was nobody there just then, as she had just finished up with a long line of people. Then she said I must be very relieved to have my suitcase back, as some people come in quite upset. She said it seemed odd that I would leave the station without it. But of course, I said nothing. I just wanted to get out of there."

Sally paused before adding, "Maybe you are right, Stefan. Maybe she's not as smart as I think she is."

"Did you want me to stop so you can open it?" asked Stefan. He was glad that Sally seemed less angry at him.

"No, I'd really like Joe to do it, in case he sees something that might help him. It would be better if I didn't touch anything, don't you agree?"

"Um, oh yes, ah—of course. Best not to touch anything." Stefan was annoyed for not thinking that himself. He should have known better. It seemed he could do nothing right around Sally.

The ride back seemed quicker, and before long Stefan had parked in the same spot and they were entering the ARD building. Joe seemed surprised to see them back so soon, and with the suitcase. Sally placed it carefully on Joe's desk, and together they contemplated it, but no one touched it. The three of them stood in a semi-circle, looking down at the blue bag as though it were a corpse or a lost treasure that held a dark secret.

"It looks as if it's locked," said Sally.

"You need to open the bag and see what's inside, maybe?" said Joe.

"Won't you want to take prints or anything?" asked Sally.

Joe shook his head. "There's no point, Sally. For one thing, it's fabric and I don't think the prints would carry. Also, there have likely been far too many people handling the bag. With any hope, inside is where you might find a clue."

Stefan added, "But I'm afraid we might have to destroy

the lock to open it, Sally. Not unless you have a key."

Sally shook her head. "I don't think I've ever locked that bag. I'm afraid I don't even know where the key is. I can't say I've ever had one, to tell you the truth. Can you open it, Joe?"

Joe picked up a metal letter opener from the ceramic jar on his desk and wedged it forcefully into the crack, as close to the lock as he could manage. With a violent twist, the lock gave way and the bag was open. The three stepped closer, but it was Joe who began rummaging through the contents. Inside the suitcase were clothes that seemed as though they had been hastily packed. Shoes were thrown on top of clothes in a haphazard fashion. Underneath a pair of sandals, he found two single passes to the zoo for two different days. He placed them to one side. Also underneath the sandals, Joe found a tightly bundled-up blouse. Sally looked up at Stefan, who was looking at her.

Joe picked it up carefully. It felt heavy. He was sure it was wrapped around an object. "Something's inside this blouse. Does it look like Hanna's, Sally?" asked Joe. When she nodded, he carefully unwrapped it. Inside, he found a bloodied knife.

Sally's mouth flew open. "Now do you believe me? Tell me again there's nothing wrong and I have nothing to worry about."

Nobody spoke. Picking up the letter opener again, Joe lifted the corners of some other items in the case, not wanting to disturb the contents any more than he already had. Lifting something blue, he revealed a small white piece of plastic. Flipping it over, he saw it was an employee tag from the Blackpool Zoo. Imprinted on the card was the name Ian Crossley.

"That's him! Crossley. That's the name of the man she was going to see. She said he is really nice, and that he invited her to come back for Illuminations in September." At the sight of the blood, Sally's behaviour had become almost manic. She began babbling excitedly. "She was excited about going there. I remember now, she said he wanted her to come down to meet his mates, and to see the ocean and the amusement parks and take a ride on the Big One roller coaster and all. He said he had a friend who worked the rides at a place called Pleasure Beach, and he'd give her rides for free." Sally's expression darkened. "I'm trying not to panic here, but that knife. Whose is it? And whose blood is it? And why is it in Hanna's bag? I don't understand." There was a faint hysteria in her voice.

Stefan again stood in awe at the way Joe could deal with people and control the situation. Speaking now, his voice had an almost sedative sound to it, which seemed to calm Sally. "Easy, Sally. We don't know anything yet. But this changes everything. Now I do need to call the police, and now we might get their help. We will need to check for prints and try to see whose blood this is. Perhaps someone snatched the case in order to get rid of evidence, and that could explain why it's not with Hanna. But Sally, a police officer will likely need to come over and get Hanna's prints from around the apartment. Also, they will need a hairbrush or perhaps a toothbrush so they can check her DNA. The good thing is, we may now have

Blackpool police on board to help look for your friend."

While Sally was clearly shaken, she managed a smile. "So it's not necessarily Hanna's blood, right, Joe?"

"I don't know any more than you, Sally, but let's try not to jump to conclusions. There are no absolutes. And trust me, I will now make this happen as quickly as I can. Will you be okay for now?" Joe stepped forward and, firmly grasping her shoulders, stared at her until he was sure she understood.

Sally nodded. "Yes, thank you. I'm fine now." She picked up her purse and headed towards the door, somewhat in a trance. Seeing her attempt at bravery, Stefan offered to drive her home. "Sally, wait. I'll take you. It's on my way."

She quickly shook her head. "I need to be alone right now."

"But you're shivering," he said, wanting to comfort her but also afraid to touch even her arm, as her body signals loudly suggested *leave me alone*.

She smiled weakly at him and said, "No, I'll be fine, really. I just need a bit of time to digest this, that's all. And I do want to walk; it will do me good." Stepping back into the room, she approached Joe with something that came close to a hug, and then she was gone. Stefan stood rooted, staring at the contents of the suitcase.

Once Sally had left, Joe promptly closed the lid and moved the case to a spot on the floor behind his desk. He sincerely hoped this was not Hanna's blood. All he could think of was Blackpool and the probability that he would need to go there. With heavy feet, Joe walked out into the front office area to speak with Barry, who was just preparing to leave for the day.

"Barry, have you ever been to Blackpool?"

Barry looked at him with an apathetic expression. "I went there once. It was about twenty-five years ago, I think. It was an experience never to be repeated. Luckily, I don't remember much about it other than I wouldn't be going back. So, I don't think I can be much help."

Joe answered with a similar deadness. "Funny, it was like that for me as well. I know it used to be the greatest place to go to when I was a kid, but I was there with my family less than twenty years ago and I felt the same as you did. I know the kids loved the beach, and the teens liked the rides and theme parks and all, but there was just something about the place."

Barry nodded in agreement. "Yes, that's it. There's just something about the place. Hard to say what, but it's there just the same. The seaside culture seems to have no rules, does it?"

"It's more *seedy-side* than seaside," agreed Joe. "So, Barry, we need the police involved. I'm going to call DI Wilkes so he can get his forensic team over to Hanna's to get some prints and DNA samples from her room. I'd like it if you could get in touch with David at the police department as well? Someone will need to come here and pick up the suitcase. We don't want to disturb its contents any more than we already have."

Joe had not spoken to DI Harry Wilkes for some time. More specifically, not since the trial of Simon Hamilton, who had been found guilty of the rape and subsequent murder of Stefan's only sister, Rita. The memories now came flooding back, thinking of Harry Wilkes.

"Will do, Joe," answered Barry as he reached for the phone.

Sally closed the front door with a bang and immediately turned on the radio, needing to hear music and voices. Strangely, she could barely remember the walk home, her head was in such a fog. She ached all over—had she really spent the entire day walking? Before she could catch her breath, she heard a knock on her door.

"Now who the hell could that be?" she muttered, padding back down the hallway. She opened the door cautiously, only to find two policemen standing there.

"Sorry to bother you, miss. We're here to check the place for prints and such. Can we come in?"

"You lot wasted no time in getting here," Sally blurted out.

She showed the two officers to Hanna's room, where they instantly got to task. She stood in the doorway watching as they probed, dusted, inspected, and examined. They penetrated literally every inch of Hanna's private world. From time to time, they would take small items, put them into plastic bags, and label them. After what seemed forever, they finished in Hanna's room. Sally was ready to open the door for them and bid them a good day when they turned towards the bathroom. There, they started again, dusting and packaging. One officer turned to Sally and said, "You'll now need to come to the station, miss. We need your prints and DNA so we can eliminate you from what we find here. You can come with us, and someone will drive you home afterwards."

Hanna, where the hell are you? she silently screamed in her head.

Chapter 8

Joe had spent the early part of the morning shuffling appointments, and before long, he and Stefan were on their way to Blackpool. Joe planned to drive directly to the zoo, and hoped to arrive around ten, when the doors opened. During the drive, they passed the time discussing Sally and Hanna, and eventually the conversation landed on Blackpool. Stefan settled back comfortably into the seat, happy to be a passenger. He recounted bits from his visit a few days back, providing a basic lay of the land between the zoo and the pier from his perspective. He had sensed that Joe was less than pleased at the prospect of needing to make multiple visits to the area.

"I haven't been there in a very long time. Simon had tickets to a Premier League game at Bloomfield Stadium about seven years ago, and I turned it down. That's how badly I didn't want to go to Blackpool. Yet here I am." Joe's scowl caused his brows to take on a whole new shape that Stefan had never seen before.

He studied Joe, a curious expression on his face. "But when I drove through, I thought it looked pleasant enough. The ocean and all."

"Things are not always as they seem. It's not just about

having the distraction of the sunniness and the ocean, with fun tacky storefronts and crass T-shirt shops, not to mention the beach and the music. Nor is it about its being run-down, in disrepair, and washed up. Or the fact that more than a tenth of the working age live on state benefits paid to those too sick to work. It's what you don't see that bothers me. It's the poison of the riffraff that have started coming, bringing drugs and sex shops and gangs that are killing each other. Blackpool used to be a very respectable place, full of working-class and middle-class families. They were decent, hard-working people, proud and independent. Then things slowly changed. Antidepressant prescription rates are too high, and life expectancy is too low. Janet once told me that local doctors say people here die of 'shit life syndrome.' The place has lost its essence; now it's gangs, drunken stag and hen bashes, cheap drinks, and bingo."

After driving in silence for the next few miles, Joe finally asked Stefan, "Okay, what's bugging you? You seem a bit off today."

Stefan smiled feebly. "Didn't think it was obvious. It's just the knife, you know? Since seeing that knife that killed my sister—actually, all knives since then. They just scare me at what they can do to a person. Then looking at that knife yesterday with the blood—well—I thought I would be physically sick. I was hoping you don't see a lot of that in this line of work."

"Well, not usually, I don't. In my personal experience, I've only seen it the one time, but you can never tell what this job might bring. Try not to think about it. That's all the advice I can give you." Joe wouldn't mention the time he was stabbed, as it would do no good to bring that up again.

Arriving at the zoo, Stefan directed Joe to the parking area. The spacious and cheerful entrance led to a large and bright lobby, with creamy white tiled floors and white ceilings generously filled with a myriad of pot lights. They entered the building and walked down the long, wide corridor to the ticket counter. Joe headed directly over to the ticket clerk and asked for the manager. She nodded and picked up a phone located on the wall behind her. After the clerk hung up the phone, she smiled at the two men and directed them through the gates to an area just inside the zoo, where they were instructed to wait. A few minutes later, a portly man approached them, wearing a big shiny tag labelled "HANK. MANAGER."

After introductions, Joe asked if he could speak to an employee named Ian Crossley. Hank the Manager snorted sarcastically. "I, too, would like to speak to Ian. There has been no sign of him. I let one absenteeism after another slide for that bloke too many times, but now I'm properly pissed because he hasn't shown up for work since Saturday."

"Okay then, could I perhaps speak with any co-workers who knew Ian well, or maybe shared shifts with him?" requested Joe.

Hank replied obligingly, "Yes, that would be Charlie. They usually work together in the same area. Hang on then, I'll get him for you." He took a few steps away and spoke into his radio, which he removed from his belt clip. Before long, a man approached them with an employee nametag similar to the one they'd found in Hanna's suitcase.

Charlie appeared nonchalant—more curious than concerned. He was very tall and rakish thin, and he had thinning dark hair that looked an unusual shade of black bordering on purple. His uniform hung slack, and Joe imagined it would be difficult to find one that was both tall enough and narrow enough to fit properly. Charlie claimed he saw Ian leave the zoo on Saturday with a girl. When Joe showed Charlie a photo of Hanna, Charlie nodded affirmatively.

"Yeah, that's the girl I seen him with. Well—she looked exactly like this person, is what I mean."

Stefan, who had remained quiet, leaned in and asked Charlie, "Where would be a likely place to find this Ian bloke, do you think?"

"I don't really know for sure, as Ian is not one of my mates. But I know he sometimes hangs out at the chip shop by Central Pier. I might have seen him there before." Charlie looked nervous. His top lip was twitching, and he kept crossing and uncrossing his arms.

"Do you know where he lives, by any chance?"

Charlie answered, "No, like I said, I don't really know him well. He's not been here that long." Then looking at Hank, he added, "But I'm sure the manager knows." Charlie was looking around to see if anyone was observing the conversation.

Hank nodded and told Joe he would retrieve the information from the girls in the office and would send it to Joe. "But it will have to be tomorrow. There's no one in there until later this afternoon. Having said that, you'll need to excuse us now. The day's just begun, and we've a lot to do." Hank turned to Charlie and nodded. Charlie took this as permission to leave, having already started taking a few steps backwards in a slow retreat, still looking around to see if anyone had noticed them talking.

"Well, here's my card. Perhaps we could speed this along, yes? I will be waiting for the information to be sent to me this afternoon, either to my phone or to my office." Joe could see no reason for this man to use a delay tactic.

Hank took the card and muttered compliance. As he turned to leave, Joe thanked him. Charlie had seemed only too happy to be done and by now was nowhere in sight. Joe would bet he knew more than he was willing to say; it was abundantly clear by his actions. Joe watched Hank walk away, and then turned towards the exit, motioning to Stefan to follow.

"But we can't just leave! Not yet, Joe, we've only just arrived. Did you know they've got fifteen hundred animals in here?"

"Excuse me, but we are looking for Hanna, right? Remember her?"

"Yes, but Joe, they've got pink birds and all. Can't we just have a bit of enjoyment along the way?"

Stefan continued his protest as Joe took hold of his shirt and pulled him towards the exit. "Come on, Peter Pan, we've work to do."

Once seated in the car, Joe pointed at Stefan's phone. "I'm sure there are lots of chip shops in Blackpool, but can you look on that thing and see if there's a mention of a chip shop close to Central Pier?"

Stefan had not noticed a chippy on his last visit to that area, so he checked his phone to find the way there. "It's that way, Joe. Just off Talbot Road."

Joe drove slowly through the streets until they spotted the building. The day had turned cool and a light drizzle had materialized. There were not many people about, and this particular area looked quite subdued at this hour. Nevertheless, there were a few inauspicious-looking types around—men hiding behind dark sunglasses with their heads down, others sitting on benches looking half asleep.

Stefan noted nondescript silhouettes withdrawn into doorways and shady areas, some bodies lying down, likely still sleeping off the effects of the night before. "I guess we'll not see much here at this time of day. Chip shop's not even open yet."

Their next stop was to the Blackpool North train station, where Joe was hoping to request CCTV footage from a week ago, on the Sunday that he believed Hanna's suitcase was placed on the train. Showing his card and asking for the security department, Joe and Stefan were led up a flight of stairs to a small office. The security chief rose from his chair and shook Joe's hand as the men entered the room. He then nodded at Stefan, who stood back a few steps. "You say footage from last Sunday?"

"That's the day the suitcase was likely put on the train, and the ticket showed this station was the point of departure. Are the suitcases carried on by the passengers, or are they loaded by personnel?"

"Could be either, depending on if the passenger wishes to check the bag or carry it on themselves. I will order the footage for you. It will be ready in a couple of days."

The visit was brief, and Joe thanked the man. Upon leaving the building, they found that the wind had picked up and the drizzle had turned to rain.

Their final stop was to the Blackpool police department, where Joe wanted to introduce himself to the local DI, as was common courtesy when investigating in another region outside one's own. They were greeted by a kindly desk sergeant, who declared, "Nobody's in just yet. Can I have someone call you?"

Joe shook his head. "We need to be back here in a couple of days to see the CCTV footage, so perhaps we could stop by then. Here's my card. This is just a courtesy visit. I believe Sheffield Police will be in touch before then, if they haven't done so already, so the DI will be informed by the time I get back."

The constable took the card and read the name. "Okay then, Mr. Joe Parrott. When you come back, be sure to ask for either Inspector Edey or Chief Inspector Andrew Hall. Either or both of them are generally here."

Driving back to Sheffield, Joe was thinking aloud.

"We will need to order CCTV from Sheffield train station as well. Just in the off chance she did come back to Sheffield, but for some reason has not gone home." He was tapping the wheel in rhythm to some music that Stefan had turned up.

Just as Joe was exiting the last roundabout into

Sheffield, his phone rang. Stefan turned down the volume while Joe set his phone to speaker. The call display indicated it was the police station in Sheffield calling.

"How do, Joe? David here. So, we still don't know whose blood it is, but the prints on the knife are Hanna's. There's another set of prints on there as well—possibly two, that we will run more thoroughly through our databases. Then we'll send the items to Blackpool to see if they can match anything."

Disconnecting the call, he and Stefan exchanged concerned glances.

Two days had passed. There had been no further news regarding Hanna's disappearance. Joe was sitting in a small room at the Sheffield train station, checking the CCTV footage. He had left home early, wanting to get a good start to his day. There was nothing of note on any of the tapes. That afternoon, Joe was again on his way to Blackpool to check their CCTV tapes, which were now ready for him. Stefan had again asked Joe if he could accompany him, and Joe again had no objection. There was an undeniable comfort being around Stefan, and Joe was reminded of the way they had bonded when they had first met. The drive seemed considerably faster today, for whatever reason. Perhaps, as they say, one simply becomes accustomed to the distance. Joe parked at the south car park behind Pleasure Beach, and they walked the distance along the Promenade to the Blackpool North train station.

Stefan seemed to be almost in a state of shock. Today was hot and sunny, and this section of the Promenade was bustling. Joe looked at him with amusement. Stefan seemed addled by the sounds of car horns and engines and the deafening yells and laughter from the people. Moving along the Promenade, his head turned in every direction as he took in an endless sea of flashing signs, penny arcades, and tacky tourist shops offering T-shirts, little flags, and tiny plastic seagulls. Windows were full of purses, backpacks, dreamcatchers, lava lamps, postcards, and water bottles etched with rollercoasters. He had never seen such grand Ferris wheels, and of course, he craned his neck as he marvelled at the Tower. Hordes of tourists were walking along what was known as the Golden Mile, which had been named after the high concentration of slot machines that once lined the street. His eyes panned the sandy beach as he enjoyed the spectacular views being offered on this clear day. Young families sat while their toddlers played in the sand, couples walked hand in hand.

Joe could scarcely believe this was the same charming place he had visited as a child. For sure the quaintness was gone, replaced by extra lanes of traffic, billboards, neon signs, casinos, and a spirited sense of edginess. Hearing the screams coming from the Big One made both men turn their heads. The roller coaster had climbed slowly to the top before now plunging down in a semi-corkscrew fashion. It seemed out of place here. Until a few years ago, the coaster, the tallest one in the UK, was known as the Pepsi Max. Four people had been crushed as two of the cars collided, and it was only one of many mishaps. The coaster was eventually renamed, but troubles persisted.

Next, they walked past the Big Dipper to the sounds of more screaming. Joe shuddered as he watched the coaster plunge down the track. Over the years, there had also been accidents on this coaster and lives had been lost. Even refurbished, he couldn't understand how anyone in his or her right minds would get on and willingly prepare to die.

At the train station, Joe and Stefan were directed to the same small room up the flight of stairs, where a small, pleasant woman greeted them. She instructed the men to sit in front of a monitor and left them alone. They had better luck with the footage here.

CCTV footage showed that Hanna had been there with her luggage, presumably to drop it off before the train was scheduled to depart. She was not alone. In the CCTV image, there was a man with her who looked like it could be Ian. He was grabbing her by the arm, and they appeared to be arguing. Hanna had looked around nervously, and they had both left suddenly, as if frightened by something.

They suddenly disappeared from view. On another camera, they were spotted exiting the building with a third person that was only visible from the back, so hard to describe. Hanna appeared to be going with the men willingly, and they didn't seem to be forcing her. She no longer had the suitcase.

Joe then shifted his focus to the tapes of the train platform cameras, fast-forwarding to minutes before the people were instructed to board the train. There were no further images of Hanna, either on the platform or boarding the train. Joe checked all angles again, but it was still unclear if it was a porter who had loaded the suitcase along with the other bags, or if someone else had placed the case on the train. Thanking the woman, they left the station.

Joe suggested they walk to the police station, and as they began heading along the walkway, his phone rang. He answered quickly and simply mumbled, "I'm on my way."

Turning on his heels, he called out to Stefan, who still stood facing the other direction. "I need to go back to Sheffield, Stefan. I've just had a breakthrough in another of my cases. This will need to wait for another day."

"What about the police?"

"This part of it can wait. You will eventually become familiar with this part of many investigations. They still need to run the data, and it might take time, so it's not essential we go and see them today. We can see them another time, sorry. Remember, this was only a courtesy visit to let them know we were in town. Besides, if there's any news, I'm sure they'll call us."

Chapter 9

It had taken Joe longer than anticipated to finish up at the office that afternoon, but before he left for the day, he called Sally to ask if Hanna had by chance mentioned where she and Ian had spent their time while she was last visiting him.

"She's really never said too much about him. We don't talk about it a lot because she knows how I feel. But that does ring a bell. Hang on, Joe, while I check my messages." A moment later, Sally was back on the line, mentioning a pub at the end of the North Pier. "Just past the north tram station. I remember because she said they took the tram and she ate something good there," she said. "Hang on again, I think I have a photo on my phone." There was another pause, then, "Here, I have it. In the pic, I can only make out part of the name. 'Duke,' I think it says; then in another photo, I can only see 'RK.'"

"Can you send it to me, please. And look, I don't want you to worry, Sally. So far, we have no indication of foul play. There have been no reports of anyone being injured, and no bodies have shown up. There might be a perfectly good explanation for what we found."

Sally admitted to Joe that she was worried. "I know

what you are saying, and I know you are trying to make me feel better. There's nothing to worry about until there is something to worry about, yeah? I'm telling you, Joe, something is off. If she's okay, then why isn't she calling me? This isn't like her."

"That's what we are trying to find out. Okay, I won't sugar coat it. There appears to be something off, but not necessarily with Hanna. If she inadvertently became a part of something, she could be frightened and have gone into hiding. Maybe they are both hiding. Something bad obviously could have happened, and maybe she is hoping someone will find out what it was. We had anticipated getting some clues from the suitcase contents, and maybe we still can, just not as quickly as we thought."

Joe said good-bye to Sally, then conducted a few searches on his computer. Based on the information and the photo, Joe came up with Duke of York, on Banks Street. On his map, he saw that it was a short walk from the north tram. He needed to go there. He also needed to pay a visit to this Ian Crossley's house now that he had the address. The girls at the zoo office had been prompt about getting the information to him. He made a few notes, closed his computer, and left the office, closing the door behind him.

On his way home, Joe was becoming increasingly aware of the fact that he had been avoiding speaking to Ray Lawson. As much as he wished he didn't have to, he needed to call in on him right now and give him an update. He hated doing it with the news he had, but on the other hand, he would not keep things from the man. While driving, he dialled the number that Mr. Lawson had given him. There was no answer, but Joe left a message to say that he was on his way, and he hoped someone would be there when he arrived. This may not have been the most courteous approach, and he wouldn't want them to think he was purposely calling in when no one was at home, but hopefully they were home and simply not picking up.

The Lawsons lived just outside of Heeley, and Joe found the terraced house easily. After ringing the bell, Joe stood casually, surveying the pleasant neighbourhood. A man was in his front garden, planting a row of colourful flowers. The street was otherwise quiet, but one could see the care that people took with their homes. The only sound was the mellow, unhurried song of a pair of duel-ling blackbirds, melodious and elegant in their repartee.

The door was answered after two rings, much to Joe's relief. There stood a stocky woman, who smiled when she saw Joe standing there. She looked about Joe's age, and the first thing he noted was her beautifully smooth skin and large glassy eyes. She was wearing a blue print blouse and a navy skirt. She had blonde hair, cut in a short bob, and was impeccably groomed. "You must be the detec-tive, Mr. Parrott. I'm Mary, Hanna's mother. Please come in." Her manners were note perfect, like her appearance. There was something about her perfection that Joe found strangely irregular.

Mary Lawson led Joe to a sitting area immediately inside the entrance. Ray was seated in a chair at the far end of the room, legs crossed and arms folded in his lap, looking like he had been posed for a photograph. Seeing Joe, he rose as if on cue. Mr. Lawson did not smile as he walked over to shake Joe's hand, but he did greet him cordially. "I hope you are bringing us some news," he said quietly.

Joe felt a subtle tinge of uneasiness around the Lawsons. Both were dressed to faultless precision. Were they expecting company, or did they ordinarily dress this way? Or perhaps they had just returned from a function of some sort. Also, their gestures were perplexing, every movement controlled, almost robotic. Their phrases sounded scripted, insincere.

The room was decorated in fashion-magazine elegance, in deep shades of plum contrasted with teal accents. The furnishings were various shades of grey. On all the walls hung pictures of a religious nature: a large picture of *The Last Supper* over the fireplace, another of Jesus on the cross, and a few others that he didn't want to turn to look at. He also noticed a collection of small crosses and chalices on the mantle and more on nearby tabletops. Joe could somewhat understand why Hanna wanted to break away from here and experience a bit of adventure.

Accepting the invitation to sit down, Joe could feel the two probing sets of eyes on him, making him uneasy. His throat felt dry, but nothing was offered, not even water. He proceeded to tell the Lawsons what little he knew. Mrs. Lawson seemed momentarily startled at the mention of blood but remained quite placid. The room was excruciatingly quiet. Even the sound of a ticking clock would have been welcome.

When the Lawsons offered no response, Joe continued, "I don't really have much to add since the initial discovery, other than to say that the blood found in the suitcase was not Hanna's. The fingerprints were hers, but that was to be expected. But we still have no idea where she might be."

Mr. Lawson had by now resumed his pose in the same chair. "But why on earth hasn't she called? She knows better than to do this to us." His expression of concern was expertly pasted onto his face.

"Someone could have taken her phone, or perhaps she lost it. Being cut off like that, she could be frightened. The battery could have died, and she has no means of recharging." Joe leaned forward, hands on his elbows. He had Mrs. Lawson's full attention. "If she's hurt, she would be disoriented, confused. And if Ian is with her, he's likely her only friend and they are protecting each other. These are all things we don't know yet." At the mention of the name Ian, the couple exchanged glances, a look of disbelief or bewilderment on their faces.

Joe carried on as if he hadn't noticed. "Or it could be that the whole thing is a prank, and she has no idea where her suitcase is." Joe again sat back in his chair and crossed his legs. "Perhaps she's simply not ready to come home." Then Joe thought to himself, *Or Ian's a twat, and he is stopping her from speaking to anyone.*

Ray cleared his throat. "I assume this Ian person is male, then. So you are telling us our daughter is out there with a strange man?"

Mary, who had remained standing, walked over and sat delicately on the arm of her husband's chair, tucked her hands neatly into her lap, and then spoke. "Thank you for helping, Mr. Parrott. My husband feels so relieved knowing you are on the case." Her voice sounded very Stepford-like, which made the hair on the back of Joe's neck prickle.

Joe was taken aback by the woman's profound lack of any real emotion. For a moment, he thought he had reached her, but then it seemed not. He imagined how Janet would respond if it were their daughter who was missing—particularly under such circumstances. While it was true the woman was wringing her hands, something seemed missing. Joe found the apathy of both Mary and her husband a little frightening, like they'd just lost their dog and not their daughter. Promising to call with any updates, Joe bid them both a good day.

As Joe started his engine, he imagined that Hanna might well want to stay missing if it meant returning to this scrutiny. He noticed on his phone that David from the Sheffield police had been calling him. He called David right back.

"How do, Joe? Chief Inspector Andrew Hall from the police department in Blackpool just called. Someone's been murdered over there. They just found the body."

"Please tell me it wasn't Hanna," said Joe.

"No, their victim is a male. Come in, and I can share the details."

Joe turned the car in the direction of the station. Fortunately, he had not received this news before his visit to the Lawson residence. However, he wondered if it would have mattered. In his head, he heard Ray Lawson's voice saying, *"She knows better than to do this to us."*

Chapter 10

David was waiting in the front office when Joe arrived. The men greeted each other familiarly with a handshake before moving into David's office. David walked around his desk and retrieved a file, which he opened.

"I have received this," he said as he handed Joe a sheet of paper. "They believe the deceased is Liam White, but of course, the CI is waiting for the coroner's official report. He says if it is Liam, he's well known to police. He's a member of the Fylde Snakes, a border gang that's apparently often causing problems with the local boys. Oh—and he was stabbed. And they haven't recovered a knife."

"Where did they find him?" asked Joe. "And did he say when it happened?"

"A passerby found the body behind a sign, near the Nickelodeon, wherever that is. The body was hidden under some broken boxes. They are still trying to establish when it happened, but the coroner is speculating that it could have been as long ago as last Saturday night."

Joe met David's eyes, and in doing so, they jointly acknowledged not only was there a missing murder weapon, but also that this was the day before Hanna was to get on the train. David sat on the edge of his desk and continued.

"They are using a blood sample from the body to see if it matches the blood on the knife found in the girl's suitcase. They will check the prints as well."

Joe read the initial report that David handed him, nodded, and asked, "Could you ask them if the results could be ready by tomorrow?" He handed the report back. "I need to speak with police in Blackpool, and I hope to drive back some time tomorrow. Hopefully they will have the results, along with any other news that could be helpful."

"Will do, Joe, and hey, come along to the pub one night. It's been a while, hasn't it? The boys have been asking. It's that new lady of yours, isn't it? I'm sure she's a sight more interesting than we are, eh?"

Joe smiled and slapped his old friend on the back. "I will catch up with you soon, David. And thanks."

Back in his car, Joe called Stefan and asked if he'd like to join him on the drive to Blackpool some time before noon. An excited Stefan was at his office by eleven. Once they had started the drive, Stefan turned to Joe and asked if he'd had a chance to think about his proposal to work together as partners.

Joe answered matter-of-factly, "I'm not saying no, Stefan. Really, I'm not. Let's try to get this done together and see how we get on. But I'm not a cop, and you aren't my partner. I'm a private investigator. We don't typically go about in pairs. You would need to have your own cases, and you would work alone. You see, I only work alone—it's what I love about my job. I don't know how else to do it."

Stefan sat listening to him, nodding intently in agreement, but before he could say anything, Joe spoke up again.

"And before you ask me, yes, so far things have been good. I know you've come along with me in the past, but this will be very different, actually working together. I could help you get on your own feet; maybe that's all I could do. So honestly, we will talk about it. Soon." Glancing out the window to avoid Stefan's eyes, he added, "And another thing—yes, there might be knives."

Once back in Blackpool, Joe and Stefan made their way to the police station so that Joe might at last introduce himself to Chief Inspector Andrew Hall. He knew the station would appreciate this common courtesy to let them know he was working a case in their city. He decided he would introduce Stefan as his assistant on this case. As they climbed the front steps and opened the large glass-paned door, Joe spotted a man inside watching them.

Chief Inspector Andrew Hall walked towards them with a cordial smile and an extended hand. He looked a very handsome young detective, who announced he himself was new to the area. "Fresh off the press and very keen," he described himself. Joe found him to be extremely helpful and very friendly. Chief Inspector Hall had no problem letting Joe and Stefan conduct their investigation and offered the assistance of the force, provided Joe gave them full transparency. Andrew and

Stefan hit it off, sharing a reciprocal sense of humour and timing. Following formalities and introductions, Chief Inspector Hall took them to a large windowless room where they could sit and have a proper chat. The CI filled Joe and Stefan in on the goings on in the area.

"We have two main rival county line gangs. The Best Boys are locals here. The county line gang is called the Fylde Snakes, and they have been coming around causing trouble for years. This man whose body was discovered, he's one of the key members of the Snakes. Their main kingpin is a man called Monty. A big man, and not one you'd want to have walking behind you. They call him the Black Python within their circle. Get it? Monty Python?" He chuckled at his own joke, then he continued, "We just call him a piece of meat with a mouth. He's not an easy man to deal with. We have reason to believe he's come here from the Manchester area."

The inspector walked across the room and partly opened the door to let in some air. "Did you hear about the bombing a few months ago at the Manchester Arena concert? It was that Ariana Grande person. That turned out to be the deadliest bombing we've had around here in about ten years. Rumour has is that Monty had a hand in it, although it's never been confirmed. The way the story went is that a certain Islam group was involved, although it's never been confirmed. Apparently Monty was in pretty tight with some of the relatives of the bloke who offed himself. And now he's been bringing his trash down here. He ought to just go home to Jamaica or wherever the hell he's from, the wanker."

Joe opened his file and showed him a picture of Ian. "I don't know if you are aware, but we are looking for him. Perhaps you know him? We believe the missing girl may be with him. Do you know if he is connected to either of these gangs, or to this Liam White?"

"Aye, he's with Best Boys, although he'll probably try to deny it. Carl is the gang leader here for the Boys, and wherever you see Carl, you know Ian is not too far away. Monty has always had it in for Carl, and we'd all laugh if it weren't so pathetic, the way Monty and Carl try to prove which of them is the toughest. Your Ian bloke, he tries to stay low key, but he's been connected to events too many times to hide his involvement. I know he's got a temper and he knows how to use a knife."

Andrew Hall was playing with the pencil behind his ear. Joe noticed two large jars of pencils on the desk, one at each end. The chief inspector continued, "And now that this Ian's gone missing, he's become a person of interest in the case. He's had run-ins with Liam before, so to me, it's not odd that Liam is dead and Ian's conveniently not around."

Stefan then handed the photograph of Hanna to Joe, who in turn showed it to Andrew Hall. "Have you by chance seen this girl around town?"

Andrew looked at the photo and said, "Well no, I haven't, but I'm not on the streets much. Like I said, I'm new, and I don't live here in the city. I'm a short distance away, in Poulton-Le-Fylde. Who is she?" He had begun tapping the pencil against his knee, either from nervousness or possibly because he had a good rhythm playing in his head.

"This is our missing girl, Hanna. Hanna Lawson. She was reported missing by her roommate almost a week ago. The bloody knife we are checking was found in her suitcase. The same suitcase that somehow took a solo train ride from Blackpool to Sheffield."

"May I have this photo? I will make sure we post it on our board. Might also distribute copies to the officers who work that part of town, particularly if there is a chance she's involved—either intentionally or simply being in the wrong place at the wrong time. There's a slight chance one of the boys may have seen her."

There was a knock on the office door, and a small man in uniform walked in and placed a piece of paper in front of Chief Inspector Hall. Picking it up and reading it, he nodded his head and whistled. "Well, we have our answers. The bloody knife in the suitcase matches the blood of Liam White. And the other set of prints on the knife match our Mr. Ian Crossley."

Joe's interest had grown considerably. Ian had now become more than a person of interest. How did Hanna get involved in all of this? "So, just who is this Liam White? Can you tell us any more about him?"

"Let me just say that Monty wouldn't be too pleased about losing Liam. He'll be looking for revenge. Liam was one of his so-called soldiers, and he'd have done anything to protect Monty. And believe me, Monty will feel unprotected now. And it's likely Carl will get blamed for this. Liam was just born wrong. I don't know if he's ever done a decent thing in his life. Monty figured he'd hit the jackpot when he took him under his wing, knowing he'd do whatever was asked of him. And he had a long way to go—he was just twenty-five when he died."

Andrew again stood to open the door, which had been closed by the officer when he left. "One of the biggest problems is that Monty and Carl have always rubbed each other the wrong way, so this won't go down too well. The two of 'em once had it out, right here on our streets, and Monty sliced Carl's cheek open with a blade. He cut him pretty bad. Carl just stood there staring at the sky and screaming at the top of his lungs, didn't even put his hand over the gash to stop the bleeding. They're a couple of mad men, them two. I wouldn't be bothered if someone topped 'em both. And because that had happened here on Carl's turf, it further antagonized the hatred between the gang leaders. And now it seems Liam has been killed here on Best Boys' turf."

"And how about this fellow here?" Joe showed Chief Inspector Hall a photo of the mystery man. "Do you have any idea who he is?"

"I've not seen him before, but I might be able to find out who he is. I will ask around the station and try to get any information I can. How is he connected?"

"We don't know that he is. He's just showed up in a few of the photos from the girl's phone, and we aren't sure if that was just a coincidence." Joe continued, "Speaking of photos, I'd appreciate you sharing any mug shots you might have of Monty, Carl, and Ian. Can you look after that for me? I need to know who I'm looking out for."

"Sure, I'll get Sergeant Thom on that right away. You'll

hear from him soon."

With the business conducted for the time being, they sat for a while longer while Stefan asked the inspector about crime rates. "Is it really so bad here?"

"So far this year, we have had two hundred and twenty-eight crimes here in town centre and three hundred and forty in Claremont. The violence and sex offences numbered ninety-six already in this year. Drug offences were higher."

Seeing the shocked look on Stefan's face, he went on to explain. "This is probably the most depraved seaside town in all of Britain. It wasn't always like this, and following the recession, the town has been trying to reinvent itself. One problem is the decline in visitors coming for holiday. It left a glut of rented accommodation, which then attracted people on low incomes, coming out of prison, or with drug problems. So now one of our biggest issues is discontent and frustration, which leads to anger and a lot of anti-social behaviour."

Stefan responded with a whistle. "I still find that hard to believe, walking by the sea."

"I know it looks lovely now, the sun and the sand and all, but believe me, when the sun goes down, these streets are transformed. All the decent people are home in their beds or hotel rooms, but out here, the rats come out to play. You've heard the expression 'where fist meets face'? Well, it would be a most appropriate expression around here. But you should know," said Andrew, more optimism in his voice, "we're trying to turn that around now. Things will change. Not to mention, we've got the best hot pot restaurants in the country," he added with a cheeky grin.

At this, CI Hall stood up, indicating the visit had come to an end. "Okay, there's now work to do. We will put out the word that we are looking for these two. And I will try to find out who this third person is and get back to you."

Joe thanked the man and stood to take his leave, Stefan following close behind. "Cheers for that. And of course, I am going to be around here looking. I will be in touch if we come up with any new information."

Moving out into the sea air, the two walked towards the Promenade. The day was bright and the breeze was mild. Upon Joe's suggestion, they sat on a bench by the beach, overlooking the street.

"Show me Sally's photos again, to see if anything around here looks familiar."

Stefan took his phone out and opened the photos he had sent to himself from Sally's phone. He handed the phone to Joe. Looking around, he tried to match up pictures on the phone with places within their line of sight.

"Wait a minute," said Joe. "Sally sent me something yesterday." Handing the phone back to Stefan, he took out his phone and read Sally's message again before suggesting they walk further north along the pier. Within a short space of time, Joe was able to identify a pub from the photo, possibly the same pub Sally was referring to. As they neared the building, Joe recognized the overhead sign, which read "The Duke of York." He nodded to Stefan as he crossed the road towards the building.

They entered the modern, brightly lit pub and were met with a smile from one of the employees, who was filling napkin dispensers on the tables. The men walked towards the bar to the beat of Sade singing "Smooth Operator." The music was soft and seemed to come from everywhere. The pub was nearly empty at this early hour, so Joe was pleased that he would have the bartender's full attention. The man looked up and smiled as Joe and Stefan approached.

After ordering a beer, Joe struck up a conversation with the man, who now stood washing a few glasses. He began with a casual, "So, have you seen Ian lately?"

Without looking up, the man replied casually, "There's plenty of Ians about, isn't there?"

Joe smiled casually. "Crossley. My friend Ian Crossley."

"Yeah, saw him a few days ago. Can't say I remember exactly when. Who's asking?"

Stefan showed the man photos of Ian and Hanna. "Was she with him?"

Joe silently groaned at this, having wanted to hold back on the interrogation for as long as possible. A man is more likely to speak with you if he doesn't suspect an ulterior motive.

"So, are you the cops, then?" A scowl appeared on the bartender's face.

Joe exhaled and gave way. He had no way to stop Stefan without making it obvious.

"No, we are not the cops," Stefan continued. "We are not from around here—we just drove in from Sheffield, and my uncle here is helping my family find my sister. She's not called us for a while, and we think she's with Ian."

This seemed to work, for the bartender responded

favourably. "Yeah, he's been here with the girl. I saw them together, I think, last Sunday. No—it was Saturday night. I remember because it was a madhouse that weekend. There were big stag and hen dos . . . two of 'em going on at the same time. That night we had a bunch coming in and out of the pub on their way to the beach. I think these two might have had a run-in with some other guys and left in a hurry."

Joe, realizing Stefan's tactic may not have been so bad, rejoined the questioning. "What about him? Do you know this guy?" He held up a photo of the mystery man, and the bartender leaned forward to have a better look. The man then looked away and said, "No, I don't know who he is. Are you sure you're not the coppers? Aren't you guys tired of kicking this bloke around? I've seen him, but I don't know him and I'm not at liberty to say anything more about him. Good day, gentlemen." And with that, he walked down to the other end of the bar to shelve the glasses he had just washed.

Stefan thanked the man, and then Joe motioned to the door. Leaving their half-finished beers, they walked back out into the street.

"That does it. You watch—this will get back to Ian. And from now on, when people hear us asking, they'll have nothing to say. When they see us coming, they'll run the other way." Joe's tone echoed his frustration. Perhaps in the end, it was he who asked too many questions—or the wrong one, it seemed.

"What happened?" asked Stefan.

"We were too obvious. Like I said, this usually works

better when I do it alone. Two guys look more suspicious." As they moved away from the pub, Joe was uncertain of where to try next. Thinking aloud, he muttered, "I think we need to go to Ian's house. We are done here. His fingerprints being on the knife may change things. Perhaps we can now assume that whatever happened might not have had anything to do with Hanna directly. For all we know, she too could be in an alleyway or in a ditch somewhere."

They started walking back towards Joe's car when, without warning, Stefan sprinted across the road, narrowly escaping the front bumper of a passing car, and started running down a side street. Joe, caught off guard, began to run after him, no time to ask questions. Stefan ran as if he knew where he was going as he darted down a side lane, Joe following close behind.

Chapter 11

After what seemed like endless minutes of running, Stefan suddenly stopped dead, Joe nearly running into the back of him.

"What is it, Stefan? What happened back there?"

"I saw a bloke back there, and he just went into that door—there, into that shop. It looked like that odd fellow in the photos, Joe." Stefan was leaning forward, his hands resting on his knees. His cheeks were red, and he was breathing hard.

"Well done, Stefan. And look at this. You're getting in shape at the same time," Joe playfully remarked. They walked on a bit, then crossed the street, choosing an obscured location where they could wait for the man to come out. Within a few minutes, the man emerged from the shop. It was definitely him—the same man from the photo. The excitement showed in Stefan's face.

"What do we do now, follow him?"

"No," countered Joe, "we go talk to him. And we ask him about Ian."

Stefan looked at Joe beseechingly. "Let me go, Joe. I'll make out like I'm Ian's mate and I'm looking for him. Look at me—I'm younger than you and more casual. You look too . . . I don't know . . . dignified. All official-like, 'specially with the clothes you picked today."

Joe looked down at his pressed trousers and his Harry Rosen loafers. Ignoring his striped shirt and tie, he naively questioned, "What's wrong with my clothes?"

"And your hair. It's too perfect."

Joe touched his hair, saying nothing. Stefan rolled his eyes and, mumbling to Joe to wait where he was, crossed the street, meeting the man head on. Joe had no objections this time.

Crossing the street and approaching the man, Stefan noticed that he was not tall. And while not unattractive, he was somewhat rough looking; his flesh hung limp and soggy, perhaps from lack of exercise. His greasy brown hair was cut in a shag style, reminiscent of an early Rod Stewart look. He wore a thick tin chain around his neck. One of his shoes had a raised sole, indicating that one leg was likely shorter than the other. He wore a threadbare sweater that was too small and faded denim trousers that were too big. He was in every way dishevelled, and he appeared startled upon being approached.

Stefan strolled up casually. He had his hands in his pockets and walked on the right, as if to pass; then with a nod of his head, he spoke to the man, "Hullo there," he called out casually. He then stopped, feigning recognition. "Hey—do I know you? I think I recognize you. Have you seen my friend Ian?"

"Who's asking?" the man remarked.

"I am, mate. I'm a friend of Ian's and a friend of Hanna's."

"Don't know you, and I don't know any Ian or Hanna."

"Are you sure? I thought he was your mate. Hanna has told me so."

The man began backing away as he said, "So then if you know, why are you asking me? I don't know what you want, and I don't know them, okay?"

The man looked scared, like he was about to run. Stefan, not knowing what to do, calmly said, "Thanks anyway. Sorry, I must have you confused with someone else."

Stefan picked up his pace and walked past the man, as though he had a destination and had not approached the man purposely. Without looking back, his eyes panned the area, trying to spot Joe, who was half-hidden behind the alley next to the building. Joe softly whistled to Stefan before grabbing him by the arm and pulling him into the laneway behind the building.

"He said nothing," said a disappointed Stefan.

"Okay, I suspected as much, watching you and him interact. So, he's seen you. Now I'm going to follow him. I'll meet you back at the car in about an hour. Keep your phone on."

Stefan asked, "What should I do?"

"Keep poking around. Maybe show Hanna's photo at some of the shops around this area, but not Ian's at this point. See if perhaps anyone recognizes her, but don't mention him yet. And be casual . . . not too many questions. Maybe stick with the family story."

Joe followed the man along a few streets, making many turns along the way. He tried to memorize the return route, as he hadn't a clue where he was. Joe esti-mated they were now about four blocks from the beach. The man then sharply turned a corner and disappeared into a doorway at the far side of a building. The build-ing was on the end of a narrow street near a small photo shop. The photo sign was still visible above the door, but the windows of the business were papered up, the place unoccupied.

Joe waited a minute before walking around to where the man entered. Inside the dark recessed doorway was a single door. It was likely a staircase that led to a flat on the upper floor. Joe made note of the location and continued walking in the same direction. Turning around and going back the same way might raise suspicion, in the event that anyone was watching his movements. After walking around the entire block, he quickly made his way back to where he had left Stefan.

Joe called Stefan on his cell, and he walked as he spoke. "Sorry, but you need to turn back and meet me. We need to come back here, to that man's flat right away. We must try to talk to him, no matter what. So that means we need to stake him out. Let's meet at the same place where we split up," he said, and then hung up.

As the two men approached one another, Joe noticed that Stefan was walking close to the wall and was looking very cagey as he eyed every passerby and car that drove by. It was an odd spectacle—this tall, lanky boyish young man with his crumpled linen shirt and khaki Bermudas, his pale blonde hair blowing around his face. He peered over his sunglasses in a not-so-subtle fashion. As Joe approached, he asked Stefan, "What are you doing?"

"Stakeout," was his furtive reply.

Joe was amused. "We don't need to look so obvious. Besides, what are you staking out here? We need to watch the door where he entered and wait for him to come out."

"How long will that take?"

"As long as it takes. That's what a stakeout is. We wait."

As they walked back towards the building where the man was last seen, Stefan's demeanour switched as he surveyed the neighbourhood. His expression quickly changed to one of aloofness—something verging on displeasure.

"Okay, now what's wrong with you?" pressed Joe, feeling rather humoured by Stefan's sudden lack of enthusiasm.

They had now reached the intersection, and Joe was examining their surroundings.

"Just how long will this take?"

"You mean the stakeout? Hard to say." Joe was purposefully cryptic in his reply.

"I don't like it around here, and I'm hungry," Stefan lamented in an unapologetic tone.

Joe, without missing a beat, replied with, "No problem, we can eat across the street, at that magnificent-looking kebab place, while keeping an eye on that doorway." He pointed to the building across the street.

Stefan frowned. He seemed to have lost another degree of his enthusiasm. Joe was now laughing. "But you want to be a PI. This is what we do. Besides, I'm good at stakeouts. There's a lady in Sheffield called Mrs.

Rutledge; you can go ask her," he added, instinctively rubbing his ribs.

They entered the Kebab Palace. The windows were covered with what were likely years of grease spatter. The door was filthy, and Joe regretted having to touch the handle to enter. The mirrors at the counter were covered in film, and the barstools had seen better days. Joe felt his shoes stick to the tile floor as he walked across the room to the counter. It seemed like even the grime had grime. But as he approached, he saw that the counters themselves were clean, as was the waiter. Stefan perused the menu while Joe ordered a coffee. Looking around the small interior, Joe suggested they take their order outside to eat at one of the wooden picnic tables that had been set up on the front walkway. Also, Joe had noticed on the walkway next to the tables, there stood an A-frame sandwich board, which would do nicely to partially shield them from the view of their target.

Once settled with his kebab, Stefan began talking to Joe in between bites. "That man Andrew Hall, he's got a good job. He has a lot of power, sits in his nice office and has all of those police at his beck and call. We sit here on a bleeding stakeout, where the chief inspector would just go in and grab the guy. Maybe I should become an inspector? What do you think, Joe? Chief Inspector Stefan Nowak. How does that sound?"

"How about Chief Inspector Stefan No Way?" Joe shot back.

"Well, that's not sounding like a very good attitude, Joe. What happened to positivity?" Stefan retorted. He was clearly enjoying this banter. Things seemed back to how they should be.

Joe chuckled warmly at his eager companion. "It's not that easy for them either, trust me. They could never just grab him—they'd have to wait for permission, for warrants, they have to show just cause . . . they have to answer for all their actions, and there's hell to pay for the poor decisions. They have to account for all their time, so wouldn't be caught sitting here like us. Lucky us, I say."

Joe then directed the conversation to their target. What was his story and how was he connected, if at all? Stefan was wistfully speculating, not really trying to establish the connection, if any.

"He seems older than this Ian guy that we are looking for. And we don't know of any link between them. Perhaps they may even be related. Maybe it was just an odd coincidence that he was in the photos—he could have been a nosy bystander looking in. Or perhaps he's following Ian as well. Do you think he knows something, or do you think he's telling the truth?"

Joe watched Stefan devour the last few bites of his morbidly offensive-looking kebab. He was recently fascinated at what Stefan was prepared to eat. From what Joe remembered, Stefan usually ate decent food. Without warning, Joe sat up and kicked Stefan under the table. "You are in luck," he whispered, as the man finally emerged from the doorway and headed down the street in the direction opposite where they sat. Joe and Stefan hurriedly left the table and began to walk after him, quickening their pace as they neared the corner.

"Stay back," ordered Joe. "Don't let him see you if you can help it."

They caught up with him a short block away. Hearing quickening footsteps behind him, the man turned, a look of fear on his face when he realized this person seemed to be coming after him. Stefan had stayed a few paces behind, trying to remain unseen.

"I just want to talk," Joe uttered slowly as he walked ahead to stand in front of him in a casual, non-threatening manner. When it was safe to do so, Stefan slowly walked up behind the man, unseen. He would position himself in case he might try to run.

Joe attempted a smile as he said to him calmly, "Listen, mate, I really don't want any trouble. But please help me out. This girl Hanna is missing, and her family is worried. I know Ian is your friend because I have photographs of the three of you together. Hanna sent them to her friend, and she gave them to me. I'm not the police. I'm not even from here. I've driven here from Sheffield, where Hanna lives. I'm a friend of her dad."

Aware of someone standing behind him, the man turned to see Stefan. Rather than panic, he seemed to somewhat relax. He may have been calmed by the fact that the younger man had not in any way been threatening during their last interaction, and he was not likely to be mugged by these two.

Joe continued speaking calmly. "My name is Joe, and this here is Stefan. What's your name?"

"Hero," he answered quietly, not making eye contact. "They call me Hero."

"Well, Hero, please be one. We could use a hero about now, couldn't we, Stefan?" he said, without looking away from the man. "So, tell me, do you know my friend Hanna?"

"I might have seen her before," said Hero, shifting from foot to foot. Then he quickly changed his mind. "Maybe it was her, but maybe I'm not sure what she looks like."

"Well, I can show you her picture, but I'm sure I don't need to do that. We need to know where she is, Hero. I promised her father I would find her and see to it that she was safe. Can you help me do that?"

Hero said nothing. Joe then asked, "Can I show you her picture?" To this, Hero shook his head no.

Stefan then made a wide circle around Hero as he repositioned himself beside Joe and asked, "Do you know someone called Liam White?"

Hero closed his eyes and shook his head from side to side in a frenzied manner. "I can't say. I don't know."

Joe knew at that moment that they had lost him. He looked at Stefan and motioned for him to back away. "Here's my card, Hero. Can you please call me if you change your mind? We mean you no harm; we are here as friends. We are just worried about Hanna. Her friend Sally is worried about her as well. I think you can understand that, can't you, Hero? You look like a good man, and we thought you might be able to help."

Reaching over to pat the man on the shoulder, Joe changed his mind and instead placed his card in Hero's trembling hand. Stepping to the side and taking Stefan by the arm, the men backed away a few steps before turning to leave.

"Remember, Hero, you can call me," Joe repeated.

When they were out of earshot, Stefan spoke. "That's it?" he whispered, feeling defeated. "We did the stakeout, and that's all we got?"

"That's all he would give us for now, Stefan. What did you want me to do, take him around back and beat the crap out of him? This way he won't be afraid of us. I'm optimistic he may call."

Stefan managed the smallest of smiles. "So, retreating at this point is a good thing. Earning trust and all. I get it, but it seemed like we were so close. Still, I want to know why he reacted so strongly when I mentioned Liam White."

Joe agreed but mentioned it might not have been a good idea to talk about Liam so soon. "I would have liked to first try to gain a bit of trust before asking more of him. It might not have been important to mention Liam. We were asking about Hanna. We go slowly, Stefan. Sometimes in order to spot a weed, you have to wait for the grass to die."

Chapter 12

The men deliberately walked at a very slow pace back to their car, Joe wanting to give Hero a chance to come after them should he have a change of heart. Sensing that wasn't going to happen, he eventually quickened his pace. They arrived at the car park and got into the car without a word, each man lost in his own thoughts. Joe drove along the coast for a few blocks, happy to be taking in the salty air of the Irish Sea. Eventually, he turned off the Promenade and drove to Grange Park, a council housing estate where Ian lived.

"I believe this is where we left off," he muttered as he pulled into the entrance. "Before we got sidetracked." Joe was taken aback at the size of the estate. Driving the streets, he estimated nearly two thousand dwellings in various sizes of red brick and white stucco exteriors.

As they slowly drove on, they were welcomed by an eerie silence. The streets were quiet and the buildings looked tired. It looked as if everyone had left. Fencing was falling in places, in dire need of repair and a coat of paint. A few of the upper railings were bent; many held makeshift clotheslines, with items that looked like they had been hanging for a long time. An abandoned bicycle lay at the end of one street in an area that looked like it was used as a dump. However, rounding the corner onto the next street, the buildings seemed better tended, with freshly scrubbed brick and brightly painted doors. Many of the flowerbeds were full of blooms.

Finding the block corresponding to the address he had written down, Joe drove slowly past Ian's house before parking a short distance away. Stefan stayed in the car while Joe walked around the block to have a look at the back. Coming around the other side, he then knocked on the door. After a few minutes, he knocked again. Nothing. The curtains were drawn, making it difficult to tell if anyone was inside. Turning, he headed back to the car. Joe started to say something but changed his mind. He started the engine and proceeded slowly around the same block, unsure of what he was looking for.

Coming back to Ian's place, Joe pulled over, slammed the car into park, and, with the engine still running, got out of the car. He walked to the front, vaulted up two steps at a time, and knocked again, harder. This time he left his card crammed into the doorframe. He did the same for the two units on either side. He then walked back to the car and shook his head at Stefan. Turning the car around, the two men headed back to Sheffield. Stefan was looking at Joe, who seemed to be wearing a similar look of dismay on his face. He rolled the window down for some air, turned up the radio and sat back for the ride home as Freddie Mercury belted out "The Show Must Go On."

They were nearly in Preston before Joe spoke. "I will

need to speak with Sally again. Also, I wonder, did Hanna have a computer? And if so, did the police take it? I will need to ask Sally that as well. I believe it was a big deal that we found that man called Hero. I feel good about the contact. But did I do enough here today?"

The rest of the journey consisted of insignificant chit-chat until Joe dropped Stefan off near his home.

It was still light outside. Joe sat alone, absorbed in reflective contemplation in the quiet of his office. He was waiting for Aisha to finish work, as they had plans for a meal with friends. It had been a long day, and at this point he felt quite unenergetic. As he sat waiting, his eyes panned his office. He looked at his old green banker's lamp and, leaning forward, ran a finger over the dust collecting on the shade. He had books on the shelves that he'd never once referred to. The walls of his office remained pictureless even after all these years. The large window was covered with a dusty film and had never closed properly. The view was further obscured by years of ivy growth on the outside. This place was worn out like an old shoe. Worn out perhaps like his old ideas. He had made such progress in other areas of his life. Selling his house had been good for him on so many levels. And Aisha had rescued his disheartened, cynical spirit.

Perhaps his career needed revitalizing as well. Maybe, just maybe, Stefan was right. At least this had given him some food for thought. It could be a good idea to start fresh. Perhaps it was the right time for a productive, modern workplace with modern technology and clean windows. Speaking of windows, when was the last time he had tried to open it? Or even the blinds, for that matter? They had remained in that half-open position for as long as he could remember.

Stefan had always grimaced in horror at the outdated computer systems at ARD Investigations. His theory was that new smart technology combined with large whiteboards and modern workspaces would induce creativity and better thinking. He must have learned that at school. Joe leaned back in his squeaky black leather chair with thoughtful deliberation. Did a new office necessarily mean a partnership? He might not be ready to make such a bold move, but he would nonetheless give Stefan's plan some thought. Still, the thought of giving up the freedom of working alone did not appeal to him.

He heard the door open and shut, and he felt his heart swell as Aisha's radiant face peered around the corner; her mouth twisted into a comical grin. She laughed.

Aisha Hunt was born and raised in Luxembourg, amongst an affluent and musical family. But she had dreams of her own, and so her career as a social worker had brought her to Sheffield, where she had settled and married. Joe had met her while tracing Rita Nowak's movements in his attempt to solve the mystery of her death. Theirs was a chance meeting, as Aisha ran a homeless shelter for women where Rita had stayed during her pregnancy before she again disappeared.

At the time that they met, Aisha was still recovering from trauma of her own, having lost her husband and only child in a fiery crash while on their way to pick her up from work. Although it had happened many years before, she had clearly still been in mourning. The moment Joe laid eyes on her, he had been quite taken with the compassionate and beautiful woman. Over the ensuing months, their friendship had grown. Then gradually as they got to know each other, it began to blossom into much more. It was the easiest thing he had ever done, falling in love with her.

Looking at her now, standing in the doorway, he still could not believe his good fortune that she had quite easily fallen in love with him as well.

"Come on, you. Why are you still sitting there? Let's go," she whispered as she walked over to where he sat and kissed him gently.

Chapter 13

Joe absolutely loved mornings. As much as he often found it hard to get out of bed, it was his favourite time of day. Today, he was awakened by the sound of the wood pigeons, which were unusually vocal at this early hour. It was at this time of day that his brain seemed the most active—absorbed in thoughtful contemplation over the days before and planning his strategies for the day ahead. If only he could find a clue—any clue. Certainly, Hanna hadn't vanished off the face of the earth. He needed to find out as much as he could about Ian, and quickly.

The sun was slowly creeping into the room, and Aisha was curled up in his arms breathing deeply. He kissed her on the cheek, then quietly rose to make coffee. He was looking forward to spending the morning at home with Aisha, as often the demands of her work took her away at an early hour. Joe knew firsthand how seriously she took her job, having watched her during his investigation. She was competent and loved what she did, and her work was having a positive impact with abused, homeless, and unwed young women.

At the time they had met, Aisha was, without distraction, completely absorbed in her work. Joe discovered later that it was mostly to keep occupied as she was recovering from her personal loss. She had found solace at the shelter; it helped her to no end to be helping others. Gradually, as she recovered from her own grief, her work took on a new meaning as she grew attached to these young women, and through the process, it helped her as well as her clients.

He padded to the kitchen and set about preparing the coffee. Once the aroma hit his nostrils, he was completely awake. He soon returned to their room, carrying two steaming mugs of the fresh brew. Aisha was now sitting, propped up by her big fluffy pillows. With a smile, Joe handed her a coffee and sat beside her, leaning up against the pillow she had prepared for him. Together, they talked about Sally and Hanna, and about Stefan.

Sipping her coffee, Aisha looked at Joe and asked, "So, what is it like there, in Blackpool? Would I enjoy it?" A strand of raven hair fell across her face, and she absentmindedly tucked it behind her ear.

"Well, it's certainly not Southwold, or Tynemouth. I can't say that it would appeal to you very much. It's not at all as I remember, but if I'm honest, I don't think it was very appealing even when it was better." He added soberly, "It seems as though life has not been very kind to Blackpool."

Joe moved a little closer to Aisha and nudged her playfully. "Oh, and by the way," he said, "Stefan thinks we should move in together."

"But we already have done," Aisha replied, a confused look on her face.

"Yes, we have," Joe answered with a big smile. "But he doesn't know yet. I've not told him."

Aisha laughed. "You do like having a go at him, don't you?"

Joe was smiling. "But I will tell him soon. We need to speak more about this business plan of his. I was thinking I would see him next week some time," he answered decisively. "I need to put some serious thought into the idea of doing things differently. I might actually call him today to set it up."

"If you were to ask me, I would say it's a very good idea," Aisha offered as she rose to take the cups away. "As long as he isn't in too much of a hurry. I know you, Joe. You won't want to make any big decisions over night." She left the room, still talking. "I'll be right back, and we can discuss it. Perhaps we can discuss other things as well, if you know what I mean."

It hadn't been an easy decision for them to move in together. It was something neither had taken lightly. Joe had been on his own for many years following his divorce from Janet. They had parted on relatively good terms and remained friends, mostly because of their daughter, whose well-being had always been their biggest and most significant focus.

Aisha, on the other hand, had lost her husband and young child in an untimely crash—a sudden explosion that changed her life in a split second. She'd had no control over the accident and had no time to prepare herself. She felt unsafe in her own body and had learned well how to hide from herself through her work. As a result, she was terrified of falling in love again. It didn't help, Joe being in this line of work. She feared for his safety constantly. Somehow, together, they had helped her get over her feelings of separation, and she felt ready to move on.

By mid-afternoon, Joe had taken the time to call Stefan, and as expected, the call was well received. The conversation was brief, and the two arranged to meet on Wednesday at Nonna's. This would be Joe's first time back there since Simon's arrest. He shook off the memories and busied himself with something else.

Joe was already seated and waiting with a coffee when Stefan arrived. He was visibly excited as he entered the restaurant with a big smile. Joe had to hand it to the kid—because he still seemed like a kid in so many ways—he was forever upbeat and unflappable. He was like that toy, the roly-poly man, or whatever it was called. Try as you might to lay it down, it always bounced back up. Or as his dad always used to say to him, *"Remember, son, cork always floats to the top."* Following a positive discussion, Stefan seemed almost unable to control his enthusiasm. Joe calmed him down.

"Don't make me change my mind. And please remember, we are still only exploring this idea. I am absolutely making no promises."

"Thank you, Joe. It's all I ask. You need to think about it, I understand that." Stefan tried to contain his grin. He agreed that over the next few months, they would slowly begin their search for appropriate business locations, Stefan saying he'd be happy to put in extra time looking since he had very little to do when not helping Joe with his case. Joe, on the other hand, had oddly become busier now that he had begun thinking about uprooting. He needed first and foremost to spend time working with Stefan to see what his gut told him. He would aim his attention on the idea of a move before speaking with his colleagues and employer at ARD.

The men parted, agreeing to meet periodically over the course of the month to go over their next plan of action. In the meantime, the heavy focus would be in trying to locate Hanna. Joe remained hopeful that this Hero fellow might call him.

By the following morning, Stefan was feeling more sober minded, the effects of Joe's positive response having worn off. He would make all attempts to appear calm once he arrived at Joe's office. As he approached the corner heading towards the building, he spied Sally on the other side of the street, who seemed to be headed in the same direction. He waited while she crossed the road and looked at her with his sheepish grin as she approached. While trying to look cross, Sally found herself succumbing to Stefan. Much to her irritation, she had to admit that this man was very charming. As soon as he had begun to explain, she found herself forgiving his deceit.

"I want to apologize again and again. You see, it wasn't a true lie; it was just a premature announcement and I had perhaps been a bit overconfident. But what it boils down to is that I really had meant to help you." He didn't smile as he spoke with obvious sincerity. "Honest, Sally. Cross my heart."

Sally touched his arm lightly and responded by saying only, "All is forgiven."

They carried on down the street together, walking closely side by side as Stefan updated Sally on the newest information.

"There's been a murder, Sally. Did Joe tell you already?"

Sally nodded. "It's why I'm on my way there. I want to hear more."

"It was the same night that Hanna was last seen. Did Joe also tell you that the other fingerprints on the knife match Hanna's friend Ian? And Sally, did Joe tell you that the blood from the bloke matches the blood on the knife that was in Hanna's suitcase?"

Stefan talked the rest of the way to Joe's office, Sally listening intently to all he said, even though she had already heard it.

Chapter 14

Despite her inner dread, Sally was trying hard to get on with her life. Driving home from the Parrott farm following a meal with her parents, she felt no less troubled. She had hoped the distraction would give her brain a rest. She had purposely not given her mum and dad any updates about Hanna. Firstly, because there really were no updates available. At least, there were no updates that pertained to Hanna directly, so she felt they really didn't need to know about the bloody knife at this point. But mostly, Sally held back the information because she was worried her parents would want her to move back home. Her mother had already made rumblings about just that. So, Sally feigned calm and discussed the issue in an off-handed fashion, deliberately trying to downplay it.

"It's likely she's still with her boyfriend and feels guilty about it, so she's not saying anything. She knows if she calls, she'll get a lecture from her father. He's very strict and would be furious." Sally sat folding a basketful of laundry, which brought back memories of when she still lived at home. On laundry days, she would fold the large bundle of warm, dryer-scented clothing as her mum cleared away the dinner dishes. Her dad would sit across the room, watching her deftly smooth the clothing as he listened to the news. Seeing the basket across the room, she had instinctively picked it up and had begun folding.

"But would she do that to her parents? Her mother is worried sick." Sally's mum, Olivia, also looked worried as she came out of the kitchen to join them. "We mothers do worry; we think you girls were safer when you were living at home."

Finishing with the last towel, Sally had taken this as the best opportunity to leave. Her father, George, upon seeing Sally stand so abruptly, looked at his wife and said, "Olivia, you've got to leave our Sally alone. She's not done anything to give us concern. These girls need to move on. They can't live at home forever."

Sally had smiled and winked at her dad and mouthed a thank-you. She wasted no time in gathering her things and leaving.

As she neared her home, the sound of her mobile phone caught her off guard. She picked it up, fumbling, unable to look at the number while driving. "Hello?" she said, her heartbeat elevated. The line was quiet—nobody was there. "Hello?" she said again. Still quiet, she moved to hang up, but then, she heard it. Faintly, but it was definitely Hanna whispering.

"Sally, it's me."

Sally cried out, "Hanna! Is that really you? Where are you? Are you hurt?" She struggled to hold control of her car until she could find a spot to pull over.

"I'm here, Sal. It's me. I'm scared."

"Where are you? I'm so happy you are alive. I was so

worried. That knife we found in your suitcase, why did you have it? The cops are looking for the murderer. Why don't you come home and we can talk about it?"

Hanna said quietly, "No. No, Sal, I can't." Her voice was alive with terror.

"What are you talking about? Of course you can." Sally was now desperate, and she began pleading with her friend. "Talk to me, Hanna. What is wrong with you? Don't be afraid, they have found the body, and now they will find the murderer. You'll be safe here."

Hanna started to cry. "I can't come home, Sally. I can't . . . because I did it. I am the murderer."

"What are you saying?" she was trying to drive, in spite of what she was hearing. Sally heard murmuring in the background, two voices, and then the line went dead. Looking down at her phone, she read the display: "Number Unavailable." By this time, Sally had managed to pull over, although the location was not ideal. Even still, she sat for a moment, trembling, her foot pressing firmly on the brake. Minutes ticked by before she stepped on the clutch, put the car in gear, and hurried home.

As soon as Sally arrived at her flat, she called Joe and told him about the strange conversation.

Joe hung up the phone and continued walking in silence. *To call this a mystery is an understatement. This is downright insane,* he thought to himself. There were many reasons why Hanna would call herself a murderer: number one being she was in fact the murderer and she did stab Liam.

Or she was trying to protect someone. Or someone was forcing her to call and say she murdered Liam. But none of these things actually made her a murderer. Could it have been self-defence? Could she have been framed? What was her connection to this Liam person? What the hell had happened that night? Joe was not convinced that Hanna was telling the truth. The second he got back to the office, he would call Chief Inspector Hall and share this latest development.

"Was that an important call then?" Joe's train of thought was broken by the sound of the voice beside him.

"That was Sally. She will call me back in half an hour. She said she's just received a call from Hanna." He was talking to Stefan, who was walking by his side. The two had just emerged from a building that, so far, looked to be the best match for what they needed. They would have easy access to head out in any direction, and it had the potential for good exposure to their new business. It had just the right look and feel, and the location was superb. The building would not become available for another six months, so there was time to make a decision either way.

Upon hearing this news, Stefan was encouraged. "So she's alive. But where the bloody hell is she?"

"Well, it wasn't exactly good news. Hanna's just called herself a murderer." Joe was absentmindedly scratching his stubble. "I just don't understand any of it."

Stefan was gripped with a feeling of utter helplessness. If his goal was to be a good private eye, he felt he needed to be doing more. He spoke openly to Joe as they walked, announcing that he wanted to return to Blackpool.

"I know this is your case, Joe, and I know I'm not officially working yet. But let me keep hanging around, like I did for Rita's case. You said you were getting busier—so I can be extra eyes and an extra mind. And, I might add, a younger and sharper mind." There was Stefan's smile, big and bold. Stefan was no longer walking beside him but a few steps ahead, and he turned to face Joe, walking backwards. Joe rolled his eyes and tried hard not to smile. "I want to be more involved than just following you around."

"But you have been with me almost every day, Stefan. Your presence has not gone unnoticed. Actually, you're beginning to get on my nerves."

"Joe, I want to go back to Blackpool," Stefan announced, disregarding Joe's comment. "But this time, I want to take the train."

"Whatever for?" was Joe's quick response. The suggestion took him by surprise, and he could almost feel his jaw drop.

"I think I would like to track Hanna's route, maybe see where the train stops along the way. I want to know what's between here and there. And, just maybe I could find a clue somewhere."

"But we don't know if she was on the train, do we?"

"But we don't really know for sure that she wasn't. What if she managed to slip on somewhere? Maybe she even disguised herself? Maybe she's somewhere at a train station now. It won't hurt. I just feel I could be doing something while we wait for answers to come to us, and right now, you haven't the extra time. It could be part of my gaining experience."

Joe couldn't argue that point. He walked with his head down, his hands buried deep in his pockets. As they arrived back at ARD, Joe's phone rang. It was Sally again, asking what he was planning to do next. Joe put her on speakerphone for Stefan's benefit and proceeded to inform her of Stefan's plan to go by train.

"Stefan, are you there? Can you hear me? When would you go?" she asked aloud to both men.

"If I can get a ticket straight away, I'd like to go within the next few days. Or even tomorrow."

Sally's reaction was immediate. "May I please go with you? Please? I won't get in the way. I feel like I need to do something to help. I'm glad Hanna is alive, but she clearly needs help. I wish we knew where she was. There must be a way to find her, Stefan, and going might help me to remember something she had said."

Joe glanced at Stefan, who had nodded in agreement. Then he said aloud to Sally, "Stefan says yes, you can go along with him. I don't know what you hope to find, but it will get you out of my hair for a day. But don't count me in, as I have work to do here. I also need to speak with police, and of course, I need to meet with Hanna's parents again."

Stefan arranged to call Sally as soon as he was able to get two tickets for the train. It felt very good to be given the go-ahead to do this, and he hoped he had a chance to make some real progress this time.

Chapter 15

Two days later, tickets in hand, Stefan and Sally arrived at the station. Stefan had suggested coming early to get familiarized and get to where they needed to be. They arrived at their gate just in time to board the train, which they did like true tenderfoots. Sally followed behind Stefan, a bit nervous about making this trip with him, although eager to do so in the hopes of finding her friend. She moved aside to sit beside Stefan, then abruptly changed her mind and, in a swift undetectable motion, sat across from him instead, face-to-face, knees about a foot apart. Stefan watched her curiously. She was on her phone, head down, both thumbs clicking away. This sort of behaviour had long baffled him. What could be so urgent, particularly when you're sitting face-to-face with someone who would be perfectly happy to take part in conversation?

He watched her slender fingers as they brushed the keys. He watched the flex of her delicate wrists. He then studied the bone structure of her knees, just visible under her pale-blue printed dress. His gaze gradually progressed upwards, past the yellow cardigan and to her face. It was a funny little face. Her eyes were very large, her chin slight and delicate, and her cheekbones well defined beneath a plumpish face. Although not a redhead, her face was liberally peppered with freckles. Stefan wondered if, were he to join the dots, would he be able to create some sort of picture?

They spent the first part of the ride watching the scenery. Once out of the city, the train proceeded along the TransPennine Express route through Hathersage and Buxworth and on to Manchester. This was Sally's first time on a train, although she chose not to disclose that information. She felt herself melt into the fabric and yield to the gentle swaying motion. As the train picked up speed, she felt a rush of excitement.

She and Stefan remained silent for much of this stretch of track. The train whizzed past the small villages, the lush green landscapes moving slowly in the distance. The air hung heavy as it did every summer, and Stefan was grateful for the breeze from the partially open windows.

When the train arrived in Manchester Piccadilly, both Sally and Stefan were happy to get out of their seats and have a much-needed stretch. They were caught unaware, as the second they exited the train, they were jolted from their tranquility and transported into a burst of lively commotion. The station was rife with activity: overhead signs changing, whistles blowing, announcements over the PA, people running in different directions to catch their trains. They had experienced something entirely different in Sheffield at the smaller, more tranquil station and the relaxing first half of the journey.

Leaving the platform, they followed the signs and

made their way through an endless sea of bodies scurrying in all different directions. Sally walked in front, as instructed by Stefan, so that he may keep sight of her. Soon they arrived at Platform 14, where they grabbed two bottles of water and some crisps before boarding the next train. They were now on the Northern Line, which would take them to Preston, then on to Blackpool. All in all, the journey was just shy of two and a half hours, leaving plenty of time for something to happen to Hanna, thought Stefan. He was holding on to the notion that Hanna had somehow managed to slip on to the train, unseen by CCTV, but that maybe something happened to her along the route. Could she have disembarked in Manchester? Was someone after her and she was forced to flee the train without her suitcase? Maybe he should talk to Joe about checking CCTV in Manchester.

Sally broke his thought process. "I've never been on a train before," she suddenly admitted, hoping to draw some conversation from the pensive-looking man seated across from her. He smiled, unsure how to respond. After all, it was she who had her face buried in her phone for the first leg of the journey. Sally was looking at him. "Are you quiet because you didn't want me to be here with you?" she then asked.

Stefan sat up, his face full of contrariety. "No, not at all! I'm quite happy to have you here. I'm sorry, it seemed as though you were busy. Anyhow, I was just thinking about Hanna. Do you suppose she could have somehow got on the train, then got off back there in Manchester?"

Sally thought about it, and then shook her head. "I'm

sure Hanna would have said so when she called me. I think she was saying she was still there, in Blackpool. Maybe she is still with Ian. I wish she had said more!"

Stefan let out a big sigh. "I don't know, Sally. This whole thing seems hopeless. Have you counted all the stops? It would be impossible to find anything here. Especially when I don't know what I'm looking for."

As the train rolled to a stop at the Blackpool North depot, they queued to make their exit. Numb from inactivity, they were glad to be walking again, even though the line was moving very slowly. As they stiffly moved along the platform towards the signs showing the way out, Stefan turned to Sally. "So, if you're okay, perhaps we should walk to the Nickelodeon area, or whatever it's called. To where Ian supposedly had this friend who would give your friend free rides."

Sally nodded in agreement, by now feeling more comfortable being here with Stefan. She was actually glad she had come, now that the train ride was over. As they moved out into the street, Sally inhaled this entirely foreign environment, with its strange buildings and winding streets. The scenery soon changed from tall buildings and vehicles to open sky, seagulls, and surf. She tried hard to look alert, as she wanted to feel she was playing an active role in the search for her friend, however small it was.

As they made their way to the Promenade area, they were again distracted by the bustle in the street and noise of the traffic. This was a far cry from Greystone's and Ringinglow. They both looked around, necks craned, eyes as big as saucers as they approached the waterfront. The sandy beach stretched for miles and, with the tide out, seemed to push halfway into the ocean. Today the beach was littered with bodies: walking, sunning, playing, and swimming. The sky was full of seagulls gliding and hovering like kites on the wind. An excited Sally grabbed Stefan's sleeve as she pointed to the Ferris wheel that sat on the pier, jutting out into the sea. Her words were carried on the wind and lost in the sound of the surf and seagulls.

After some initial confusion, they decided to walk from North Pier, past the Blackpool Tower, and on to Central Pier. They crossed the road and followed the arrows to Bonny Street Market, for which Sally had seen a sign and had given Stefan a beseeching look. Stefan kept a keen eye on everyone as Sally poked around a bit, peering into shops long enough to have a glimpse of trappings ranging from small crystal replicas of the tower, assorted postcards, retractable plastic daggers, to fancy ladies' scarves. They made their way back to the Promenade, and before they knew it, they had arrived at Central Pier.

"I wonder if this is the right place," asked Stefan. "Does it seem like it's more for kids?"

Sally agreed. "I see that Ferris wheel there, but Hanna had mentioned a massive roller coaster." She wore a huge grin. "I can see how she found this place exciting. It's brilliant!"

Looking further down the coast, they noticed in the distance another amusement park area with what appeared to be a very big roller coaster. Asking a pass-erby, they were told that was the bigger, more popular amusement park, and they could likely walk there in about fifteen minutes. Stefan looked at Sally and nodded; she nodded back, so off they set. They walked past a huge sandcastle waterpark before arriving at Pleasure Beach Amusement Park. The entrance was easy to spot, even from a distance, with its large white arch and looming roller coaster. Stefan suggested they buy tickets for the fun fair, as this was likely where Hanna had her free rides.

Entering, they were unsure which way to go, so they randomly walked straight on towards the Big One roller coaster. When Stefan looked up to watch the activity to the left, he spotted a man operating one of the rides. He wasn't facing them, but Stefan knew right away who it was. The man was wearing a Blackpool FC soccer jersey—different clothing but definitely the same person.

"See that man there? I've met him, his name is Hero," he said to Sally, his voice filled with spirited enthusiasm. "He's the third man in all the photographs. Do you recognize him?"

Sally looked at the man and nodded. "I-I think so. It does look like him."

"But he refused to say anything to Joe and me when we questioned him." Stefan stopped walking. "He can't see me again, Sally. He might run. Joe says backing off him is the best way to make him come around."

Sally said, "So, are you thinking this guy must be the friend who gave Hanna rides? Okay, we won't let him see you, but please let me give it a try. He might have heard of me."

Without waiting for Stefan to answer, she walked right up to Hero and began speaking to him. "You have a good job then, don't you? Do you ride yourself after work?" She smiled shyly.

Hero looked around to make sure Sally was in fact speaking to him.

"Yeah, it's all right," he said. "Good job, but I don't ride."

"I've never been here before. I heard it's not really a safe place, Blackpool, so I didn't want to come. But it seems okay to me."

"Well, all you tourists see is cotton candy and soft ice cream. But I live here, so it's not special to me. It's all right and that's all. There are people who say these streets can be mean, but I think it's only if you go in the wrong places."

"Well, I think my friend might have gone in one of these wrong places. Do you know my friend? Her name is Hanna, and I think you might have met her. I believe she's with someone else you know, named Ian."

Hero looked at her suspiciously before asking, "Are you with the Fylde Snakes?"

Sally raised her chin and answered him emphatically, "No, I don't even know who that is. I'm not from here, like I said. I came here from Sheffield to find my friend. Hanna." She paused, uncertain whether Hero believed her. "I'm Sally, her flatmate. You might have heard of me."

Hero shrugged his shoulders and bit his lower lip. "Then you must be with them two blokes that was here a few days ago. I don't know anything. And I'm not stupid.

You shouldn't talk to me like I'm stupid, and besides, it's like I told them other men, I don't have to talk to you."

"I'm not with those two men. I'm here alone," she stuttered nervously, unsure what to do but realizing she was making a mess of it.

Stefan, seeing that Sally had managed a conversation, slowly began walking up behind them, but before he could cross the walkway, he realized that Hero was looking his way. Again, he had acted too quickly.

"Wait right here for a minute," Hero said to Sally before disappearing behind a building. Sally waited reluctantly but soon realized he wasn't coming back. Having reached the same conclusion, Stefan loped over to her and said, "Shit!" The two ran in the direction Hero went, but it was very clear that he was gone.

Sally turned to Stefan and screwed up her nose. "You're not very good at this, are you?"

Stefan looked at her with a twinkle in his eye and said, "Give over, we're trying. Learning a bit every time. It's called trial by error. They taught us that, you know. The real problem would be if I tried the same thing each time and hoped for different results. That, they said, would be called stupidity."

Sally smiled and said, "I don't mean it. After all, it was me who likely said too much."

"You were doing fine until he saw me coming. You are right—I'm not very good at this. I should have waited longer."

As they walked away, past alleyways littered with broken furniture, they didn't notice Hero, who was peering at them from his hiding spot above. He was watching intently as Sally left with Stefan, and he watched them as they walked together towards the water. He watched until he could no longer see them.

Chapter 16

Directed by Sally, the pair began making their way towards the water. She motioned to the stairs that led down to the beach. "Tide's out!" she shouted over the noise.

"Where are you going?" Stefan called out to her as she ran down the stairs and onto the sand.

Sally turned her head sideways and called to him, her eyes sparkling. "Come on, Stefan. Let's have some fun." Taking off her sandals, she ran into the warm sand and towards the gently lapping water. "The tide is going out further, look," she said, by now barely audible.

Stefan could only smile. It was exactly what he had said to Joe only a few days ago at the zoo. Far be it for him to now appear stodgy, as Joe had.

"I'm coming," he called as he hurried after her, stumbling as he tried to unlace his shoes. He felt a bit embarrassed by his lack of coordination.

"Why do you look so uptight?" asked Sally as he at last caught up to her.

"Well, remember when you said it was your first time on a train? Last week with Joe was my first time seeing the ocean. And today is my first time on a beach."

"You should have said so right away! So come on, take off your shoes then," ordered Sally, "and let the sand and water squish between your toes." He obediently did as she said.

"It's actually not the ocean but the Irish Sea. Still, there's something very romantic about being by the water," she said, then quickly blushed. "Oh, I'm sorry. I didn't mean . . ."

Stefan shook his head. "I know. It's okay."

After a moment of walking in silence, Sally continued, "I haven't been here for years. My parents brought me once, with Joe and his family. It was for the Illuminations."

"What's that?" asked Stefan.

Sally explained, "It's a light festival they have every year. It's huge! People come from all over. They put lights on everything, from the street cables, trees, lampposts, and signs to the boats and the buildings. Even on all the wires that cross the streets. About six miles of lights that shine from September to November. I think it's their way of refusing to give up summer. The entire area is lit up like a Christmas tree. And there's music, and partying! We were here for Switch On. That's the first day, when a pop band or a movie star comes to turn on the switch that lights everything up."

They stood facing the land as the breeze blew from behind, pushing their hair into their faces. Sally brushed her hair back from her eyes, then turned to face Stefan. Speaking loudly enough to be heard but not to be overheard, Sally asked what would happen now that they hadn't been successful in speaking to Hero.

Stefan could only shrug his shoulders. "We'll have to come up with something else. Joe still wants to try to find Ian. Maybe we'll try the zoo again. I really need to hang about and take my time speaking to more people. Someone must know something."

"What if you don't find anything? I mean, what if we never find her or know what happened?"

"Well, there's always a chance of just one lucky break-through. One small clue—an off-chance revelation or something. It's like I once said to Joe: even a blind squirrel finds the occasional nut."

Sally giggled, and she looked up at him. He led her back to the street. They sat on one of the huge concrete steps to dry their feet before putting on their shoes. Walking back up towards the Promenade, Sally pointed to something in the distance. A huge, mirrored ball stood high above the crowd in all its reflective glory. "Look, Stefan. There's your crystal ball. Why don't you look into it and solve this thing?"

He jammed his hands into his pockets and said nothing as he shook back his already tousled wheat-white hair, which was partially covering his eyes.

Sally and Stefan shared a hot dog and a bag of crisps before agreeing it was time to go home. They walked slowly back to the train station, feeling drained of energy from all the walking and the sun. Stefan felt very reluctant to be leaving and, for a moment, regretted bringing Sally. For no other reason than if he was alone, he would spend a lot more time searching every dirty, littered alleyway and every pub on the Promenade. He would have stayed at Pleasure Beach, hidden, and waited for Hero to return. He sighed as they lined up to get on the train.

This time, as they found their seats, Sally waited for Stefan to sit and promptly sat beside him. "Thanks for bringing me. I know we didn't get off to a very good start, but today was real nice." Sally's words hung in the air. Stefan also thought the day was very nice, but he wondered if it was the same sort of nice for both of them.

As the train pulled out of the station, Stefan finally replied, "You made me feel like a kid today. I know I'm only twenty-four, but I mean like a little kid. I lost my youth somehow, and I don't remember quite when. I lost Rita when I was young, and in part my childhood left with her. My family was all over the place in terms of mental state. I think I grew up with humiliation, so I grew up fast and left home as soon as I could." He then smiled his trademark smile. "But then I met Joe. And I found out about Aidan, and I met Susan and Nigel. I now have a new life, but a grown-up life. But today, I felt like a boy again."

"You must feel sad sometimes. Do you miss them? Your family, I mean. Do you miss Rita?"

Stefan shook his head. "No, we can't grieve, Sally. That was a long time ago. I did grieve, but I can't grieve for that long. That's not why we are here. We need to struggle, then survive, and then find ways to be happy again. That's what it means to be alive. I want to be happy for those that aren't here to be happy for themselves; otherwise it'd be a waste. I don't want to go through life with a calloused heart."

Sally left Stefan to his quiet thoughts. She leaned her head back and closed her eyes. She felt dusty and damp after being on the beach. Although they had accomplished nothing, she felt okay.

The train arrived back in Sheffield around six in the evening. It had been a long day, and Stefan noticed that Sally looked extremely tired.

"Let me drive you home, Sally. I know today took a lot out of us."

Sally gratefully accepted, and Stefan led her towards the car park. On the drive home, Sally sat with her head leaning back on the headrest, her face turned towards the window. Neither of them spoke, although Stefan frequently glanced at her. He couldn't tell if she was asleep or awake. The streets were quiet by the time Stefan pulled up to her door. With the engine still running, mostly due to lack of parking, Sally jumped out of the car and said good-bye. With a smile and a wave, she quickly ran up the steps and soon disappeared behind her door.

Chapter 17

Stefan had been in a deep sleep when his phone rang. It initially sounded like an alarm in a dream, causing him to wake with a jerk. It was Sally on the phone, whispering, "Are you awake?"

He answered, "Why do people always say that? Of course I'm awake. I answered the phone, didn't I? And I'm awake because you phoned me, right? At . . . let's see . . . at around twelve thirty at night, I might add."

"I'm so sorry, Stefan, but someone's outside my flat. It's been happening for about half an hour. I saw the shadow, and twice I've heard someone trying to open the door. Can you please come over?"

"Now? Don't you have anyone you can call?"

"Yes, I do. And I'm calling him." There was an edgy sarcasm to her voice. Then softening, she added, "I can't call my dad. Besides, Hanna is usually here, so I'm scared now, being alone."

Thinking this could have been his sister, Stefan re-evaluated his reaction to Sally's situation. He would like to think that someone would have gone over to help Rita as well.

"I'll be right there, Sally. Hang tight and don't go

near the door or windows." Stefan walked across the room, blinking away the sleepiness. Dressing quickly, he grabbed his keys and headed out the door.

Stefan arrived as quickly as he could and found parking easily, likely due to the late hour. He quietly walked up the steps to the front door, looking around and behind him as he did. Sally must have been watching out the window, because the second he tapped and whispered her name, he heard the latch click.

The small room was dim, lit only by the streetlights. There was a faint smell in the air of something dainty and feminine, like lavender or vanilla, he wasn't sure. Sally ushered him to the sofa and motioned for him to sit before she left the room. He remained standing; still quite groggy and amazed he had managed to drive here while feeling so out of it.

Sally reappeared carrying a blanket and a pillow, which she placed on the sofa. She mouthed a thank-you and disappeared into her room. Stefan looked at the couch, which had been opened into a small bed. He had not intended to spend the night, he thought he was only here to check that Sally was safe. With some reluctance, he lay on the sofa fully clothed, using only the pillow. He lay awake for what felt like hours, his eyes taking in his surroundings, using what little light the outside streetlamp afforded. All was quiet but for the hum of an appliance. A thought had occurred to him. Why did Sally think it would be impossible for him to be romantic on the beach or anywhere else? While aware of the fact that he'd never had any sort of relationship before, he didn't realize that maybe it was obvious. Did he look unromantic, or worse yet—did he look unattractive? He fell asleep thinking about that.

After a few hours of deep sleep, Stefan slowly woke, for a minute forgetting where he was. He estimated it was around five in the morning, as dawn was just breaking. He quietly stood up, smoothing his ruffled clothes and finger-combing his hair. Placing the pillow and blanket on a nearby chair, he tiptoed out of the flat. Assuming Sally was still sleeping, he took care not to make a noise. It took him three or four minutes to shut the front door in his effort to prevent the latch from clicking in place too loudly.

Arriving home very tired, he called Joe and filled him in on their trip. He withdrew his earlier theory about Manchester—or any other train stop for that matter—realizing it would be nearly impossible to find anything out, due to the size of the stations and the sheer volume of people.

That same afternoon, after a few more hours of sleep, Stefan headed to Joe's office. He found Joe seated at his desk. Joe motioned for Stefan to sit down as he covered the receiver with one hand and whispered that he was trying to reach Chief Inspector Hall in Blackpool. "He's not available, so I'm waiting to speak to a Sergeant Michael Thom."

Once the sergeant was on the phone, Joe asked if he would mind being put on speakerphone. Sergeant Thom agreed, so Joe settled into his chair and hit the speaker button. After introductions, Joe asked if they had found any new information on Ian, or even Hero for that matter. Joe was curious to know who exactly this Hero person was.

"Yes," answered the sergeant. "I have updates here. Up until now, we have not seen any trace of Ian. Dodgy bloke, he is. We've searched everywhere, and we are currently working on a warrant to enter his home. He's not been seen around since last Saturday, and he's not answering his door. He seems to have vanished off the face of the earth. Unless he's come to harm, he could be hiding out at one of the Best Boys' homes." He cleared his throat, as if waiting for Joe to say something, then continued, "In case you don't know, the Best Boys is our local gang, and is headed by a bloke called Carl. He's a right nutter, that one. Thinks he's Elvis Presley or something. Walks around in these black cowboy boots. He's got these ridiculous-looking sideburns, and he sports a big scar on left side of face. I suppose the sideburn helps to hide the scar, and he'd look more ridiculous with just one, wouldn't he?" Another pause, as if waiting for laughter. Joe remained silent, so the officer continued, "Anyway, I think even his own mates are afraid of him. Ian is one of his obedient co-conspirators. Point being, if Ian's anywhere around, we will find him eventually."

"And hopefully Hanna along with him," Joe commented, more to Stefan than to the inspector, then louder, "I'm also waiting for mug shots. I was told you were the one who would get them to me."

"I'm working on it, I am. As for Hero," the man continued, "we know he is mates with Ian, who for some reason protects him. I'm not sure about that one, though. Some of the boys here don't trust him. They think he's hiding something, acting so innocent and all. The word is that he's no saint. He doesn't directly participate in their acts, but he's always covered for Ian. He'll turn a blind eye and help Ian get safely away. And he always keeps his mouth shut."

"What else do you know about Hero?"

"Well, when he's not working on the rides, he can often be seen around town watching local football matches at Watson Road Park or Fishers Field. Hero is known, but left alone, by both gangs. He's kind of 'off limits.' But some of our boys like to give him a hard time, slap him around a bit and all. They like to keep him afraid, and the hope is eventually he'll talk. They get fed up with his persistently useless replies to their questions. The overall hope is that their pressuring might keep him honest."

Joe frowned, not afraid to make clear to Stefan his disapproval and distaste for this man. "That doesn't sound very sporting, hitting the bloke if he's done nothing wrong."

"'Guilty by association,' that's my motto. Every one of 'em we can get rid of is good news. There's a saying, and don't quote me, but it says something like, 'tragedy is when I cut my finger. Comedy is when these arseholes fall into an open sewer and die.'"

Joe was glad he was not facing the man, or he just might be tempted to hit him. "So what else about Ian?"

"Ian lives in Grange Park housing estate, somewhere behind the school. But like I said, we've not seen him around in some time."

"Yes," said Joe. "My partner and I drove by the place last time we were there. We didn't find anyone there either."

Stefan's heart felt like it would burst at the sound of Joe calling him a partner. He sat up a little straighter in his chair.

Sergeant Thom continued, "These county line gangs are bad. I mean, fourteen-year-olds kill each other around here. We have nearly a crime a day—just in one neighbourhood. It's a shame what's happened around here; it was once a great place to be. I've been told this was the birthplace of the Industrial Revolution, and now it's the most deprived seaside town in Britain. Young folk here are rife with antagonistic behaviour—plenty of defiance and hostility. It was a long time happening, but because of the industrial decline, Lancashire is now the seventh poorest area in Northern Europe. I'd cut 'em all down any way I could, if I had it my way."

After the line had disconnected, Joe's gut told him there was something off with Sergeant Thom's "holier than thou" sermon on all that was wrong in Blackpool. It sounded disingenuous at best, and he thought the man's concern to be a tad deluding.

Hours passed and still the conversation with Sergeant Thom was fresh on Joe's mind. He was still thinking about it later that day when Ray Lawson called him for an update. This was the second time in as many days. Joe tried to choose his words carefully. "I know this is likely a bit of a shock to you both, but this has turned into a criminal investigation. I'm thinking perhaps this is the time to let the Blackpool authorities deal with it."

Ray pleaded, "No, Joe, now is not the time to stop. You know they'll not make my Hanna a priority. They've no reason to look for her if they have no proof that she's involved with them. She's just missing. Even you said her fingerprints on the knife mean nothing at this point, since it was in her suitcase. She has no record, has committed no crime—so what's their motivation to keep looking for her? Sure, they say they will keep an eye out, but that's not the same thing. But you, Joe. You're the one who finds people. You must promise me you will keep looking."

Joe reassured Ray that he would continue his search and wouldn't abandon hope. Joe also mentioned that he would work on finding another lead, as he was not yet ready to tell Ray about the seriousness of her prints being on the knife. On his way home, he called Sally again and asked if she could please remember to drop off Hanna's computer. In case her status changed with the police, he wanted to be sure it was in his possession and not theirs.

Chapter 18

Spurred on by Stefan, Joe began to slowly wrap his head around the idea of beginning a partnership. The two would often meet late in the afternoon, after Joe had finished work for the day. Joe was still a little unsure as to how the arrangement would work. Sitting in a pub following one of their outings, Joe swirled the dregs of his pint.

"I don't want to get ahead of this, but if it did happen, I would need to contribute to this venture as well."

"You will," argued Stefan. "You have the name, the clientele, the reputation. I will have nothing but an empty building. And from there, I will learn. I can begin in the office and work my way out. We can bring some of your things from your old office if you like, but in all seriousness, I think we can burn most of it."

Joe had agreed to a degree. "Fine, but we are just looking at this point. There is plenty to consider." He quickly added, "But again, if—and only if—it happens, I'd like to buy the new furniture."

"Not on your own, you won't. You need to take Susan. Or Aisha. Her office is wicked. She'd have some good ideas for ours."

They left the pub together on a light note. There was an unusual chill in the air. Saying good-bye to Stefan, Joe walked back to his car. He had missed a message from Sally, who had called to say she had just dropped off Hanna's computer.

"I went to your office and gave it to Barry. He looked at it and confirmed it is password protected. But he says he has a man in place that can help with the problem, and he can likely get by the password. But he said he'd have to pass the computer on to Blackpool once he's done with it. It might help them as well."

Joe called and thanked Sally as he made his way home. He knew this might well be in vain, as he remained skeptical as to whether they would actually find anything of importance before handing it over to Chief Inspector Hall.

He arrived home to find Aisha curled up watching *Jeopardy*. She was wearing leggings and a cozy-looking sage-green jumper. Her hair was swept up and clipped on top of her head. She looked absolutely and completely alluring. Joe always did find cotton far sexier than silk. He smiled and sat down beside her.

Since moving in together, Aisha had also become hooked on the game show. She and Joe would themselves compete—although it was surprising that for two somewhat intelligent, seasoned people, they struggled with so many of the general knowledge categories.

"Have you told Stefan about us yet?" They had a minute to chat before Final Jeopardy.

His lips brushed her forehead. "I am trying to pick the

right moment. I will soon. Maybe we'll invite him over for dinner so he can run his ideas past you. Oh, and I haven't told you yet, but he wants to name us 'Pole and Parrott Private Investigations.'"

"Tell me it's not true," she said, stifling laughter, unsure whether Joe was taking the mickey.

"That's what I said as well. And trust me, it will not be true," said Joe, a hint of dread in his voice.

"It sounds more like the name for a pub, not an investigations business."

"We may as well just open a pub. Stefan will likely drive me to drink anyway."

Aisha laughed. "Don't look so serious."

Joe smiled. "But I should warn you, he has asked for your expertise in decorating."

Aisha wrapped her arms around Joe and said, "I'd be delighted to help. Maybe I could help him name your business as well. Or, if that doesn't work out, I could help decorate your new pub."

Joe looked at her as if to say something, then changed his mind. Smiling, he wrapped one arm tightly around her waist and gently lifted her face up to meet his. "You truly are a beautiful soul," he said as he bent down to kiss her. "Not very funny, but definitely beautiful."

Pushing him away, she laughed. "It's time for Final Jeopardy. Shush now."

He could hear the television show in the background, but what was really nagging at him was his difficulty in finding a solid lead. The trouble was in getting through to anyone. Every time he opened his mouth, he was being treated like a pariah, and he had to figure out why. It would be impossible for him to discover anything when there seemed to be a tight network working against him. What he would like to know is why the secrecy? Was it on behalf of Ian? Or Carl? Or Hanna? Or Hero? Or even Liam White? Something was connecting all of them, and someone—or something—was stopping anyone from speaking out about it. Perhaps even Sergeant Thom knew more than he was letting on. Blackpool wasn't his turf, so he would need to tread carefully.

Hanna was another curiosity. Joe wasn't sure what to make of her. On one hand, she could well have run away and had no plans to come back. On the other hand, she could be hiding, or she could even be dead by now. Her one impetuous act of getting on that train may well have changed the lives of not only herself, but of her parents, her friend Sally, and anyone else who was close to her.

When the game was over, there seemed to be nothing else to add to the conversation about Stefan, and Joe was not in the mood to further discuss the case, so he changed the subject.

"Are we still walking in Hathersage on Sunday?" he asked Aisha.

"It's due to rain on Sunday. I'll hazard a go, but not if it gets muddy," she said as she switched off the television and stood up.

Agreeing to appraise the situation when the time came, they made their way to the kitchen where Aisha had their dinner warming. Although he tried hard to stay engaged, he did find his mind slipping back to the conversation he had with Sergeant Thom. He decided he didn't like the man, nor did he appreciate his comments. Was this perhaps the reason why Hero was so reluctant to speak with him and Stefan? Joe needed to find a way around that, to convince him that they were not a threat. He was eager to find out exactly what Hero knew, and he was fairly certain he knew a lot more than he was saying.

Joe cleared his mind and turned his attention back to Aisha, suddenly aware that he'd nearly cleared his plate. He didn't remember tasting anything, and he hated to admit he had not been fully listening to her. But he was not about to spoil the evening, so he smiled warmly and accepted the seconds she offered, and while she did so, he refilled his wine glass to the very top.

Chapter 19

Quite unexpectedly, Chief Inspector Hall called Joe the next day. "Someone has spotted Ian this morning. At least we are led to believe it was Ian; we had a few reported sightings last week that didn't pan out, but this one sounded more believable. We have our men out now, searching the area and all places nearby."

"Was he alone, or with Hanna?" asked Joe, putting down his pen.

"No, he appeared to be alone, walking down Talbot Road. He had his head down, and he was described as walking with purpose. We have a description of his clothing, so have something to go on this time. Whoever reported it had no idea in which direction he went once he left Talbot. We're also checking all CCTV in the area to see if we can pick him up anywhere else."

Joe tried hard not to feel discouraged. He was also aware at how inept he felt, being here in Sheffield when he would do more good in Blackpool.

Andrew Hall sensed the quiet on the end of the line. "That doesn't mean anything bad has happened to her, just might be he's left her somewhere. We will get in touch again when we know more. I've had word from

Sergeant Thom that he will look for Ian personally, so we might hear something soon." There was a brief stillness on the line before the inspector cleared his throat and continued, "Have you spoken to DI Wilkes yet?"

"No, I haven't. Should I speak to him?"

"Well, it's up to you, but I thought it might shed some light on your case in terms of the girl perhaps not wanting to be found. Apparently there wasn't much on the girl's computer, as you speculated when it was given to us, but we did manage to access something else on her search engine site. She had been extremely active on these dating sites. She's used quite suggestive language and with a wide range of men. She was definitely looking for an adventure. There were a few messages exchanged between her and Ian Crossley. Much of her language was, I'd say, coarse—bordering on indecent. Ian was teasing her about not having the balls to get on that train, a good girl like her. That seemed to be the incentive that encouraged her, as her tone changed, and she was saying things like, 'Who says I'm a good girl?' and 'Maybe good girls aren't so good.' She may have thought it would be fun, but then when things went wrong, her involvement made it difficult to return home. Maybe it's a case of *be careful what you wish for*. Or it could be she's willingly involved and enjoying it. She seems to have an appetite for this sort of thing."

Joe looked up to see Stefan coming through the doorway, and at Joe's mention of Hanna, he had quickly walked over to the desk to listen.

"Or she has no way to back out of it now. But like you

said, too many 'what ifs' as yet. I really appreciate your call, thank you. I will be in touch."

Joe's eyes were on Stefan as he hung up the phone, an expression of grave concern on his face.

"Was that about Hanna? Have they found her?"

"No, and I less fancy our chances at this point," said Joe, the helplessness coming through in his voice. "Think about it. Just over a month ago, a Myanmar military plane went missing and lost one hundred and twenty-two people. They were able to locate the bodies after a few days. And yet I'm not feeling very optimistic about finding one girl." Joe kept his conversation with Inspector Hall to himself. He didn't want this new information getting back to Sally, or to Hanna's parents.

"Should we go back there?"

"And do what? I'm afraid it's difficult to assess what is needed at this point. There are so many unknowns, too many hostile and unfamiliar faces, and absolutely no cooperation. And because Hanna is not from there, it's not like I can check with her friends and place of work. She seems to have this private side to her that people here in Sheffield aren't aware of." Joe was thinking of Hanna's call to Sally. According to Sally, she hadn't sounded buoyant and full of pep. She had sounded frightened and panicky, saying she was in need of help.

Stefan sat down, his face markedly bent into a thinking expression. "But it doesn't sound like you, to not want to keep trying."

Joe leaned back in his chair and reluctantly added, "That's not the case. I'm trying to decide what's best at this point." Joe stood up. "But I think you are right. I do need to go back. I need to dig aggressively. I need to take what I do know and simply buckle down and tackle it. I should have knocked on Ian's door loudly, and more than twice. Hanna may have been inside. More importantly, I should have spoken to the neighbours right then and there. I don't know what I was thinking."

"It's because of me," Stefan said emphatically, his words heightened.

"What do you mean, it's because of you?"

"You'd have been more careful if you were alone. You'd have spent more time evaluating and questioning. I think you would have done it right if I wasn't there distracting you. It's true what you said about working alone, Joe. Maybe I'm holding you back."

"I'm still not sure I follow," Joe slowly answered, although he was beginning to understand.

Stefan delivered his explanation. "When I went there on the train with Sally, I thought the same thing when it was time to leave. She wanted to go home, but I'd have stayed longer. I'd have walked more streets, hung about the unusual places. I should have hidden and waited at the spot where Hero disappeared, because certainly he would have had to come back if he was working. I wouldn't worry about time or food; but being with Sally, I was distracted by wondering if she was hot or cold or needed food or perhaps was tired. When she said she wanted to leave, I didn't object, yet I felt I could have done more. Maybe I needed to sit on that bench for decidedly longer, until I came up with a new idea. I think you might act the same with me, so you don't concentrate on what's important."

Joe was quiet. There was a lot of truth to what Stefan was saying, yet he wasn't sure how to respond. The one certainty was that Joe, up until now, wasn't doing his job. Whether or not Hanna wanted to be found, he needed to find out where she was and assure her parents that she was alive and well—even if he couldn't bring her home.

Stefan almost looked guilty as he continued, "I know I'm not professional, and I know I go on about feeding my stomach and complaining about other things. I'm big with my opinions, but from now on, I'll try to not get in the way. You are good at this, Joe. You have a deftness, an ability with your thought process, and I don't want to balls it up for you."

Joe slapped his desk. "Okay, that's it. I am going back, and you are coming. We need to know if we can do this together."

Chapter 20

Before Joe and Stefan had the opportunity to organize their return to Blackpool, they were greeted with more bad news. CI Andrew Hall called to tell Joe that Ian had been found murdered. During an early morning search, an officer on regular patrol in another area of the city had discovered Ian's body partially concealed behind a skip.

"Any idea what might have happened?" Joe motioned for Stefan to lean in and listen.

"He was stabbed, and not just once. The coroner suggested there may have been more than one assailant, as the wounds on his chest and stomach were different than the ones on his lower back, indicating different weapons. There were no defensive wounds, indicating he may have been stabbed first in the back while he was facing someone else who perhaps was distracting him. Also, the angle of the stab wounds would suggest that the person behind him was much taller."

"And I don't imagine someone would stab him, roll him over, switch weapons, and stab him again," commented Joe.

The CI continued, "Rightly so. Drag marks show us the body was moved, but not far—only about ten feet.

Just far enough to partially conceal him."

"When did this happen?"

"The initial estimation is that he must have been killed early last evening, maybe as early as five. The patrol officer found his body around seven this morning. The rats were on him by then."

Stefan's stomach heaved, and he felt he might lose his lunch. "Rats?" he asked aloud.

"There are plenty of rats around here. It's a chronic problem. Not only do they cause issues for businesses and homeowners here in Blackpool, but they also leave droppings, spread disease, and build nests. They gnaw through pipes, wires, woodwork, and insulation, and occasionally they will treat themselves to a face or two if they happen upon a dead body."

Joe looked dismayed but unconcerned with the grue-some news. He regretted the news of the death for one reason alone. "That dashes our hopes of speaking to him about Hanna. Now we've our work cut out for us. Thanks, Andrew. I will get back to you soon."

Stefan spoke as soon as the call was disconnected, sounding almost frantic. "We can't just sit back and do nothing, just wait for things to go from bad to worse. It's time to go and talk with Hero and stop with the nice-ties. He's clearly not hiding from us, so we will have no problem finding him."

"Yes, and with Ian gone, things may have changed. He may be far more willing to speak with us, less afraid of being disloyal to Ian."

"Or he's the one who killed Ian. Maybe he killed Hanna

as well. So, how will you handle him, knowing that?"

"Ease up, Stefan. Let's not let our imaginations get the better of us. So far, there's been nothing by his actions that might suggest he did it. I do have some experience at reading people, so grant me some credit for that. But yes, we do need to get going. There's no time to lose."

The drive to Blackpool was quicker than expected. Traffic had been light. They took the exit and headed directly to Pleasure Beach. The area was becoming more familiar to them as they parked the car and proceeded to the cashier to pay the five-pound admission at the park entrance. As they were entering, Joe caught a glimpse of something behind him, out of the corner of his eye. There, plain as day, Joe grabbed sight of Hero walking down the street. Hero had seen Joe at the same instant, once within his range of vision and, spinning on his heels, was now headed in the other direction. Joe ran out of the park, shouting at Stefan, who had not seen what just happened. Stefan followed a few steps behind. Joe easily caught up with Hero a block away, as the man's handicap prevented him from running quickly. He walked up to him and took him gently by the shoulder.

"Now you're going to talk to me. I have no guns or knives, so I can't force you to come with me. But I'm not going to hurt you."

By now, Stefan had caught up with them. Joe continued, "We just want a friendly little chat. As I've already said, I'm a friend. I'm not the police."

Hero emphatically objected. "They can't see me with you. Besides, I need to go to work. I should go now, before anyone sees us." He flinched, trying to break Joe's grasp. "I don't have to talk to you."

Joe released his hold and softened his tone. "All right, Hero, but we are going to follow you in. And don't try to run. I'm bigger and faster, and we will raise attention. Then someone more than likely will see you. As for speaking with us, you are right. You are under no obligation. But I could call Inspector Edey to come and do it if you prefer."

At that, Hero seemed to calm down, and he walked on without a further word. Stefan walked alongside Hero but stood well apart. Joe remained a few paces behind. Joe noted that Stefan was trying hard to be sociable and make conversation. He was trying to be helpful.

As the admission fee had been paid, they held up their tickets and followed Hero into the heart of the amusement park, to a small building in the centre of the Thrill-O-Matic ride. Hero opened the door and reluctantly waved the men inside, then swiftly closed the door, peering out and having a quick look to be sure they weren't observed.

Joe stood looking at Hero, having time now to be close and study his face. Hero would not look at Joe but sat down awkwardly and remained staring at his feet. He wore the look of someone who had grown accustomed to being poorly treated.

"Will you please talk to us? Ian is dead, Hero. Do you know why?"

Hero nodded his head and muttered a barely audible "Yes." Whether he was saying yes to either question or both didn't bother Joe, and he carried on talking.

Joe crossed his arms and leaned against the door. "Let's start at the beginning. First, we have a knife with that bloke Liam White's blood on it, and Hanna's prints. Then we can't find Hanna or Ian. Then you pretend you don't know them when we both know that's not true. And now Ian's dead. What else do you know? Please help us, Hero."

Hero sat up defiantly and straightened his head. "I'm not daft, you know. People pay no attention to me—they think I don't know much. So it's easy for me to know what's going on without letting on to anyone that I know."

"So what do you know?"

"I do know Ian. Well, I did know 'im, and I know why he is dead. And yes, I met Hanna, when she was with Ian. I was at the zoo with Hanna on Saturday morning. We were meeting Ian after his work shift was over. Hanna wanted to go early to have another look around. She loved the animals. It was nice watching her. She was so kind, and I liked being with her. She was nice to me, like a friend. Ian finished his shift and came to meet us by the orangutans. But then these guys walked up because Ian had his uniform on. They started calling him a creep, keeping animals locked up this way. One was saying they should be free. I told them maybe they should leave. They were laughing and shoving me, and that made Ian mad."

Hero stood up and walked across the room. "But I knew it was more than that. It had nowt to do with the animals. That bloke there was a mate of Liam's, and he knew that Liam's girlfriend, Jude, had been stepping out with Ian. She even told him she was breaking up with him because of Ian." Suddenly Hero couldn't stop talking. He sat up, eyes wild, and finished his story.

"They had a bit of a barney, Jude and Liam, and Jude finished up with a broken nose and wrist. She said she fell down some stairs, but Ian said the bruises on her arm and neck were saying different. He knew Liam had had a go at her. Then Ian shows up with Hanna, and now everybody is upset with Ian. He's a wide boy, that Ian. Used to hang out at this sex shop called the Moon. Always was a bit of a skirt chaser, he was. So anyway, Liam was right pissed at him. Stole his girl, Jude, and now right away had a new one. So anyway, the bloke, this friend of Liam's, pushed Ian, and Ian cut him."

"What do you mean 'cut him'?" asked Joe.

"Sliced his leg. By then, the security blokes came, and Ian took me and Hanna away through the employee exit. They told Ian he needed to go to security office and settle it and all. But he didn't go. None of us was feeling very good and Hanna was upset that Ian used his knife. She was surprised he had one."

Then Hero stopped talking. Joe and Stefan exchanged glances. Joe shrugged his shoulders.

"So then what happened?" asked Stefan. He was leaning forward, but not too much as to appear too excited. He looked at Joe then added, "We need to know what happened that evening, Hero. Saturday night after the zoo."

"Well, it was stag and hens do that night in town. It was a crazy night, that Saturday. Not the usual crazy—there was like, you know, an electricity in the air. It was real unsettling. The blokes at the stag party had been on the assault course all day, so by evening, they all felt like Rambo or something. At the hens do, the girls had moved their absinthe party to the beach. Sometimes these dos are on nights apart from each other, but when there's both on the same night, everyone ends up on the beach."

"Get to the point, Hero. Please," said Joe, a little more harshly than he intended.

Hero's words were coming slower. "That night, Ian brought Hanna to the pub to meet me for a nosh. Ian was in a bad mood the whole time. He told me to take Hanna outside, and he'd go settle up at the bar. We went outside and there was this commotion, and then we heard that someone stabbed Liam. But Hanna didn't do it."

"Wait—why did you just say Hanna didn't do it?"

"Because there's some who thinks she did." Hero stood up quickly, acting distressed, rubbing his hands together and stamping his feet.

"Hanna confessed to someone that she did it."

"I don't believe it. She wouldn't do that." Hero covered his face with his hands.

"Okay, let's move on. And that bloke who got stabbed, you say that was definitely Liam?"

Hero nodded. "I heard it was an accident. But I didn't care because he meant to harm her. I never liked Liam. She didn't know they were from the Fylde Snakes. She just thought they was stag blokes. But Ian, he knew they were Snakes, and he should have looked out for her."

"So why would they think Hanna did it?"

Hero sat down again, calmer now. "Well, they might have blamed Hanna or Ian. By the time we all got our heads around it, it was already morning. We told Hanna she had to get out of here, go back home, and she needed to take the knife with her and hide it. Get rid of it somewhere at home."

"How did you get the knife? And why didn't you just toss it into the water or leave it where it was if none of you were guilty?"

"I don't know. I suppose Ian got it somehow. I won't say any more about that. I don't know."

Hero was again becoming agitated, and Joe was afraid of losing him, so he changed the direction of questioning.

"That's good, Hero. So, what did you do next? What happened to Hanna after that?"

What Hero told them next explained the entire scenario at the train station as they had seen on the CCTV cameras. Hero had told Hanna he was going to make sure she caught her train. Then chaos ensued.

Hero explained, "I took her, and Ian came along, even though he didn't want to. Ian got her luggage checked in and got her a ticket; then he gave the ticket to me. He wanted to wait outside, to hide. Then two of the Snakes, they came into the station, as if looking around for us. They must have seen us on the street and followed us. So bloody Ian, brave Ian, he tried to run. One guy made a phone call; then the other 'un took off after Ian. I grabbed Hanna; we ran the other way and went round the corner, slipped out another door, and I took her back to my flat. Ian was already there."

"You acted fast to help her," added Stefan encouragingly.

Hero looked at him, all seriousness. "It's like a good football match, when you have the ball and the opponent comes right at you, all aggressive like, and they try to force you to give up the ball. But I wasn't going to do that. So I had to think fast, like David Beckham or Wayne Rooney, and use fancy footwork and go the other way. I was not going to give up the ball."

The two men nodded as Hero continued. "So there we was, hiding in my flat, the three of us. Ian was wild with anger, and Hanna just cried. But then, I think after about three days, Ian said he wasn't gonna do this anymore—he didn't do anything wrong. So he left. We didn't know where he went. I'd go walking about looking for him. It wasn't long before the Boys picked him up. Ian likely thought Carl would protect him, but what I heard was that Carl was the one who killed Ian. Carl had to keep the peace with Monty and the Snakes. It was like payback for what happened to Liam. I heard about it almost right away."

This time Hero looked right into Joe's eyes as he said, "Ian had no business bringing a girl like Hanna here. He ought to have known better, and then to take her around at night? I might look stupid, but I'm not. She should not have been here, should have not been around his mates."

Standing up, Hero said, "I have to go inspect the ride. I was meant to do it as soon as I arrived, and I need to do it now."

Stefan stood as if on cue. "I'll go with you."

Once the men had left, Joe took this opportunity to search the small, cramped office, although he doubted he would find anything here. He didn't know whether to believe Hero. After all, Sergeant Thom had said that Hero would do anything to protect Ian. At this stage of the game, there could be many theories and Joe could not discount any of them. Hypothetically, Hero could have gotten rid of Hanna as payback for Ian. She could have been dead shortly after the news of Ian's demise. Or even before.

Chapter 21

Once the inspection was complete and the two men had returned to the room, Hero appeared calmer, almost friendly. Stefan wore that familiar grin and added a wink, suggesting to Joe that he had made some headway in befriending Hero.

Once seated, Hero continued, "Okay, I'll tell you another thing. Before Ian died, I heard he ratted Hanna out, told them it was Hanna who did it. Now they're all over this place looking for her. They came at me then, but Carl says to leave me alone for now, coz I wouldn't have done anything. I'm too daft, they said. But then Carl looked at me with that look, like he wasn't too happy. He says if I knew she did it and I was hiding her, I'd be in big trouble." Hero shook his head again. "Ian didn't care about her; he didn't even run out after her when one of the Fylde boys was after her. He only cared about himself."

To which Joe responded, "But you care about her, don't you, Hero?"

"She's always been nice to me. When I gave her rides, she even kissed me right here," he said, pointing to his cheek. "And she took my arm once when we were at the zoo. We was walking and she just grabbed my arm, all natural-like. And she's got them big brown eyes; I don't want to see any harm come to them eyes, that face."

Oddly, Stefan found himself thinking of Sally's eyes.

Joe knew that Hero was tired. They had held him up for quite a while, but he was afraid to let him go. Afraid he might run before they could get the whole story from him. He pressed Hero.

"Where were they hiding? Where is your place? We need to find her."

"She's not there anymore. She ran too. This morning."

"But were they staying at your flat?"

Hero looked down. "They were close by to me, but it don't matter now, does it?" Hero sat quiet for a moment. "When she heard they got Ian, she panicked. I shouldn't have told her about that. I shouldn't have told her that Ian said she did it. That set her off."

Joe then said to Hero, "So a minute ago you said you didn't know why they blamed her, but now you are saying that Ian accused her of doing it? Which is it?"

"You are confusing me. I don't remember."

"Okay, forget that for now. So when we asked you about her that first time we met, she was really with you?"

Hero nodded without looking up. "I didn't know who you were. Why would I tell you?"

Joe sat back in frustration. It was hot. He ran his fingers through his hair, now damp with sweat. His clothes were damp, and his shirt clung to him. At least he knew she was alive. Up until this morning, that was.

Hero looked at Stefan. "I thought maybe she went back to Sheffield, so I went to her flat to see."

Stefan stared at him incredulously. "How did you know where she lived?"

Hero spoke matter-of-factly. "I followed you that day, on the train. When you were here with that other girl. The one who said she's Hanna's flatmate."

"You followed me?"

Joe looked at Stefan, and couldn't resist saying, "You didn't know he was following you? I thought you were a PI?"

Stefan looked from Joe to Hero and back at Joe before directing his comment to Hero, "How did you do that? Was it that easy to do? How did I not know you were there? Bloody hell, you're a better PI than I am."

Hero looked down and chuckled at that comment. "No, I'm no PI. But yes, it was easy. You weren't paying attention; you were more interested in the girl you were with. Nobody ever suspects me of anything, so you wouldn't be looking."

Stefan blushed. "I was just concerned for her. She was quite upset."

"Like I was for Hanna, right?"

Joe spoke at that. "Yes, Hero. Like you were for Hanna. She was lucky to have you looking out for her."

Hero had tears in his eyes. "I would have taken her to the train sooner, but they were watching. I knew it wasn't safe. They'd have taken her right from me."

Hero stood up again. "After that, the Snakes roughed me up a bit." He lifted his shirt to show Joe and Stefan a badly bruised torso. "But some of the Boys caught them and stopped them. They told me they roughed me up because I likely know more about Ian. But Carl told them I was harmless. Now I'm showing them that I'm not so harmless and I can take care of myself. The Boys never saw me near them that night, so they think I wasn't involved."

Stefan looked at Hero with concern, and he spoke with kindness when he said, "You need to be careful."

Hero shook his head. "Folks leave me alone. I run the rides, not much more. But they should not think me daft. I pay attention, and I know what's what."

Then Hero smiled. Not a big smile, but nonetheless it was there. "And I never miss a local football game—I love our lads. Blackpool FC, you know? The Seasiders are brilliant. Sometimes I would go out with Ian to the pub. He would hang out with 'is mates and I would just watch." He paused as if still thinking. "And I like going to the zoo."

Joe agreed with Stefan. "You might not be safe. They may find out Hanna was with you."

"I would be safe if you'd just stay away from me. They will figure out who you are, and then ask why I am talking to you."

Stefan again reiterated, "This place is bad, isn't it, Hero? Even though there's some who will say it isn't."

"Yes, it is. It can be very bad for some. It's not all sunshine and chips. That's why you need to stay away from me." But with an expression that faintly resembled another grin, he added, "But it's not all bad, not to me. It's my home."

Joe had long wanted to ask Hero this question: "Why

do they call you Hero?"

"It was my mum that named me Hero. I was a young lad, she said, and she had put me to sleep. Then she fell asleep with a cigarette. Dad was out at the pub with his mates for their Friday night drink." His eyes took on a sorrowful expression as he added, "I always said my dad was my hero, but that day, Mum and Dad called me their little hero. She would tell everyone how her little hero saved her life. She was asleep, and there was a lot of smoke and I cried and cried, like really loud. There was a story in the local paper; it called me the hero of Blackpool because all the row of houses could have burned up if it weren't for me crying and waking up me mum. She kept the clipping in a book by her bed. I've been called Hero ever since. I don't think anyone's ever used my real name. I was too young to know what I had done, but my dad would talk about it every now and again."

"You must really love them."

"My mum used to tell me I could be anything I wanted to be. But when she died, my aunt told me that she were lying. She told me I was nothing but a waste of space." He bent over to pick up a wrapper that had wedged itself behind the leg of the small table.

Wanting to now leave the man in peace, Joe said softly, "Thank you for speaking with us, Hero. Please call us if Hanna contacts you. I think she will if she doesn't know where else to go."

Hero nodded his head. "The Snakes have their guys all over the place. And the coppers are watching for her, too. She'll not want to go to them. She says she's a murderer, but I told her to stop saying that."

With nothing left to do, Joe stood to leave. He felt maybe now they could get Hero over to their side. "We need to convince her that she's not."

Touching Hero on the shoulder, Joe added, "Let me know if you change your mind. We can help. I can do things to help you, Hero. I don't want you to be in any danger either. Without Ian here to look out for you, you too may become a target."

"I can look after myself, you know. They only wanted Ian, and they got him. But now he's made it unsafe for her, hasn't he?"

"Hero, who exactly is *they*? Is it one man or many men?"

"The Snakes. From up coast. Fylde Snakes. Monty wants blood for the death of Liam. And Carl, he needs to keep the peace with Monty, so I think he had to have it done with Ian, as payment for killing Liam."

Stefan also stood. "But if they want Hanna also, and if they think you helped to hide her, they could come looking for you. So again, be careful."

"It's not just them, you know. I think they have a friend copper. He has a go at me sometimes, and I've seen him with Carl before."

"Can you tell me what he looks like, Hero? And do you know his name?"

"Don't know his name. He just looks like a copper. Bigger than me, a podgy old bloke, he's got a head of skin—no hair. He spit his gum on my shoe."

Shaking Hero's hand, the two men left. As they walked

away, Stefan said to Joe, "Do you believe him when he says she's gone? Do you trust him?

"I'm not sure. I don't think Hero is a danger, but I don't know if he is lying or if he's being truthful. I'm just not sure what lengths he would go to in order to protect certain people. If Carl is protecting him, he may in turn be helping Carl to locate Hanna."

"Maybe Fylde Snakes didn't give Hero those bruises. It could have been Ian, as Hero was knifing him. Or it could have been that bent copper."

Joe said nothing to Stefan, but he had a watchful eye on a figure that had followed them from the park. The darkly disguised form made no attempt to hide, which bothered Joe to some degree. He quickly steered Stefan towards the Promenade and the crowds of people.

As soon as they had gone, Hero sat back and closed his eyes. He now felt like he could breathe. As soon as he could, he would go back to his flat and tell Hanna about these men, to see if she knew them or who they were. He still didn't completely trust them. He didn't trust anyone right now. He would tell them anything they asked. Everything except that Hanna had come back this morning. There was no chance he ever would have told them where she was, hidden away at his flat, watching the telly. But now he needed to go home and take care of her once and for all. This needed to end.

Chapter 22

Stefan finally understood Joe's reluctance towards this case in Blackpool. The drives were long and tiring, what with the frequency of their trips. And he knew this wasn't their last. Once back in his flat, Stefan called Sally to see how she was doing. He wanted to tell her about their visit with Hero.

"So I guess technically Hanna would be scared. But with Ian dead, she might want to find her way home. If only we knew her situation. But if someone has her, it could be why she's not calling."

Sally agreed, but then quickly asked, "Are you all right, Stefan? It sounds terrible, your day. And that poor man, will he be okay? It's not just about Hanna anymore, is it?"

"I think I'm okay, but it is a different life there, and it leaves me unsettled each time we've come away. And I'm not sure I'm of much use to Joe." Stefan left out the part about Hero having followed them back to Sheffield. He wasn't about to share the news for fear she would think less of him. Dealing with his own feelings of inadequacy was enough for now. Hanging up, Stefan leaned back in his chair and closed his eyes.

Joe received an early morning call from Inspector Edey, advising him, in his good Yorkshire accent, that they had found what might be Hanna's phone. It was found not far from Hero's flat.

"It has been given to our guys to unlock it and retrieve pictures and anything else that might be there. We will check her texts and phone calls, both outgoing and incoming. We will also check it for prints. I will know more tomorrow. But," he paused, "I don't mind saying, I'm not sorry about what happened to Ian. That one had it coming. And I think this Hero bloke might be better off without him. Now if we can just keep him away from Carl, he might fare better. It'd be good for him to be free of their dealings—the gangs and the drugs and being at their beck and call."

Joe quickly added, "Before you hang up, what can you tell me about Hero?"

"Ah, yes. Hero. I did some digging. His mum, Lily, and dad, Frank, lived meagrely but were very well liked in the neighbourhood. Lost their first child in less than a year, but then soon had another. Hero was a good lad. He had a slight deformity, which made people want to take care of him. He grew up adored, not only by his parents, but by neighbours and friends. They called him their guardian angel because he had saved his mum from dying in a fire. The neighbours that lived there at the time still remember Hero as some kind of effigy—a symbol of protection." Inspector Edey cleared his throat.

"Here, listen to this bit. Hero's mum, Lily, worked part-time as a piano teacher, and his dad worked for a moving company. Decent folk, they were. Slowly over the years, more thug types started moving into their neighbourhood, but Hero's dad always treated everyone the same. The story has it, he once helped Ian's dad off the road where he'd dropped drunk. He might've got run over if it weren't for Frank, who picked him up and drove him home. Lily wanted to move away, but Frank said no, he wouldn't be chased from his home. He said they could all live in peace.

"Then Hero came home from school one day. It was winter. The lad was about ten or eleven years old, it says. That day, the entire street in front of his house was surrounded by police tape. The Boys had a big fight with the Snakes, and that fight somehow ended up on the street in front of Hero's house. Hero's mum ran out to meet Frank, who had just come home from work. He was outside trying to break up the gathering and talk the boys into leaving. Mum and Dad were pleading with them to go away, and they ended up dead at their front door. Someone was shoved into Lily, Frank shoved back, a gun went off, then another. Turned out they were both fatally shot by someone from one of these gangs, don't know which one. Anyway, a few minutes later, Hero walked up and saw 'em both lying in the street, dead and bloodied."

"Bloody hell," said Joe in disgust.

"Police records show that two members of the Best Boys were arrested, one of them being Ian Crossley's older brother. Yes, the same Ian—Hero's mate. A member of the other gang, the Snakes, was also arrested for having a pistol. The bullets were matched to those that killed Hero's parents. One of the blokes was sentenced and went to prison. Carl had some kind of modified air gun that grazed Hero's mum, but it wasn't the pellet that killed her. They didn't have enough on him to put him away, so he was placed on probation. From then on, the hostility and antagonism between the two gangs increased even more.

"With both parents dead, Hero was put in the care of his uncle, who was rumoured to have either physically or sexually abused him, no proof, but aunt treated him like a lodger. One day, about a year later, he ran away and lived in anonymity back here on the streets. He blamed himself for the deaths of his parents, saying he wasn't much of a hero after all. He managed to get by somehow, doing odd jobs for some of the shopkeepers, and eventually he got his job at the fair. Since then, Ian and the Best Boys always looked out for him. Ian did it because of guilt I suppose, for his brother killing his parents. But none really went near him or bothered much with him, so odd to me why he would need this so-called protection.

"Hero was different when he reappeared. I've heard he became like a zombie. Couldn't get much out of him for a long time after that. So pretty much everyone left Hero alone. There was an unspoken understanding that Hero just didn't matter to anyone. Ian would never get over the guilt of his brother having been involved, as he had always been grateful for Hero's dad being good to his own. That's what likely bent Ian the wrong way. But after Ian joined the Best Boys, Carl started to groom him. Said he was soft, so Ian tried to prove him wrong by doing his bidding. Ian was pathetic in how he has cow-towed to Carl ever since, dragging Hero along as well to share in the dirty work."

Thanking the Inspector, Joe hung up the phone. Edey had promised to call back in a day or so, once the phone had been examined. With a sigh, he unlocked his file cabinet, grabbing a handful of paperwork before sitting down at his desk. Sombre and uninspired, he continued with his work, but at the back of his mind was the ghastly thought of how profoundly Hero's life had been changed. He was decidedly more interested in Carl.

The next day, Joe received a message saying it was indeed Hanna's phone, but there had been absolutely no call history; it had been wiped clean. Joe called the station and was passed on to someone he wasn't familiar with. "Yes, it was me that left you the message. The phone is clean. Also, the battery was dead. The history would have been wiped clean before that."

Chapter 23

"But I really am afraid. It might be something real this time," Sally said on the phone to Stefan. "Please come over. There are noises outside my flat again."

"I'm sorry, I can't keep doing this," Stefan replied, with no attempt to hide his frustration. He was thinking it was likely nothing, or possibly Hero again, keeping watch. But then, he thought again. Maybe Hero was here to harm her, to keep her quiet. Or what if Carl had also followed Hero to Sheffield? Surely he wasn't the only stupid one who could be followed without being detected. Sally's breathing was uneven. Did he dare leave her unprotected?

"All right, I'm on my way," he said at last. "But this is the last time, Sal. You need to sort it out."

Sally was nearly crying as she thanked him. So once again, Stefan found himself heading out his door at midnight. He got to Sally's flat quickly, and this time, Sally was very awake when she answered the door. She spoke with him briefly, describing her concerns and thanking him again. Stefan sat on the sofa bed, shaking his head.

"No need to thank me, but you will need to put a better lock on your door or call a friend to come and stay with you. I can't keep coming here, Sally. I mean, I don't mind, but surely you will need to have a plan."

"I know I do, and I promise I will. But how was I to know it would happen again? I just wish it was Hanna, coming home without a key."

"Have you told Joe? Perhaps he needs to know about it. And maybe even the police. They might put a patrol car in the area."

"You are right, Stefan. Tomorrow I will let Joe know. It's just that you live closer, and you live alone, so I'm not disturbing two people. But I will deal with it, I promise. I just wasn't thinking it would happen twice." She left a cover and pillow and wished him a good night.

He waited until she left the room before he lay down, his back to the wall. The streetlight outside cast a beam across his bed. A shadow moved across it, likely a tree branch in the wind. It seemed to be waving at Stefan, beckoning—or daring—him to come outside. He shivered, turned on his side, and fell asleep.

Part way through the night, Stefan was awakened by the sound of Sally moving around the flat. The footsteps seemed to roam about, but then he could sense that she was in front of him. He kept his eyes closed. Suddenly and quietly, Sally slipped under the blanket and curled up in front of him. She moved stealthily, with barely a sound, and she seemed to glide under the covers like a ghost. Shivering, she pressed her body against him softly as she spooned, being careful not to wake him.

While Stefan pretended to be asleep, he had never been more awake. This was the closest he had been to another human being since his mum held him as a child. He could barely breathe for fear of disturbing Sally, yet he wished he could move even closer. As close as was physically possible so that no air, no crack of light remained between them. He lay that way until her breathing levelled and he was sure she was asleep. Then ever so slowly, he leaned his head forward and gently buried his face in her hair, smelling the sweetness of her scent. Was it vanilla? He fell asleep that way.

Stefan woke to Sally stirring. Daylight was slowly flooding the room. Neither had changed position since she had crept under his covers. Sensing he was awake, she began speaking, making no attempt to move. It was barely a whisper.

"You know, what's happening to Hanna really doesn't surprise me much. Something inside her wanted adventure. I told her to get an adventurous job. I mean, what excitement did she hope to gain from sorting parcels? But more than adventure, I also think she wanted danger. When she first started doing online dating, she would scroll through the profiles and show me her prospects. A few were nice, but she said they were boring. When she picked Ian, I told her she was daft. What do you want with a potty-mouthed zookeeper from Blackpool? Seriously? And his profile pic was a bit creepy to me."

Stefan commented, "It looks like she picked the worst possible man, and he's now involved her with some very dodgy people." He then asked, "What about you? Online dating, or do you have someone?" Both seemed comfortable lying this way, and neither made an attempt to change position or to get up. It felt strangely natural. Stefan certainly didn't want to move, although his arm had fallen asleep.

"Who, me? Oh no, I have no one. Not online or anywhere. I've liked boys before, for about a minute, until I got to know them. It's not that I wouldn't like someone, but I can't help it. None around here appeal to me."

"Why is that? What are you looking for?"

"I guess it's more what I'm not looking for. I'm not keen on blokes around here. Too many have the long pub nights. They seem to live in the pubs. And I quite dislike all the sport, the beer, the bad jokes, and the calling out at every pretty girl that goes by. They act like they are still twelve—it makes me crazy. I once started to see a boy who seemed different, but he turned out to be very controlling. And I don't want that either."

"But I'm sure not all guys are like that," muttered Stefan, almost defensively.

"Well, it seems most of the blokes my age are like that. So then, what are your mates like? Are they different? I must admit you seem quite different from other blokes."

"I don't have any mates, really. I haven't lived here for very long." He then quickly added, "I guess Joe's my mate."

Sally giggled. "But Joe's not a mate. He's a father, or a boss. To me, he's like an uncle. Did you not have mates where you moved from?"

Stefan became quiet. "Well, not really."

Sally sensed his discomfort, so she thought she'd change the topic. "Okay then, do you have a girl?"

"Well, I liked a girl a long time ago, but it didn't work out." Stefan sighed. He felt uncomfortable and had begun to twitch. "It's a long story, Sally. I didn't grow up around here. And my life didn't really leave room for mates or pubs or sports—or girls either, for that matter. But that's a conversation for another day."

Sally thought it best to change the mood, and so she sprang from the sofa and opened the curtains. It was the first time Stefan had been here in the daylight, and he was very impressed with the style and warmth of the flat. Most prominent were the art pieces on the wall, exotic and vibrant, yet not gaudy. A large red bookcase stood against the far wall, fronted by two large gold armchairs. At the opposite side of the room, a smoked-glass globe lamp hung over an oval wooden table, which was surrounded by five rattan chairs. Overall, the flat was minimalistic, but what was here was tasteful and functional. Sally disappeared through a doorway. "How about a cuppa coffee then? I need to get going soon, I'm sorry. I'm on shift today!"

In the kitchen, Sally set to making the coffee. Stefan could hear running water and clinking cups. He stood to fold away the bedding. He still felt a little uncomfortable. While making coffee, she turned on the music. "Do you like Robbie Williams? Yeah, you will do," she added. "Here, have a listen."

Chapter 24

Seated by the window in Susan's front room, Joe carefully held his granddaughter, who had fallen asleep in his lap while listening as he read her a story. Her name was Emma. She had been named after Joe's mother. Emma Elizabeth had just turned eighteen months, and before she had fallen asleep, she had been more curious about Joe's ear than the story, tugging at it gently, running her finger across the lobe several times. He had not been to see Susan and her family in a long time, as his cases were keeping him busy. But today being Sunday, he did set aside time for an unhurried visit.

Emma was at a curious age, learning to form words and how to put the pegs in her board game. She had recently begun walking, and it brought back memories of Susan at that age. Odd, but it seemed not that long ago that Susan had learned to walk. Seeing Susan and Nigel as new parents had brought back memories of he and Janet, when their life had also felt like paradise. But Susan and Nigel certainly had a better grip on things, and for that, Joe was pleased.

Susan came in and motioned for Joe to carry the sleeping child to her room so that they could have a visit themselves. Nigel had just returned from a farm visit to see to one of his client's sick horses and was now ready to catch up with a conversation and a glass of beer.

While listening as Nigel and Susan whispered about the shiny mobile above Emma's bed, Joe couldn't help but think of Hero. Emma had a good chance of faring well, would have every opportunity for success. Whatever Hero's successes might have been, he had lost all chance of realizing any of them. And again, he couldn't imagine what it must be like for Hanna's parents, knowing their daughter was out there somewhere and very likely in danger. Joe silently hoped that she was still alive.

Joe looked over at Nigel, who was looking very relaxed. It had been a good visit with his relatives from Canada. Joe had enjoyed meeting Nigel's stepbrother, Adam, and his aunt, Claire. During the visit, Nigel's father, Paul, and his sister, Claire, had spent a lot of the time together, having obviously missed each other's company. They would disappear onto the moors for long stretches at a time, walking while reminiscing about their childhoods and the different directions their lives had taken them. Adam had enjoyed questioning Joe about his private investigations, recounting his experience in helping two young people to reconnect, while Adam's father, Ben, had enjoyed playing with the baby more than anything else.

"So?" Susan nudged her dad playfully, bringing his thoughts back to the present. "How's it going, you two living together? It really was about time." It was as if she had been waiting to ask this question ever since Joe had arrived. He saw it in her face and was impressed that she had managed to wait this long before asking.

He answered assuredly, "It's very good. I was feeling that living alone was no longer satisfying without someone there to share it with. You were absolutely right, Susan. What was the point of having nice things if there was no one to appreciate them with? As for cooking a nice meal, it had lost its magic when I was eating alone. It just needed to be the right time; then suddenly it was."

Joe was thinking of the evening he had shown up at Aisha's door. It had been raining, and the wind had picked up. It had only been a few weeks since having exposed Rita's murderer, and Joe had been distraught, feeling he had nowhere to go. And he really needed someone to talk to. She was the first and only person he thought of. Aisha had opened the door with a curious look on her face. They hadn't known each other long, but at that point in their relationship, their connection had become quite powerful. He stood there, not knowing what to say, but she knew what was wrong. She had taken a step towards him just as he felt his legs give out. She held him tightly, and there was so much in her embrace. He held on to her for a moment, his body shaking with grief. Within a few minutes, she had led him to her room.

Susan broke him from his reverie. "I think you met Aisha at just the right time. Back then, you were both reluctant to move on, but your attraction for one another was apparent. And look at you now—your lives are blissful and rosy."

Joe smiled at her description. Then nodded, adding,

"Even after I'd sold the big house, it didn't seem a big enough change. By then, we'd both sold our perspective homes, and we slowly found we didn't want to be apart. Family means a lot to her, and she'd lost hers in the most unspeakable manner. And I, the fool, had almost lost mine." At this, Susan smiled warmly at her dad. "And although Aisha's work means a lot to her, as does mine, suddenly work wasn't enough for either of us."

"You are different, Dad."

"How do you mean?"

"I always thought the way a person is born is the way they stay. I suppose I'm somewhat different since being with Nigel. And I know that fundamentally, you are who you are, but I can really see something else in you. You were one person with Mum, and it was a good person from what I could tell, but with Aisha, you've changed a lot. I see all the little nuances of you that I never noticed before—whether they are new or not, they have certainly surfaced. You are calmer, more thoughtful, and many of your focuses have shifted."

Joe laughed. "Well, I am older. That alone usually can calm one down. But she is good for me, on so many levels. While I don't exactly feel different, I do know I see many things differently."

"Do you ever think of Simon?" asked Susan, the question so off topic it threw him for a moment.

"It's funny, but I never do. Maybe an image will occasionally flash through my mind—but the image is more of a particular moment or event that stands out, and not necessarily of Simon."

Even as he spoke the words, Joe thought about his and Simon's lives back in their youth into their adulthood, before Joe had started to distance himself from his friend. And that had even been before the arrest. Joe knew the direction he had taken had been something palpable in his life. It was as if he had stood at the edge of a precipice and stepped off the ledge, and fortunately found himself on the other side. Simon, on the same ledge, had lost his footing and fallen into the abyss. Joe smiled with gratitude as he realized he was no longer that man.

Susan stood to refill their glasses. "How is Sally holding out? I hear her friend has gone missing and that you are looking for her?"

Joe scratched his head. "I must say I'm a bit baffled. I'm reluctant to speculate about Hanna's whereabouts, and I'm hesitant to trust this bloke we've been talking to. I need to sort this out quickly. I don't like how much time has passed."

"Mum knew when you were onto something. She said you would have this look about you. Your whole body would change. She used to show it to me sometimes when you weren't looking. I can see you don't have that look, so I think you haven't figured anything out as yet."

Joe's face contorted into a scowl, and he didn't look over at his daughter. He was thinking about what Stefan had said, about his being a distraction. He needed to pay attention to that and, if necessary, work around it and sort it out. It annoyed him that he seemed incapable of dealing with Hanna and Stefan at the same time.

Chapter 25

Stefan had felt very appreciative when Sally called and asked him to meet her for a meal. She had explained, saying she owed him for staying over. But it was also more than that. Waiting for news, she said, was driving her crazy and she could use the company. Stefan felt the same way and, though she didn't owe him anything, was happy for this pleasurable distraction. It was true that while the case was moving relatively quickly, new developments didn't seem to be happening fast enough.

Stefan offered to pick Sally up after work, and following his suggestion, the two had agreed they would drive to the Prince of Wales on Ecclesall Road.

When Sally walked out of Tesco, she looked around for a moment before spotting Stefan's car. Stefan was standing by the front of the vehicle. But at that same moment, Sally recognized one of her co-workers standing awfully close to Stefan. Sally felt the hairs on the back of her neck bristle with anger. Giggling and touching his arm, this girl was clearly sweet on Stefan. Sally felt her cheeks burn as she approached the vehicle. Without a word, she got into the car and slammed the door. The girl took a step back but batted her eyes sweetly and waved, apparently unfazed by Sally's unexpected arrival.

"You always know where to find me," she called as Stefan made his way to the driver's door. But the girl had glanced at Sally, so it was obvious for whose benefit she had made the comment. "Hi there, Sally," she teased.

Stefan groaned audibly as he quickly climbed into the car and started the engine. This scenario had made him terribly uncomfortable, not just because of the actions of the other girl, but more so due to Sally's reaction.

"Hi, Sally, nice to see you," he remarked, peppering the greeting.

"Hi, Stefan, thanks for picking me up."

"That girl back there, was she your friend?"

"I was about to ask you the same thing," she replied, courteous yet clearly displeased. With head turned, she was looking out the side window, avoiding his gaze.

"Come on, Sal. You know better." Stefan was confused by her behaviour.

She sighed and slackened her stance but still didn't look at him. "I'm sorry, Stefan, I'm just tired. You're right, I know better." But the fieriness she had felt at the sight of that girl standing near Stefan had taken her by surprise, and she was very confused by it.

Stefan kept his eyes on the road and his hands on the wheel. This was all new to him, dealing with female emotion, and he didn't quite understand what had just happened. As soon as he had parked the car, he got out as quickly as he could and ran around to open the door for Sally. She exited the vehicle, smiling, obviously pleased by this gentlemanly action.

Once inside, Stefan seated Sally at a quiet table just inside the door and went to fetch them a drink. Sally watched him as he walked to the bar, warmed by his easy smile and mannerisms while in conversation with the bartender. Sally had only been in this pub a few times. She looked around at its finery; the booths all had padded leather cushions, the bar was polished, the mirrors went to the ceiling, and blue glass bottles were on display all along one side. The plush carpet added incredible warmth to the room, which was warmed with red tones throughout.

Stefan returned just as a girl came over to light the candle at their table. The flame flickered to life as it greedily lapped up the cold wax.

Stefan leaned over and said to Sally, "I think I should tell you it was Hero who was outside your house the other night."

"Hero was here in Sheffield? How do you know that? And how did he know where I live?"

"He told me as much." Stefan was ready to confess. "He followed us that day on the train, apparently."

Sally turned to face him with a *you-got-to-be-kidding* look as her mouth popped wide open. "And you didn't know he was following us? Blimey, he makes a better . . ."

"Yes, yes, I know. Joe already told me as much," said Stefan, shrugging his shoulders but smiling, albeit somewhat shamefaced. "But he made the remark innocently enough, not like he was trying to hide something. He only thought Hanna might have returned home, and he said he was anxious to see if she was safe."

Sally lamented, "So that means he doesn't know where she is either."

"But we know she's alive, and we have a good chance of finding her."

"Should I be worried that he knows where I live? Maybe he was lying and was just trying to get to me?"

"I'm sorry it happened, but I don't know what we can do about it now. I don't think he means to harm you. I'm certain he wouldn't have said anything if he did."

"I suppose you are right." Looking into his eyes, she added, "At least I hope you are right."

They had soon fallen into their new level of comfort with one another, and when the meal arrived, Sally asked, "Well, we now know you're not a good detective, but you must be good at something. So, what did you do before you came here?"

"I worked with metal, and yes, I was good at it. I was working my way into a partnership in a small business in Leicester. I say partnership, but what that really means is that I basically worked for three years for free. I had a room above the shop, and that was my life. When the business owner wanted to retire and I wanted to buy him out, I had no idea what I was taking on. The business did well and all, but I knew at that point that I would be working forever for free. Then I met Joe."

"It's brilliant that you have a trade. I've done nothing for myself that way, but I know there's still lots of time. I'm still young, my dad says. But right now, my parents are upset over this Hanna thing. My dad wants me to move home, but I can't do that. It'd be like going backwards."

Stefan quickly interjected, "You have to realize that you are so lucky to have parents who love you."

"Yes, I know, you are right. But I have always wished they had me when they were younger. You see, my parents had me really late. I believe my mum was in her mid-forties, and Dad, well, he was already fifty. So now I'm twenty-three, and they are in their seventies, so more like grandparents. My whole life, it's been like being raised by grandparents. There weren't many outings or vacations, and neither of them got me interested in any kind of sport. My friends were always on about where they went on the weekend, or family nights at the movies or theatre. For me, it was just sheep farming and early nights. I was what you'd call a tomboy. Wouldn't get caught dead in a skirt. I was climbing trees, mucking hay and manure, running through fields, helping Joe with lambing, and such. It was only when I started school again after the summer break when I was about fifteen that I began to feel self-conscious. Some of the kids at school would turn away and snicker at me. Girls were all dressed up pretty, and I looked like a boy. I never had the kind of mum who took me out shopping for nice things."

"I notice you wear mostly dresses now. I suppose it makes sense after you've explained it. There are a lot of things I wish had been different with my parents as well," Stefan responded, shaking his head. "Thinking back, I don't have a clue who they were; it was such a mess."

Not really listening, Sally carried on with her account, "When I have a little girl, I'm going to dress her up in frilly little dresses."

Stefan shuddered in horror, remembering images of little Rita prancing about in her frilly dresses that his mum loved to buy for her. He also remembered the way his father would come in the door after a trip to the pub and leer at her.

"Just make sure they're not too frilly," Stefan said to Sally, trying to hide his frown. "Subtlety is better than flowery."

"Of course," she said, still only half-listening. Sally took a sip of her beer and, sitting back in her chair, asked Stefan, "Where are your parents?"

"They are both gone now. My dad has been gone for a very long time. And my mum died just over a year ago."

"I'm so sorry. It must be hard, having no parents. I mean, I complain about mine, but I can't imagine not having them around."

"When my dad left, I was really young. Actually, he left shortly after Rita disappeared. We thought he'd gone to find her and bring her back, but he never returned. I never heard from him again. My mum, well, I moved away from her when I was eighteen and would visit her once in a while. It's funny, but I never really got close to either of them. They lived in the same house, yet it felt like we were countries apart. My mum, she seemed to live in a fog."

Sally studied his face as she said to him, "You're different from anyone I've ever known."

Wanting to change the subject, Stefan looked at Sally and asked, "Did Joe tell you what happened to Hero's parents?"

"No, why would he?"

"They were murdered, right in front of him. He was just a boy, coming home from school."

As they sat finishing their meal, Stefan recounted the story. Sally had to remember to chew her food; she leaned forward, her eyes riveted on Stefan. When he had finished, he said to her, "We take what we have for granted until we don't have it anymore. Especially parents. You ought to hug yours next time you see them."

Stefan sat back and casually threw one arm over his head. "But he's clever, that Hero. The way he followed us that day. I'll never be a private eye if I don't know who's following me. I'll need to do better than that!"

"But maybe you don't really want to be a private eye."

"Meaning what?"

"Well, it sounds like you want to help this man more than you want to see him arrested for doing something wrong. Maybe you need to rethink what it is you really want."

"I want to work with Joe to help people. He helps them, you know. He helped me. But as I'm finding out things—many of them quite disturbing—I want to make sure I'm not losing something of myself at the same time. How do I do that?"

"You will have to ask Joe. Besides, he only helped you by default. He sure didn't help his mate Simon, did he? 'Cause you see, somebody has to go down. Maybe Joe has learned how to lose bits of himself and not worry about it. There's always a price to pay. I don't think you could do that. Maybe you can work with Joe but not do what he does, if you know what I mean. If you ask me, I believe it's Joe's friend Aisha who really helps people. Maybe you ought to do her work."

Stefan shook his head, disagreeing, but the expression on his face said maybe this was something to consider.

Chapter 26

It was one of those picture-perfect mornings. The sun was shining and the sky was bright blue. There was just a wisp of a breeze that brought with it a dusting of light clouds, as if painted across the sky with faint brushstrokes. The leaves on the tall elm next door were dancing and twirling, some detaching and fluttering to the ground. Stefan was standing in his bedroom, looking out his window. Never had he seen mornings like this from the confines of his room above the workshop in Leicester. All that was visible was the side of the building next door.

He walked into his kitchen only to be greeted by a sink full of dishes. In his bedroom, he had tried to ignore the basket full of laundry. It was obviously going to be a home day. Regardless of the state of his flat, Stefan could not be happier. His life was fertile, and his future was looking bright. Not a day went by that he wasn't grateful for what his mother had done for him, and as it turned out in the end, also his father. His conversation with Sally last night had been enlightening. He had a new understanding about his parents. He was slowly acknowledging the internal struggles his father and mother must have had.

He didn't think he could have handled being in either of their shoes, and he rather pitied them.

But also nagging him was their conversation about his career choices. He tried to ignore any feelings of apprehension as he realized being a PI would require greater adjustments if he were to succeed. And he felt certain he did want to succeed at this. Hadn't he wanted this for quite some time now?

Busying himself, he became aware of the silence. What was that music Sally had been listening to? Robbie somebody. He would need to ask her so he could set something up for himself here. It was time to make his home feel a little more lived in. Since he was in this domestic mood, he decided it was time he finish unpacking his last few boxes of personal belongings that never seemed to have a "place."

Opening the first box, he smiled as he unwrapped a standard-sized metal tin. It was a Reading London biscuit tin—Huntley and Palmer's to be exact—that depicted a scene from India, of men on safari, with elephants draped in brightly coloured tapestries. It had belonged to his business partner's wife, Lydia. And before that, it had belonged to Lydia's great-grandmother, Alice. Lydia had told him to always keep the tin, as it was very rare and actually belonged in a museum. She said this tin might some day bring him a pretty penny if he ever found himself in need. It was her gift to him, as she had no one to leave it to, having no children of her own.

Stefan fondly ran his fingers over the embossed ridges on the lid. He smiled as the memory came flooding back to him. Once a week, Lydia would line this tin with a piece of checkered cloth and fill it with homemade cookies for him. How he missed those sweet-smelling ginger cookies. How often had he eaten them all before the first day had come to a close? Customers would come into the shop while he covertly brushed the crumbs away from his mouth. He had been embarrassed when she first brought them in, but before long he readily accepted them. As each new tin of cookies arrived, his new goal was to make them last at least until the end of the week. Stefan looked around his kitchen, searching for a good spot in which to display the tin. Deciding on the small shelf by the door, he gently placed the colourful tin in the centre. Standing back to assess the location, he silently thanked Lydia.

His phone chirped to life, and he saw on the call display that it was Joe. "What are you doing?" Joe sounded very cheerful.

"I'm looking at my fruit right now. I can't remember when I bought it, but I know it was a while ago. I don't trust fruit that doesn't go bad. There's something unnatural and very suspicious about permanently unripened fruit."

Joe laughed out loud. "Perfect timing, then. Come for dinner, will you? Tonight, five o'clock."

"I don't know what to say."

"Say yes. Come and join me. By the way—have I mentioned that I've moved? Here, write down the address."

"You've moved? When did this happen?"

"You've been away in London, Stefan. The world does

still revolve while you are not here. Just come."

Stefan arrived at Joe's a few minutes early, eagerly anticipating a home-cooked meal. Stefan was surprised and even a little hurt that Joe had not disclosed that he moved to Dore. But then again, he had been in London, so why would it have come up? He had heard good things about the village of Dore, such as its rich history ranging from the smallpox outbreak in the 1800s to the belief that England's very first king, Egbert of Wessex, became king here in Dore. Stefan had also been eager to explore all the varied shops and cafés, pubs, and churches. He could understand the proximity of Joe's new home to Blacka Moor, as he knew how Joe loved to ramble. He would need to come back and explore the area one day.

He parked in front of the updated vintage cottage and walked to the front door. The brick bungalow was situated in a cul-de-sac in a beautiful setting, with plenty of off-road parking. The gardens were delightful, and Stefan noted the wide path that wound around before disappearing towards the rear of the property.

He knocked twice, loudly, and took a step back, his hands folded behind his back. Aisha answered the door, drying her hands on a towel, a huge grin on her face.

"Hello, Stefan. Welcome to our home."

Standing immediately behind her, Joe looked sufficiently satisfied with the look of surprise on Stefan's face.

Once the shock had subsided and details were revealed, Stefan was given a tour of the home before moving out to the back garden. He was greeted by the finest English garden he had ever seen. On the right,

Stefan spotted a raised bed chock-full of a wide variety of herbs, which were spilling over the sides. In the far corner of the yard stood a small, lopsided shed, and beside it a large wooden bench newly painted in the same shade of blue. Delphiniums, hollyhock, canterbury bells, and sweet peas were in abundance everywhere. Still in a state of shock, Stefan looked over as Joe pressed a glass of wine into his hand.

"It took me a long time to like flowers and to want them in my garden. When my husband and daughter died, everyone bought me flowers. My home was filled with them. Then after a while they all started to die, and it made me sick all over again. They were dying just like Daniel and Ava had, and it was like having them die all over again. So for a long time I avoided them. But now I love them. It's strange how they now signify living. It's a beautiful thing bringing them to life and watching them grow. Funny, that." By the time she reached the last two sentences, Aisha was speaking more to herself than anyone else. The men watched her but said nothing. Then, with a big exhale and a smile, Aisha invited them back indoors, and she left them in the front room while she disappeared into the kitchen to fetch a plate of snacks.

Joe was sitting back, his one leg crossed at the ankle. He wore a Cheshire cat grin as he rested his arm over the back of his chair. Taking a sip of wine, he smiled at Stefan. "What do you think?" he said as he set down his glass.

"You sneaky bugger. I am utterly gobsmacked at this. Well done, Joe! This looks quite posh, doesn't it? I mean, it's perfect for you two."

Aisha returned to the room, all aglow at hearing his remarks. She placed the small plate of snacks on the table between Stefan and Joe. "So, you look properly chuffed, Stefan. That's very kind of you."

"This is the bee's knees, Aisha, I mean it. Not just about you two, which is very good news, but this place is a real gem."

They spent much of the next hour in conversation, Aisha and Stefan catching up with each other, after which Aisha invited the men to a small dining room. The room was softly lit by a vintage chandelier, which cast a warm yellow glow over the table. She had prepared tagine, a North African dish that had become a specialty of hers and a meal that had always been well received by anyone who had tried it. She always used lamb and heavily spiced it with ginger, cumin, turmeric, and cinnamon before adding the tomatoes, lemons, dried fruit, and nuts. As usual, it was served with couscous, tiny granules of rolled durum semolina. The quietness during the meal revealed how much they were enjoying it.

"How is Aidan? I hope you don't mind my asking." Aisha was the first to finish her meal and was ready for more conversation.

"He's growing. I really enjoy our visits, but I must say, I am overdue. We do text occasionally, now that he's old enough to have his own phone. He's a bright lad, brighter than Rita and me put together, and I don't mind saying he's a good-looking young lad. Did I mention he looks very much like me?" He winked at her playfully.

The three sat at the table and laughed into the wee

hours. Joe was reminded of his fondness for Stefan and the things that had drawn them together in the first place. He needed to remember this more often, particularly amid his own frustrations. Sitting here watching Stefan engage with Aisha, he was reminded of the frail, translucent-skinned young man who had travelled to Sheffield years ago to identify the corpse of his nearly twin sister—his only sibling.

Looking at him now, he saw a healthier, happier Stefan. The young man had always been cheerful and optimistic, but it was more than that now. Stefan seemed to be developing a real sense of who he was and what he wanted. He retained gentleness despite how cruel life had been to him. And although Stefan often frustrated him, Joe could not discount this man's determination to better his position in life.

Chapter 27

Gulping down his coffee while checking the time, Joe simultaneously reached over to pick up his ringing phone. He looked at his screen. "Ray," he mouthed to Aisha, who was standing nearby. Aisha nodded and left the room to give him some privacy. Ray Lawson was looking for updates. He told Joe that his wife was becoming more and more upset. This was actually good news to Joe, for he had feared the woman was quite devoid of emotion where her daughter was concerned. He sat down and began to give Ray a detailed up-to-date account. He wanted to hold nothing back, knowing he needed to be honest. It was a good sign that both Ray and Mary were worrying about their daughter, and any tidbit of information would be appreciated.

Looking at his watch and realizing the time, he appealed to the man, "Let me call you from my office and we can finish this conversation. I'm just leaving home now. I promise I'll call you as soon as I get there." Joe disconnected and, saying good-bye to Aisha, headed out the door.

Once at the office, Joe had just reached for the phone to call Ray Lawson when his phone rang. The throat-clearing noises on the end of the line made Joe sit up. He could tell it was Hero, and he felt optimism in his gut.

"It's Hanna—she has gone."

"I thought you said she was already gone?"

Hero sounded dubious with his reply. "Aye, she had gone, once, but that was just for a few hours. Then she came back. But this morning, soon as she heard Ian had bought the farm, she threw a wobbly and ran out the door."

"You should have told me as soon as she came back the first time." Joe sighed. "You told me she had already known about Ian."

"Didn't have to tell you anything. You lot think I should just trust you. I didn't know who you were, only who you said you were. I wanted to tell her about it first, to see what she said. I needed to ask her about you and this Sally person. She told me you were okay."

"But now she's gone? Where do you think she went?"

"I don't know, but I think it's not good. She was mad, and she said she wasn't coming back. She has no phone, nothing. She's out there roaming about, and she doesn't know the area very well. She's ill-protected, and I need to find her before someone else does."

"Hero, let us help you. Tell us where you are and who this 'someone else' is. Tell us everything you know; we can offer you protection."

The line went dead, and Joe cursed loudly. He immediately called Stefan, then made his call to Ray, to say they now have confirmation that Hanna was indeed alive and so far, she was well. He left out the part about her disappearing again. Joe was glad that Hero was not standing in front of him, as it would have taken a herculean effort not to grab him by the throat and choke him to death.

His next call was to Chief Inspector Andrew Hall. They spoke briefly about the situation, after which Joe asked him, "I need a mug shot of Carl. Do you have one you can send over to me? I'm walking the streets out there, and I wouldn't know this guy if I tripped over him. It sure would help."

"Didn't Sergeant Thom send you those a while ago?"

"Never got them. Your sergeant never got back to me."

"Okay then, right away. Hang on, I'll email it to you."

After a pause, Joe heard the click of buttons; then his phone pinged. The CI then told Joe he would promptly put the word out for the beat cops to watch carefully for the girl. Hall then suggested that Joe stay put, as there was nothing he could do at this point. "Best you stay and wait to hear from us, or from Hero, or even from Hanna herself. She may also try to call Sally, so keep your phone close at hand. You might come all this way for nothing."

After he hung up the phone, Joe muttered, "Not bloody likely I'll stay put. I'm sure as hell not working for you, mate. I can be reached by phone wherever I am."

He opened the file and took a long, hard look at Carl. He was a little surprised at what he saw. The face staring back at him was unremarkable in every way. With his unruly mop of sandy hair, freckled nose, and mild features, he could have been anybody. You would pass him on the street and perhaps nod in greeting, or even smile at him—not run away in fear. The giveaway was the scar; mean and glaring down the side of his face, where Monty had torn it open. While nicely healed and partially obscured behind a sideburn, it was still starkly evident under the bright glare of the camera flash.

By the time Stefan arrived, Joe had cooled down as he announced he was convinced they should drive to Blackpool rather than sit here and wait for news. Joe relayed to Stefan what the chief inspector had suggested.

"But I don't know what to make of Hero. I'm impressed that he called, but somewhat puzzled as to why he's reaching out. I think he wants us to find him; he just won't come out and say it."

Their eyes locked in chorus with a look of agreement, and as Joe nodded, the two men headed towards the door. The decision had been made before Joe had finished his sentence. So without a word, they headed to the car park. With any luck, they would find Hero.

They made their way around the city, painstakingly revisiting all the places where Hero might be, starting with his flat, back to the area where they had first spotted him, then the amusement park. Having no luck, they decided to visit the place Hero had spoken of on the night someone had stabbed Liam. A search of the area left them equally empty-handed. The place was closed at this hour, and the few lost souls hanging around didn't look helpful. Joe felt watched, but again, any attempt at eye contact with the locals proved futile.

"What if he killed her, Joe?"

"Who are you talking about, Stefan?"

"Hero. Let's just suppose he whacked her, then hid her body and called you to make it look like he's innocent, and then he says he doesn't know where she is. It's easy for anyone to say she ran away."

"Slow down there. Don't overwork your brain, Stefan. Somehow that's not where my logic is taking me. I think he's reaching out. My hat's off to him that he called. I think he does want our help—he wants us to find him and help him, but it's not his nature to say. Here, let's sit for a minute."

Walking along the Promenade, they sat down on one of the benches. Joe rested his arm across the back and turned to face the beach, lost in thought. He closed his eyes briefly as the breeze brushed his face. He let out a sigh.

"It was started by gypsies, you know."

The voice came from behind Joe, startling him. He looked up to see a grey-haired, hefty woman standing very near to him. She seemed to tower above Joe; even though he was seated, he could tell she was not of average height. She wore a pinafore smock over her dress, and her hair was done up in a very chaotic bun that seemed to have been slept in for a few days.

"I beg your pardon?" Joe asked. He lifted his chin, his eyes narrowed in the sunlight.

"This whole area," she said, spreading her arms open wide in a grand, theatrical gesture. "All of Pleasure Beach. It were gypsies that came here first, right where you are looking. They had an encampment, just there," she said, gesturing towards the beach, "back in the early nineteen hundreds. Just a few tents, a fortune-teller or two, and some simple rides. But it was already called Pleasure Beach—has been since the late eighteen hundreds. It was a man from Yorkshire, with a steam carousel, who named it that. And that there tower," she said, turning lightly and pointing towards the famous Blackpool Tower, "they built that back then."

Joe and Stefan looked at each other, then back at the woman.

Her skin was wrinkled yet glowing, and there was a lively sparkle in her eye. She held out her hand in greeting. "My name is Rose. Rose Strudwick. Who are you two, then?"

Stuttering, Joe answered her awkwardly, "My name is Joe." He stood to shake her hand, then sat down again. "And this is my friend Stefan." Stefan remained seated but smiled and nodded in greeting.

Rose Strudwick nodded to Stefan in return. "I've lived around here all my life. Seen many changes. And I've seen you around here a few times now."

"Are you a tour guide?" asked Stefan.

The woman let out a grunt. "Not bloody likely. But I do want to know what you want with that fellow I saw you talking to?"

Again, Joe and Stefan exchanged glances. Both were dumbfounded to silence.

The woman seemed exasperated. Almost shouting, she cried out, "Hero. Our Hero. What do you want with him?"

Before Joe could think of what to say, Rose sat down, practically in his lap, forcing him to shuffle over to make room for her. "So, again, what do you want with Hero? Are you the police? I've not seen you around here before last week, but now I've seen you three times in one."

"No, ma'am, we are not the police." Joe sensed he needed to choose his words.

"Well, you don't look like his friends, and he didn't look too happy to see you lot. I've seen him running and you chasing. Are you working with that copper? The one with no hair? He is always hurting Hero."

"We don't know the policeman who hurts him, but we would never want to hurt him. We really need him to help us find a girl who has gone missing. Her parents are very worried about her and asked us to look for her. We were lucky to find Hero, but he seems reluctant to help at this point," said Stefan, leaning around Joe to face her.

"I don't know if he will help you. I've known him practically his whole life. You see, I was his teacher! And my husband, Elwyn, he was the school headmaster. I'm retired now, but I taught him in grade school, right up until the accident. He used to be a bright lad, you know. Now he walks past me like he doesn't know me. He's just not been the same since he came back. He will pause occasionally with a hint of recognition in his eyes, but then he'll look away with his head down. I think it was too much a reminder of a life that was gone. I want so badly to say something to him, but what? I don't have anything nice to tell him. I'd only make him remember."

"Does he not remember you?" asked Joe.

"I think there's a lot he doesn't want to remember. The day after his mum and dad were killed, they took the lad away to live with his uncle and his new wife. And there was the lad's turning point. Hero also lost his own life that day, so to speak. It was that devastating moment when life as he knew it was over—such a tragedy for a young lad. His switch went from love to loneliness."

Rose sighed before she continued, as if she had repeated this story many times and was no longer concerned whether anyone was listening. "When his uncle took him away, that added to the problem. He wasn't a good man, and he beat the boy. His wife was verbally abusive to the young boy as well. You see, the lad suffered from brain trauma after he saw his parents lying dead in the street. Acute trauma then turned into chronic trauma because he had no help. He ran away from his uncle's home when he was fifteen and has been back here ever since, living wherever he could and finding any odd job. My husband said he'd never seen trauma so bad."

Stefan was suddenly very interested in what this woman was saying. He was relating to this on many levels—how trauma can mess with your head and how important it is to get help. Although Stefan's own trauma was, he felt, not as severe, it still struck a note with him, for he was certain that Rita's trauma would have been extreme, like Hero's.

Rose went on to explain how brain trauma can stunt mental growth and stop further development. "He just stopped developing in his head. He has trouble with boundaries, you know. And he's very anti-social and iso-lated. Did you notice he displays little empathy? It's no wonder he won't help you."

Joe asked Rose, "So you are saying the stress could have rewired his brain? Would that have also impaired his walking and coordination?"

"Well, that's partly it. He has anisomelia—we call it 'short leg.' He wears the boot, as it's meant to help against scoliosis. But the trauma did affect his gait. It's more than likely that not only did it affect the part of his brain that controls emotion, but it also affected his motor develop-ment. I think the poor lad walks around with a sort of helplessness. The trauma could have been lessened if dealt with back then, but now I just watch him and cry. I keep an eye on him. I do it for his mum, you know. She'd be happy to know I watch out for him."

Rose Strudwick's voice quieted as she continued, "She was a wonderful pianist when she was alive. I sometimes walk past their old house, and I can still hear the music. Hero was playing back then, and quite well. He used to hurry home from school for his lesson. He liked it because it pleased his mum so much when he played well."

Rose was staring off into space, as if recalling some-thing in particular. "The year it happened—when they died—we had a district concert planned, and Hero was to play at the church. That never happened, and the boy never played again. The boy's life may have seemed unre-markable on the surface, but I will always remember it as having been remarkable."

As she spoke, she played with a piece of fabric on her dress, crinkling it up then patting it flat again. "Well, that's it for me." Standing to leave, she looked at the pair and, with a big sigh, said, "Just don't expect too much from him, and don't hurt him. Help him. We need to walk towards the Kingdom with the least among us. It was Jesus who warned that the nations will be judged by what we do for the least among us."

Then as she turned and walked away, she uttered a final, "Just don't hurt him. I'll be watching."

Chapter 28

Neither man knew what to make of their encounter with Mrs. Rose Strudwick. Stefan had looked at Joe and shrugged his shoulders, and Joe had done little more than furrow his brow while still absorbing the conversation. They had walked back to the car in silence. Now that the car was in motion, Stefan was first to speak. "That's what you call a real tragedy. You know, I don't dislike him. It would be nice if someone could help him."

"An hour ago, you were ready to pass sentence and send him up the river."

"Well, I changed my mind. I was just thinking of Rita and her trauma. I think that's how Rita was. Don't you think, Joe? When I was hearing the things about how she was, her muttering and all, I think maybe she had that trauma thing as well. Maybe that's why I'm thinking different now. I'm thinking now he must be innocent."

"We have no room for absolutes, Stefan. You will need to learn early on not to think in absolutes. It won't work in this business."

"But say he was innocent . . . and think about it. If it weren't for Mrs. Hunt—Aisha—Rita wouldn't have done as well as she did. I really mean that. But Hero hadn't the same help. Maybe she could help Hero too?"

"I'm afraid it's likely too late, like that lady said. That was a very long time ago. He seems somewhat settled into his life. He has a flat, a job, things that make him happy. It could likely go bad if you tried to alter his life. And it's quite likely too late for any type of medication. Who would be there to monitor, to make sure he took his meds? Like Rose said, all she can do now is keep an eye on him.

"But Stefan, we need to worry about Hanna right now, not Hero. He could be my one obstacle if he's playing silly buggers and purposely hindering my investigation. As for Hanna, I can't figure out if she's in trouble or if she simply doesn't want to be found. If that's the case, she's not in any danger and there's nothing we can do other than try to locate her. She needs to talk to the police, and I can't understand why she hasn't done that. When she spoke with Sally, she said she couldn't come home."

"Do you suppose things could have changed since then?"

"Maybe. But we have no proof of that, and without a crime, the police won't waste time looking for an adult female who quite simply may not want to go home. Her fingerprints alone were no evidence of a crime. After all, it was her suitcase. It would be logical for her prints to be on the knife if she placed it there. I don't know what I will tell her father, and I haven't figured out yet what my instincts are telling me. Of course, if she was intercepted by someone and is being held against her will and there is real danger, I must find out somehow and alert the police.

The question is, how?"

The drive was a mix of music and conversation, and the time went by quickly. Nearing the boundary of Sheffield city, Joe's cell phone pinged. He glanced down at the screen to see if it was a call that he could leave for later but saw that it was Susan. It was unusual for her to be calling at this time of day.

"Now what?" Joe muttered as he answered the call.

"Come home, Dad. Aisha's been in an accident."

"What's wrong?"

"Well, she's had a fall and she didn't want me to call you. She says she's fine, but . . ."

Joe disconnected and stepped on the gas.

"Drop me off at the end of the road, Joe. I can walk the rest of the way. I could use the walk anyway, to clear my head. You need to get right home."

Joe thanked Stefan and the men parted; Joe sped the rest of the way home, thankful for the clear traffic.

His house was quiet when he came in. As he neared the living room, he could hear music softly playing. Aisha lay with an ice pack on her head, another on her shoulder. Her ankle was wrapped in stretchy bandage.

"It's nothing. I'm more embarrassed than anything. I fell off a small ladder, that's all. It's not serious enough to make you rush home. I wish Susan hadn't called you."

Joe disagreed with Aisha's assessment, expressing how grateful he was that she did call. "I don't know what I'd do if anything happened to you."

"Don't say that, Joe. You will know what to do. We can't stop our lives because of someone's injury or death."

Aisha looked very serious as she said, "You can't shelter me, Joe. One day something might happen—to either of us. We both know that reality all too well. All we can do is live the best life possible. We have no guarantees."

Joe said, "All right, point taken. But you need to be extremely careful."

"I will, I promise. Now go bring us a glass of wine and I'll be fine."

Joe disappeared to the kitchen, and after putting the oven on to reheat their dinner, he soon reappeared carrying two glasses of wine. Aisha sat with her eyes closed, but opened them and smiled when she heard him coming.

"Tell me, what on earth were you doing on the ladder in the first place?"

"Well, I was looking for a place to store a few boxes. I'm still finding my way around this new place, and I noticed a trap door in the ceiling above the hallway. I thought it might be a storage attic and I might find a bit of free space. I still haven't had the chance to see. As I was trying to push the door open, the ladder tipped. I may have been using too much force. Perhaps I don't know my own strength, knocking myself off the ladder," she said, grinning slightly.

"I'm just glad I was on my way home and not still stuck in some pub or station in Blackpool."

"But as you can see, I'm fine, so no cause for panic. So, it's your turn. How did it go today?"

"It was not overly successful, and I'm afraid it may have been a wasted trip. But something has me curious. We met a very unusual woman today, and she told us a story about Hero, from his school days up until now. He'd witnessed his parents dying in the street. His life apparently went from bad to worse. She was talking about things like acute trauma and age regression and such."

Aisha listened to Joe's story between sips of wine. When he had finished, she digested his comments for a moment before responding, "Then it makes sense when you tell me things about him, how he behaves and such. If he developed PTSD after the death of his parents, he could have experienced acute or chronic trauma, which in turn developed into age regression as a defence mechanism. The age regression could go back to a few years or even a decade or more. He feasibly has no self-perception, and he more than likely suffers from low self-esteem, shame, and perhaps even guilt. He may feel it was his fault that his parents died. After all, they named him Hero. I doubt he felt like a hero that day."

"It's funny, Hero himself said exactly the same thing. He said he didn't feel much like a hero, watching them die."

She leaned her head back, looking up to the ceiling. "I'm sure I went through a bit of guilt when my husband and daughter died in that crash. Why didn't I drive myself that day? I went through months of torment, blaming myself one day and blaming the lorry the next. Then other things would torment me. The memory. It broke my heart all over again as the years passed and I could no longer remember the sound of my own child's voice. So in my mind, I invented a new voice and somehow convinced myself that was what she sounded like. I got better over the years, but it seems Hero hasn't. Perhaps we share that—our hiraeth. It's our something that can never be again."

"I do view Hero differently now," said Joe. "But I'm still not sure how much I can trust him. Do you think he could be dangerous?"

"He likely has difficulty controlling impulses, so yes, I suppose he could become violent or aggressive. Do you think he could have hurt Hanna? Could he be lying about that, and about the stabbing as well? Could it have been him who stabbed Liam?"

"That's what Stefan thought—at first. Now he feels the man isn't harmful. He compares Hero to Rita in some ways. Remember her muttering?"

"He's absolutely right, Joe. There will be many different levels of trauma from person to person, but she was profoundly impacted by trauma."

"So he wouldn't necessarily have become violent and harmed Hanna. Maybe it helps him to be protecting her? He may have felt he had not protected his mother and father, but if he's now remembering, perhaps he feels a strong desire to protect Hanna. And now it's not unreasonable that, in frustration, he would have killed anyone who tried to hurt Hanna."

Nodding, she added, "It could be one of many things that you are dealing with here, Joe."

"I'm afraid I'm performing quite poorly on this case. Another is the fact that I think someone is watching us. I have spotted him on two occasions, when we have been poking around. I've never seen anything like it before. I always find someone willing to open up, if only a little. Usually even the most secretive of people will offer up at least a tidbit. But these people . . . it seems the more I ask around, the further underground everyone goes, including Hero. It's like this huge conspiracy. Like everyone is afraid of something—or someone. There's a wickedness I can't put my finger on."

"Now it's my turn to ask you to be careful," said Aisha, squeezing his arm. She turned into him and buried her face in his neck. This little part of his neck that was her favourite place.

Chapter 29

Sally looked in the mirror and hardly recognized the frantic-looking person she saw staring back at her. There were bags under her weary eyes, and her lip was swollen. She realized she had been wearing the same clothes for three days. She hadn't noticed the downward slide. When did she let herself go like this? She had always cared how she looked. Never overdone but always neat, natural, and impeccably clean. The face in the mirror had crusted mascara from at least two days ago; her hair was un-brushed and had been pulled into a careless ponytail.

The past couple of weeks had been surreal, as if living in a nightmare. Things seemed to be happening in slow motion. The inside of her lip was raw from her constant biting. Lately she'd been hearing noises; not just outside but often in the next room, paralyzing her. She needed to get a hold of herself.

Sally looked at the clock, then went back to bed. She would miss another day of work, but so be it. She couldn't go in this state, but at the same time she needed to work, so she made up her mind she would go tomorrow. Lying on top of the covers, she stared at the ceiling while remembering the day she and Hanna had met.

Hanna had been in the store numerous times, shopping. They had smiled at each other often until one day Hanna walked up to her and told her how much she loved her hair. From then on, they would often stand and chat in the aisle. One day, while on the Moor with her mum, she had run into Hanna checking rentals at the notices board by the post boxes. While her mum shopped, Hanna and Sally had coffee.

Hanna struck her as saintly back then. She came across as gentle and unpretentious, and Sally felt she was really smart and knew a lot about the world—far more than Sally, who only knew farming. Remembering Hanna back then, she realized how slowly the transformation had happened. Sally hardly noticed until she had completely changed, yet there were now things about Hanna that intrigued Sally even more.

The new, daring Hanna was never afraid to speak her mind. While usually private, she began sharing everything with Sally, and before long Sally thought her to be intensely bold. Hanna had almost hated her parents for how they had raised her. She felt there was too much God and not enough real world. If sex was a sin, where did she come from? Her parents had the advantage of a free life, marrying young, making decisions for themselves, yet they were now denying her any freedom to make her own choices.

Sally went into Hanna's room and started angrily rifling through her belongings. She tore clothing out of drawers. Tore the blankets off the bed and checked under the mattress. Feeling defeated, she clenched her jaw, sat on Hanna's bed, and covered her face with her hands.

Oddly, Sally had never really known Hanna, although she had secretly admired the rebel in her. Hanna wasn't afraid to take risks. Quite the opposite; she said she got off on the risks. At times, she had a potty mouth, and other times, she behaved proper. She said she held in a lot of anger towards her parents and would likely never get rid of the chip on her shoulder at not having had a normal childhood. She was never permitted to invite friends over; worse, she doubted any friend would want to come over, her parents being so standoffish. Although they looked flawlessly polished, to her they behaved more like the Addams Family in their weirdness. Sally had said she should not worry so much about it, as everyone hates their parents at some point and resents part of their upbringing.

One thing Sally could never understand was the way Hanna seemed to obsess over men. Hanna said it was like forbidden fruit because of her sheltered upbringing. And she had been a chubby child and mostly overlooked. As she matured and lost her baby fat, boys would look at her in a different way, and she liked it. She fantasized about the sexiness and the excitement of the possibilities now available to her. Sally would never have such audacity, for though she was brought up in quite an open and liberal household, she personally felt it improper. Actually, for her it seemed gauche and very possibly dangerous and destructive.

While she sat wondering if she even liked Hanna anymore, the sound of her cell brought her back from her thoughts. Sally walked over to the side table to pick up the phone, if only to stop the incessant ringing. Seeing it was Stefan, she answered right away. He explained he was calling to give her the latest news about Hanna being missing.

"But I know she's missing. When I first met you, I told you she was missing."

"Well, now she's missing again. Or should I say, more missing."

"What are you talking about?"

Stefan then explained about Hero's call, how he had been hiding her but now she had left and he was worried. "And if Hero is worried, it's not a good sign."

"Why would you say that, Stefan? According to you, he doesn't exactly have a luminous personality, so why believe him at all?"

"I dunno. It's hard to explain. I really like him, Sally. In some ways, he reminds me of me, about living through losses when he was young. But it sounds like it was not easy for him to try to bounce back. I thought we might have had a bonding moment after he told me this really strange story. Can I tell you?"

Sally moved to the front room to sit down and listen to Stefan's story.

"Hero had a bad time a while back, and he was out walking. He said his foot was hurting and he was tired. He met a man there on the Promenade. The man was a tourist from Panama. Hero said they don't all speak to him. You know, the tourists. But this one did. They sat on a bench on the Promenade for a long time, watching people. The man made Hero talk about himself. Then the man looked out into the crowd, and he said he thought, for the most part, people were sad. Then he told Hero about this book, called *The Dictionary of Obscure Sorrows*, that he was reading. The book, he explained, was a reference where you could search out some definitions of emotions, the ones that are not that easy to explain.

"He said the description the man had picked for him was 'nodus tollens.' I remembered the words because he helped me to say them properly. I asked him what that was, and he said—if I can remember it the right way— it was like the pain of realizing that the plot of his life just didn't make sense to him anymore. He was finding himself in places where he didn't belong. First everything seemed important, then nothing did. He was getting by on luck and charity, and when that ran out, he realized that all along, it was up to him to create his own life, not just randomly wander through it. And now he felt it was all over and he blew it. Or something like that."

"That sounds very strange," said Sally. "I wonder what it all means. What was he trying to say?"

"Maybe nothing. Maybe he was just opening up to me, I suppose. I don't know if he talks to a lot of blokes, aside from the ones that go around stabbing people."

"But Stefan, you are not to get attached to these people. You are supposed to be a PI working a case. You should only be using any information to solve the case, not talking about how you could help him."

"Thanks, Sally, I know that. And I'm trying. This isn't exactly the easiest case to be involved in when I'm just trying to get my feet wet. I have to go now, but I'll talk to you later."

Sally hung up and went back to Hanna's room to straighten up the chaotic mess she had left there—although she was conscious of the fact that she didn't create all this chaos in the first place.

Joe's phone rang. He immediately recognized the hesitant breathing on the other end of the line, although he had not spoken.

"Hero? Is that you?"

"I've done things I've not been proud of, but I've never hurt anyone. My only wrongdoing was in saying and doing nothing when I saw things. Maybe I should have said things then."

"Why are you telling me this, Hero?"

"Because this time Hanna has not come back. She's been gone for two days now. I thought she'd come back again, but she hasn't. And I think I know where she is, and this time she really is in danger. I think it's not so good." Hero's voice became aroused. "She isn't smart enough to know that how she was acting was trouble—all smiling and friendly. She didn't know what they would do to her. What they would want her for. So I'm telling you that I need to go and get her."

Joe was on his feet, almost yelling into the phone. "Not this again. What would they want her for, Hero? Tell me where you are. Let me help you. I can meet you anywhere you say."

"It'd take too long, and I don't want to be seen with you lot. I ought to have done something sooner."

For a brief second, it sounded like Hero was going to say more—something about the pause, as if he had a burden to unload. There was a brief, "I have to go now." Then the line went dead.

It was worrying, how quickly he had hung up. Was Hero testing him? It sounded like he was struggling to speak; his words had come out in choppy spurts. Why had he called?

"Son of a bitch," Joe yelled, slamming the phone down onto his paper-cluttered desk. Taking a big breath, he quickly picked up the phone again to call Stefan.

Shaking, Hero hung up the phone. He opened the cupboard to retrieve his little tin of teabags. He fished out one of the newest ones and put on the kettle. He didn't try to close the cupboard this time, as he was no longer interested in the fact that it had never closed properly. There was a thin stream of light coming in through the yellow-stained window shade. He walked over and sat at the small table that stood against the wall. He no longer noticed how badly the wallpaper was peeling, nor did he pay attention to the musty, sour smell of the small, airless room. He gazed over towards the small, unmade bed that stood in the opposite corner, looking not at it, but through it. Even if he had the energy to go over and pull up the covers, he lacked the desire to do so. He pictured Hanna, huddled up and frightened, with Ian sleeping beside her.

Once the kettle had boiled, he got up and poured water over the nearly depleted teabag. He took the cup and again sat at the table. After poking the bag around for a few minutes with a fork to urge some colour into the water, he finally stood up, no longer interested in the cup in front of him. With a sigh, he spit on his fingers and flattened his hair before walking across the room. "Best get on with it," he said as he opened the door and headed outside.

Sometimes it is better to lose and do the right thing,
than to win and do the wrong thing.

Tony Blair

Chapter 30

Hanna was walking quickly along the beach, stooping close to the wall to screen herself from the street. She doubted anyone would think to look for her down here, away from the Promenade. Since she had left Hero's flat, her heart had not stopped pounding and she had been unsure what to do. Her surroundings were not familiar. It was the second time she had left—on the first attempt, she had returned after only a few hours. It amazed her how quickly she had become like a frightened wild animal that had escaped its cage, just like the animals at the zoo that Ian had taken her to see. Leaving the flat, she had stood in the alley, her back against the wall and her head pressed into the timeworn, clammy brick, her eyes closed. Thinking quickly, she first knew she needed to follow the sound of the seagulls to the water's edge. She needed to get to the train station, although she had no idea what she would do when she got there. Still, she could find her way there once by the water and deal with the rest as it came.

She was acutely aware of the fact that she had no phone, no money, and no identification. She had no idea why she had left her bag at Hero's and felt a real twit.

But she needed to get out of there quickly, before Hero returned to the flat and tried to stop her. She couldn't stay in that cramped, grungy flat a moment longer, no matter how kind Hero had been. She wanted to go home. Hanna longed for her own bed. How the hell did this happen? Why was she here, in this predicament? Her very essence was crumbling right before her eyes; she no longer knew who she was or what she would do.

Eyes darting and fists clenched, she slowed her pace. People were looking at her strangely. She felt ashamed and embarrassed. She hadn't changed her clothes in over five days, although it could have been more. She no longer knew what day it was. She could feel her hair sticking to her neck and her forehead. Her skin was dry and dirty. She was squinting against the sun, shading her eyes with one hand.

Coming to the end of the sheltering wall, she realized she would need to walk up to the street. It was the only way to carry on in the direction of the train station. Climbing the steps, she hurried along the walkway, her head down. Not watching where she was going, she nearly walked right into a body—the big body of a policeman. He turned to look at her, and she quickly turned to head in the other direction. She felt a new panic rise inside of her.

She hadn't walked far when suddenly she heard the screeching of brakes and a car door slam. She turned and saw a man getting out of a shiny green car. He began walking towards her with urgent resolve. Terror struck as she realized it was Carl. How on earth had he spotted her so quickly? Had Hero called him?

Panicking, she ran out into traffic to cross the road. She was narrowly missed by a car, and then another. She froze where she stood, horns honking all around her. A group of people stood on the edge of the walkway, shouting at her, shaking their heads. The bald policeman stood rooted, watching her. His legs were spread wide apart and his arms were crossed. Why was he doing nothing? It was then that she felt the strong arms around her, pulling her back onto the walkway.

"It's okay, folks. Lover's spat." Carl laughed as he grabbed her wrist and led her back to his car. With firm and precise movements, he opened the car door and pushed her towards the opening, smiling at the onlookers as he nodded to the policeman. The gulls overhead were circling, their squawks escalating as if screaming in protest. Hanna climbed into the car reluctantly, not knowing how to fight. Before Carl closed the door, he muttered aloud, "It's all over folks. Just me needing to teach this one some respect." The small crowd dispersed, no longer interested in anyone else's affairs. A second later, she was crushed with strong blow to the back of her head; then everything went dark.

When Hanna woke up, her head was throbbing. She cautiously felt the back of it and found a small wound, which felt sticky and crusting. She was surrounded by darkness. She felt around and determined she was in a very cramped place. Was this a closet, perhaps? What were the lumpy things on the floor under her? She felt around and realized she was sitting on a pair of shoes. Standing up she hit her head on clothes and hangers. Plastic hangers. Not much good for anything. How long had she been here?

Just then, she heard a key in a door. Someone was coming into the room outside her closet. She held her breath and didn't move, afraid to make a sound; although it was ridiculous to do so, as it was likely the same person who had put her in the closet. Hanna sat in terror as she heard footsteps pacing back and forth, pausing at the closet door and then moving again. She heard a man softly swearing. She recognized the voice as Carl's. Eventually she heard the pop of a tin can opening, followed by more pacing and swearing.

"I need to pee," she screamed.

Hanna waited for what seemed a very long time. She thought she might faint. She was thirsty and hot, and her heart was racing. Time passed. It seemed like forever before the door opened. It was completely dark, inside and outside. The shadow grabbed her shoulder and led her to the loo, pushed her in, and turned his back but didn't close the door. Knowing she had no choice, she quickly went about her business. When she had finished and had flushed the toilet, the shadow turned towards her, grabbed her by the hair, and pulled her back to the closet.

"Ow," she whimpered. "Is this necessary?" She tried to resist, but the hand on her back was big and strong. She fell into the closet, hitting the back wall and stumbling.

Standing in the same spot, staring into the darkness, Hanna eventually sat down, wishing she knew what was going on. The apartment was eerily quiet before she finally heard his voice again.

"Yo, Dane, this is Carl. Tell him I've got the girl. Yes, yes, I told Thom, no more trouble. I'm a man of my word. You can have her, I promised you both. We need to clean this mess up and make it all go away. Yes, no hard feelings. Take the slut, do what you want to her. Don't understand why you need another peace offering for Liam. Weren't it enough that Thom got rid of Ian? Okay, fine, like I said, come and get the slag. She's worth more to you than she is to me. It's your guarantee she'll never be around to tell anyone about all of this." Then the room went quiet.

Hanna bit her knuckle to stop herself from making a noise. She lay there for hours, her legs starting to cramp. She must have fallen asleep for a time, as there was now a faint crack of light coming from the top of the door. She heard the television, then snoring. She frantically tried to wedge the door, but there was no lock or handle on the inside. She wrestled with the door, trying hard to be quiet as she struggled to push the lower corner away from the frame. An impossible task, she learned. Who the hell uses plastic bloody hangers? She sat back again, holding her throbbing head. She was certain that she was going to die.

She had let everyone down, including herself. She could never say sorry to her dad or hug her mum and explain how her rebellion had started out so innocently. Would she ever see them again? And what about Sally?

Poor Sal had put up with a lot from her lately. If only she could have one more chance to explain to Sally what had come over her—her need for adventure. Never again would she have the chance to have her old life back. She breathed deeply to stave off the panic that was beginning to grip her.

Hanna must have dozed off again, and she wakened to the sound of movement. Carl must be up. Straining her ears, she heard what sounded like the shower running. Hanna started with a desperate tug on the door before she frantically began to kick it, hard. She stopped when she heard footsteps hurrying to the closet. The door opened, revealing a stark-naked and dripping-wet Carl.

He opened his mouth and yelled at her, spit flying out. "I won't tell you again to shut up, okay?" His arm was waving in the air. "Next time I hear you, I'll rip out your throat," he said as he slapped her, hard, and shut the door again. Then the sound of retreating footsteps, and the room went quiet again. The side of Hanna's face was wet with soap and water, and it stung from the slap. She lay back, shivering.

After what seemed like forever, Hanna woke up. Again, there was no light coming from the top of the door. She had no idea whether Carl was home or not, so she dared not make a move. She feared what he might do to her if she tried the door again. She shifted her position quietly. It seemed to make no difference. She had shifted so many times, she ached equally on every which side.

Then Hanna heard a different sound: footsteps that were coming from far away. It sounded like they were climbing stairs. Then the sound drew closer; then there was a knock at the door. It must be someone from the Snakes coming for her. Her heart began to pound harder. They were here. What would happen to her now? She heard Carl walking towards the door.

"Who is out there?" he called out, barely audible.

Then Hanna heard a familiar voice, and her heart began to race with hope. It was Hero.

"Please let me in, Carl. I know what you've done. I came to talk to you."

She heard a click and the squeaky sound of Carl opening the door.

Chapter 31

Hero stepped cautiously past Carl and into the room, looking around for signs of Hanna. He turned slightly to face his host, not wanting to be caught off guard with his back turned.

"I've come to turn myself in to Monty. It were me who killed Liam."

Carl stepped past Hero as though he was invisible and spoke as he moved towards the sofa. "Don't be daft. You couldn't kill anything bigger than a fly."

"I can and I did. Hanna, she did nothing. She pushed him was all, and he fell down the steps, and I grabbed his knife and stabbed him." Hero lowered himself onto the arm of the sofa, cautiously looking around the room.

"You weren't even there. My boys watched it all, Hero. And Ian let us know just before he died. I know that's not what happened, so why don't you be a good lad and piss off." He bent over and opened a wooden box that sat on the side table and took out a cigarette. Closing the box, he walked towards the kitchen.

Hero took advantage of the fact that Carl had his back to him. He rose quickly and stepped towards Carl. He pushed him as hard as he could, but Carl barely stumbled.

He was far larger than Hero, and the push hardly moved the man.

"You are a liar. Ian wouldn't have said that," Hero sputtered. Carl turned around with a laugh and pushed back hard, sending Hero crashing against the closet door. Upon the impact, Hanna screamed out, "Hero, help me."

In one quick motion, Hero spun around and turned the knob before Carl could reach him. Carl stepped forward and punched Hero in the jaw, sending him reeling sideways. Hanna stumbled out of the closet and lurched forward into the room, her eyes taking in her surroundings as they adjusted to the light. Carl paid little attention to her as he again took a step towards Hero. Looking around, Hanna picked up the nearest object—a table lamp—and springing forward before Carl could turn, she forcibly bashed him in the side of his head, the lamp shattering into fragments.

That gave Hero enough time to get up off the floor. He stumbled to his feet and, grabbing a heavy glass ashtray from the table as he rose, smashed Carl in the face, his nose exploding into a bloody mess. In a split second, Hero pulled his knife from his belt and plunged it into Carl's thigh. Carl fell to the ground screaming. He looked at Hero with hatred, fire, and blood in his eyes.

"What the hell do you think you are doing, you little retard? You will pay for this!" He grabbed his leg tightly as his jeans turned crimson.

Hero's plan was falling into place. Without hesitation, he grabbed Carl's car keys and phone and, taking Hanna by the hand, ran towards the door. He threw open the door and pulled Hanna towards the staircase.

"You have to come back with me, Hanna. Quickly. Now." Hero let go of her hand and grabbed her firmly by the arm as together they fled down the stairs, out of the building, and into the street.

"I might have hurt him badly," he said as he whisked her around the corner and out to the main street, where he hoped to hide amongst the people and traffic. He knew where Carl's car was parked, having looked for it before he had gone to the flat. The two quickly made their way there. Unlocking the doors, he asked Hanna to please get in. A confused Hanna obeyed. She had never seen Hero act this way before. He was determined, confident. Daring.

Hero started the car and put it into gear. She sat in shock, not knowing where they were going and not caring. It became apparent that driving was not Hero's strong point, and Hanna clutched the edges of the seat, fearing they would hit something or be hit any minute. As the car lurched forward, Hanna was turned in her seat, watching out the back window for any sign of Carl. She breathed easier with each corner turned. As she turned back to face the front, Hero announced that he needed to make one stop.

The car jerked uncontrollably as Hero navigated into a small parking area behind a block of stores. Once he had carelessly parked the car, he got out without once looking at Hanna and disappeared inside a Boots store. Hanna had to decide whether to leave or stay. Something told her to stay.

He came out a few minutes later carrying a bag—full of what, Hanna wondered but didn't ask. Without hesitation, Hero opened Hanna's door and, handing her a bottle of water, asked her to get out. She grabbed the bottle and drank it down greedily. She had not had a drink in likely two days. Hero locked the car, then threw the keys into a nearby hedgerow. Hero put out his hand to hail a taxi. A dark cloud had moved overhead, and the wind had picked up. He looked around nervously, seeming unsure of this plan, when a taxi pulled up alongside Hanna. As Hero held the cab door open for Hanna, he asked the driver to head towards the marina at the top of River Wyre.

By the time the taxi had pulled away from the curb, it had started to rain. Tiny droplets on the windshield quickly turned into an intense downpour. The windshield wipers squeaked as they raced frantically back and forth. The taxi ride took about twenty minutes, and Hanna hadn't moved a muscle for the entire ride. Neither she nor Hero spoke. The taxicab pulled up alongside the entrance to a marina. Once Hero had pulled Hanna from the cab, he paid the driver, who then put the cab in gear and drove away, all with barely a word spoken. Once the taxi had left, Hero took Hanna by the hand and they began to walk along the long pier, heading towards the boats. The rain had begun to subside by now.

"Are you okay?" he asked her, to which she merely nodded. His steps slowed as they came to a stop alongside a badly weathered cabin cruiser, partially covered with a tarp.

"Why are we here?" she asked.

"You'll see." Hero walked alongside the boat and unlatched a small boarding ramp at the stern of the vessel. He held the slimy tarp over to one side and boarded before turning to face Hanna, coaxing her to follow.

"Whose boat is this? You have to tell me why we are here. I'm scared, Hero." Hanna was shivering with either cold or fear, or a mixture of both.

"Please, Hanna, we need to do this. We need a place to hide, and I know this boat. We will be safe here for a spell. Please get on the boat and I will explain."

As she nervously stepped on board, she asked, "Are you sure this thing won't sink? It don't look too healthy to me." The boat began rolling, the weather-beaten teak creaking with the motion created by their moving bodies.

He grinned his crooked grin and said, "It won't sink," as he pulled the tarp back over the entrance. She followed Hero into the cabin, then forward and a few steps down to the galley. She nearly choked from the stifling, musty odour. The galley looked old, with only one small window behind a cobweb-covered blue velvet curtain. The countertop held one small rusty basin with a badly pitted tap set. A small bench ran the length of the interior, and there was a hole in the floor that had likely held a post and table.

Hero placed the bag into the basin and, opening it, pulled out a pair of scissors and said, "This has to happen, Hanna." He began removing all the contents and laying them out on the counter.

"Why are you doing this?" she asked.

"Did you not understand what was happening to you? Carl was giving you to Monty, as a gift. Payment. Monty would drug you, Hanna—and he would keep you drugged until you liked it or needed it. And then he would sell you for sex. Or he'd make one of 'em movies with you, where in the end you would probably die."

Hanna looked at him in horror. "But what will happen to me now? Bloody hell, I don't even know who I am anymore."

"Yes, you do, Hanna. More than ever, you will know who you are. It will all come back to you as soon as you get home."

"But what will they do to you, Hero, for helping me?"

Hero stepped towards her with the scissors and said, "Let's not talk about that just yet, Hanna. Let's do this, and then I promise I'll tell you everything."

Hanna blinked against the darkness, trying to see. For a moment, she thought she was back in Carl's closet, but then she felt the motion and heard the creaking. She heard Hero moving about the boat, which was likely what woke her. As she heard him cross to the other side, his movement was again causing the vessel to gently rock back and forth. Surprisingly, she had slept soundly through the night. She could tell it was morning. The dim light was just beginning to form shapes in the cabin, and she could hear the gulls start up.

Hero came close and touched her arm. "You need to get up now, Hanna. We have to go."

It was half past five in the morning, and by the first sign of light, Hero was already standing by the hatch, waiting for Hanna to wash her face and hands. After she nodded towards him that she was ready, they left the boat without a sound. Her hands were still wet, and she wiped them against her shirt. There was no point in looking back to see if she had forgotten anything. All she owned was what she was wearing.

They walked along the pier and back to the entrance of the marina. Carrying on through rows of warehouses, they eventually came to a main road. Crossing it, Hero took her to a tram station, which read Stanley Road, where they sat together and waited. Once the tram arrived, they boarded in silence. He steered her to the back of the tram to two empty seats and sat by the window. Hanna sat beside him, and he gave her the instructions once more.

"Here's your ticket. Remember, I can't come into the station with you. Go in really quickly and try to get on the train right away, to stay out of sight. They likely won't spot you this time, but they will be looking for me."

On the tram, Hanna held on to Hero's hand firmly. She and Hero looked at each other for a long time—something that was very foreign to him, to maintain such prolonged eye contact. He felt an indescribable peace, for the first time in many years, and he smiled at her.

When the tram reached the station at the North Pier, Hero squeezed her arm and pointed.

"It's that road, right there. Remember what I told you. Walk right down to the end and you will be at the train station. Go now!"

Hanna quickly exited and waved at Hero through the window as she crossed the street. She looked back again, but Hero had disappeared. Fortunately, by the time she had walked the few blocks to the station, the train to Sheffield had arrived and was waiting in its berth. She handed the ticket to the man at the gate, almost running to the platform, and quickly boarded without daring to look around. Once seated, she burst into silent tears. She sat like that for a few minutes until she had collected herself. As the other passengers were now arriving, she tried hard to act calm. She opened the bag Hero had given her, trying to see through her tears.

Inside the bag she found various items: two bottles of water, a sausage roll, and a bag of crisps. He had given her Carl's phone, saying there was stuff on it the police would like to see. It suddenly dawned on her that Hero might now be in grave danger. She hadn't given him a second thought. She just wanted to get out of there. What he did to Carl would not go unpunished. Where could he go to be safe? She kicked herself for not asking him to get on the train with her.

Hanna cried shamelessly. Here she was, finally on the train to Sheffield—who would have imagined the things that had happened since she first arrived in Blackpool? She had been so full of hope and adventure, and now she was simply grateful to be alive. What a fool she turned out to be; a naive, airheaded twit. Sally had been right, and she would tell her so. But still, none of the things that happened had made any sense to her.

What was wrong with her? Was her brain somehow

wired wrong? All she wanted was to mean something to someone. She wiped her sweaty palms against her knees and shifted her position, leaning against the window. How different was this journey home compared to the ride to the coast all those days ago. People were looking at her as they walked past. She looked away and closed her eyes, cursing Ian.

Closing her eyes may not have been a good idea, as immediately she was back in the closet, the musty smell hitting her nostrils. She could hear Carl's voice and feel the sting of his hand across her cheek. Hanna sat upright and opened her eyes. She exhaled, her breath coming out in rasps. The back of her neck was wet with perspiration, even though she was shivering. She needed this train to go faster.

She briefly closed her eyes again, thinking if she didn't, she might faint. With shaking hands, she picked up Carl's phone and saw there was very little battery left. She knew she could make all but one quick call before the phone died. Without further hesitation, she dialled Sally's number.

Chapter 32

The streets of Blackpool were glistening from the downpour that had just passed along the coastline. Droplets of water hung from the lampposts and wires, hesitating before falling onto the street. Joe glanced upwards to the sky when a big drop hit him on the forehead. The sun was once again glaring, causing steam to rise from the roadways. Stefan was squinting against the brilliance, keeping up with Joe while dodging the puddles. An earthy smell had risen from the greenery along the streets. The two men had looked everywhere but found no sign of Hero. Joe tried to redial the last number that had called his phone. Nothing.

Climbing the steps to the precinct, Joe opened the door and the two men stepped inside. The room was empty but for the desk sergeant and another officer, who was on the phone. Both men stood behind the counter that was littered with various brochures, ranging from Senior Scams, Vehicle Burglary, Beach Safety, to Everything There Is to Know About Opioids.

Joe checked in with the desk sergeant to see if there had been any news about the case. He was told they were not actively involved in looking for a young woman that had likely run away from home, unless evidence turned up that would link her to the case—evidence other than a fingerprint on a knife in her suitcase. The other officer had hung up the phone and was staring hard at Joe, who had been trying to listen to his conversation. The voice was familiar to him, and he eventually recognized it as that of Michael Thom. Thom was a big man, and he was chewing gum. Hero had mentioned a big copper with no hair, who had spit gum on his shoe. Thom, Joe noted, had no hair.

After his brief conversation with the desk sergeant, Joe thanked the man, then turned to leave. The officers were acting odd, and Joe desperately wanted to find out why. Stefan, before turning towards the door, asked aloud if maybe the sergeant had seen or heard anything unusual. The desk sergeant looked at him over his glasses that had slid down his nose.

Holding back a chuckle, he shouted, "You're joking, right? Have I seen anything unusual? Are you a bleed-ing comedian? Have you seen it out there? Every day is unusual!"

Thom watched the two leave, an expression of impas-sivity on his big, ugly face. Joe struggled with whether he should be speaking to the man, but again thought better of it. The precinct had an eerie air about it today, and he didn't want a confrontation. He sensed that things could escalate quickly.

The sun had by now nearly dried the streets. Stefan and Joe found a dry spot on one of the sun-drenched benches and sat to observe the activity on the boardwalk.

Stefan was eating a soft ice cream cone that he had just purchased from a sidewalk vendor. Joe had, at that moment, opened his mouth to speak when they heard a scream. Both men jumped out of their seats. On the edge of the walkway, a woman stood in horror as she watched her toddler run into the path of a passing tram. He had run into the road to fetch his ball and was narrowly missed by the vehicle. The result could have been deadly.

"And that's how quickly someone's life can change," said Joe.

Stefan appeared restless and disquieted. "So let's go home," he said with an air of dread. "Something doesn't feel right."

"No," answered Joe, emphatically. "That's enough. I'm not leaving until I get some answers. Hero must be somewhere, and I'm tired of leaving here empty-handed. We need to go back to where it all started, that night at the pub where the stabbing occurred."

"But we've been there already. We found nothing," Stefan responded, obviously forgetting their conversation about his standing back and letting Joe get on with his investigation.

"Yes, but that was early in the day. Sorry, Stefan, but we need to be there at night, at a time when they all crawl out of whatever hole they hide in during the day. We need to find a hotel. I'll let Aisha know I won't be home tonight. If you feel you want to go, you can leave, no hard feelings. But I need to see this thing through."

"I'm staying right here with you, Joe. After all, we are partners."

Joe smiled at Stefan and nodded but said nothing. He was focused. Looking around, he pointed in a random direction and announced, "There must be a hotel on every block in this town. Let's go find one. If you have anyone you need to call, I suggest you call them now."

Stefan followed quietly, then slowed his pace. A red car had passed them, then had turned around and parked on the side of the road just behind them. He turned to look. The engine was still running, but he couldn't make out anyone inside as it was a fair distance back. He pretended to be looking at something else entirely. He did notice the grill of the car had a face that looked, oddly, like his father, which caused him to shiver. The car then drove ahead and parked again. Was someone following them? They walked past the vehicle, but Stefan said nothing to Joe. The windows were tinted, so it was impossible to see who was driving. Stefan again made a point of ignoring it. A few minutes later, the car drove off. Had Stefan been imagining the car was following them?

They found a small hotel around the corner, on Alexandra. The receptionist offered a room with twin beds and a shower. Not what Joe would have chosen if he was on vacation, but all they needed was a place to lay their heads for the night. Stefan wished he were at home, as he again felt something in the air—an element of danger that wasn't present before. Joe seemed a changed man. He appeared driven, with a stoic determination that perhaps surpassed logic. Stefan wisely sensed that this was not the time to express any opposition or voice an opinion.

Once they had checked in and Joe had spoken with Aisha, the men prepared to go back to the pub. Stepping outside into the dusk, Joe suggested they walk, as it would be quicker than waiting for a cab. Joe also wanted to check out the area on the way there.

It was dark by the time they arrived, and the pub was close to full capacity. The voices were loud, as was the music—Joe recognized the song as "Blurred Lines" by Robin Thicke. Some of the girls stood around with drinks in hand while rhythmically flexing their hip outward to the beat of the music. Stefan stood by while Joe walked to the bar and grabbed two pints. He tried to engage the bartender, hoping to ask him a question about Hero, but the man looked at him with disinterest as he placed the beer down. He turned away before Joe could speak again. Stefan wasn't having any luck either. Even a young, good-looking person such as himself was being ignored when trying to make eye contact with anyone.

They took their pints and walked over to the kitchen window to place their orders for fish and chips and mushy peas. Two girls stood nearby, laughing and carrying on, but as Joe turned to say something to them, they quickly walked away. He suddenly felt very old. Joe then caught sight of someone out of the corner of his eye but didn't look up, for he was sure this was the man who had been following them. He was wearing a checkered blue shirt and a black baseball cap with a bright green logo, which said *Illuminations*. Joe said nothing to Stefan for fear he might react negatively, making it obvious. Or worse, he feared Stefan, in his present state, would be hot-headed enough to approach the man. Instead, he kept an eye on the individual as they headed towards one of the only unoccupied tables.

On the way to the table, Joe tried desperately to engage some of the patrons with a nod or a smile. Nobody would make eye contact. It was unusual for regulars to ignore newcomers. Usually it was quite the opposite, and the newcomers would be stared at or even approached. But these people were going out of their way to look anywhere but at Joe.

Watching the baseball-cap man from this angle, Joe noticed the piercings on his face, eyelids, earlobes, and lips—he looked like a grotesque walking pincushion. The man made no secret of the fact that he was looking right at Joe. He slowly walked over to three men standing at the end of the bar and whispered something to them.

"This is useless," said Joe. "If I even open my mouth to speak, they are already shaking their heads and looking away." As he spoke, he noticed the four men slowly making their way to their table. Sensing trouble, Joe moved in his chair. "We need to go outside, now," he said to Stefan. It suddenly dawned on Joe that this place was a hangout for the gang members and that they would be most unwelcome here, particularly since they were looking for information.

"What's going on?" asked a flummoxed Stefan. "I thought we wanted to be here?"

"We need to go outside now. If I'm wrong, we can come back inside. Just do it, Stefan. Quietly."

As they stood and casually turned to head towards the

door, so did the other men, Mr. Baseball Cap in front. As a confused Stefan approached the door, Joe moved over to let Stefan pass. Watching Joe's eyes turn towards the men, he quickly became aware of what was happening. He took longer strides and reached for the door handle, just as the man moved in front of the door and blocked their exit.

"So, a little bird told me you are looking for Hero, is that right?"

"Never said I was," answered Stefan. Joe was quickly moving up beside his companion.

"All right, sure, but I've seen you lot here before. Word is out you are poking about, looking for him and Ian. So do me a favour—when you see Hero, be sure to give him this." With one swift motion the man pulled a blade from his sleeve and thrust it into Stefan's mid-section. Joe grabbed the man's wrist just as the tip of the knife cut through Stefan's shirt. He let out a muffled scream as he fell back, trying to avoid deeper penetration. Joe's advantage was his size, as he stood a good head above the scrawny punk. Grabbing the man firmly by his arm, he pulled back, twisting it slightly to direct the knife away from Stefan.

Stefan's shirt was turning red. As Joe's hands went for the man's throat, he stopped himself, thinking it unwise. The last thing he wanted was a brawl. He pushed the man backwards into the table behind him. The patrons had all turned away as if nothing had happened. Grabbing Stefan under his arms, Joe pushed the door open, and they escaped into the night air.

Chapter 33

"We have to move, Stefan. Fast. Over that way, towards the road." Joe had no idea what time it might be, but the streets were quiet. Stefan seemed to be okay, although he was tightly clutching his stomach, so Joe could not tell the extent of the injury.

"Are you okay?" He had been holding Stefan firmly under his arm, but he loosened his grip and took him around his waist.

"Yes, I think so. Let's just go."

Neither man dared turn around. They kept walking in the direction of their hotel. Moving quickly down the street, Stefan noticed a much older woman standing on the corner on the other side of the street. She was dressed in a tight-fitting skirt and a cropped jumper. Her hair was as red as her lips, and her heels were high. She hollered out to them in a broken, raspy voice. "Are you hurrying home to the missus? No need to hurry, boys. There's plenty of what you want right here. Come on around back. You can have your pick."

Turning his head away quickly, Stefan stumbled. From out of nowhere, a cab pulled up alongside and asked if they needed a ride. Joe gratefully accepted, and as he helped Stefan to climb into the rear seat, he felt hesitation.

"Please, not now, Stefan. We need to go." He had just spotted the men who had been walking behind them. As soon as they saw the cab, they had quickened their pace, drawing nearer at an increased rate. Joe climbed into the cab beside Stefan and closed the cab door. "Please get moving, man," he growled, and they were on their way.

"Saw them blokes, and I know who they are. For sure they was up to no good, so I had to stop. Did you two piss 'em off or something?"

"I guess you could say that. I do appreciate you stopping."

It seemed a much shorter distance with the godsend of a ride, and before they knew it the cab was pulling up in front of the hotel. Getting out of the cab, Joe leaned over to pay the driver. It was then he noticed that Stefan's shirt was sodden with the oozing, glistening crimson. The cab driver noticed it as well.

"Hold on there, you're in no shape to go anywhere. So the buggers nicked you, did they? Come on then, get back in the cab. This one's on me. There's a clinic just up the road."

Within minutes, they pulled up to a red-and-white brick and stucco building with a small sign on the lawn reading "Medical Clinic." As they stepped inside, the receptionist looked up from her desk that was partially hidden behind the glass partition. She took one look at the panicked expression on Stefan's face and, picking up her phone, pointed Joe to the back room. Before Joe could say anything to Stefan, a cheerful man dressed in scrubs came out from behind a curtained area. He put his glasses on and leaned forward, taking a hard look at Stefan.

"I've got it from here, thanks," the man said to Joe, and with that he led Stefan away. As he walked through the curtain, Stefan glanced back at Joe as if beckoning him to follow. He looked like a frightened child who wished he had a hand to hold.

Joe stood there, his eyes fixed on the curtain. He was remembering his own stabbing, in the stairwell in Sheffield while chasing after the wayward Mr. Rutledge. He seemed to recall much less blood, but he could be mistaken. After all, he was lying on the ground in a state of shock. Maybe Stefan's wound was in a different area. He took a step closer so he could overhear as the doctor spoke.

"Ah-ha!"

"What is it? Is it bad? Am I in trouble? Will I die?"

"No, my lad, you are lucky. It seems no organs were penetrated, and no, you will not die. You are bleeding out, not in, and it looks like it's already slowed. We'll just fix you up with a stitch or two and you'll be on your way. Don't worry, I'll give you something for the pain. Hold this down firmly and don't let go. I'll be right back."

"Please hurry. It hurts like hell," Stefan emphasized.

Once back at the hotel, Joe took Stefan to the room and helped him lie down on his bed. He could tell Stefan was already groggy from the pills the doctor had given him. Joe knew he would sleep well. He closed the door quietly and returned to the lobby. He walked along the carpeted corridor and saw no one. All was quiet, and the lights had been turned down so only a soft glow of yellow light coming from the reception area was visible. He could hear Joe Cocker music coming from the speakers on the wall. The lobby was sparse, with a few mismatched chairs around a small coffee table that was covered in dog-eared, well-worn travel magazines. Joe rang the bell at the front desk and asked the clerk if he had a first aid kit.

"I have one at the back, an 8599-1 kit, for the workers in the kitchen."

Joe showed the man his card and said, "I'm sorry, but I need to ask if I can use a few things from it. My partner's been hurt, and we've just been to the clinic for stitches. I'm thinking I may need to change the dressing if the bleeding doesn't stop."

The clerk fetched the kit. "I'm afraid I wouldn't know what to do with it, and I'm alone. There's nobody here until morning."

Joe was already rummaging through the kit. "No, this should be good. I can manage. Luckily there is a good roll of adhesive tape and a good amount of dressing, so I have everything I need. Cheers, mate, I'll see you in the morning."

Returning to the room, he walked over to check on Stefan, who was soundly sleeping. There was enough light coming in from the street, so Joe didn't bother switching on the lamp. Stretching his back for a moment, he turned and sat in the only chair in the room. It stood partially jutting into a niche, close to the window. He stretched his long legs onto the coffee table and sat looking out at the dark formidable clouds that were still hanging about. He knew there would be people upset by what had happened to Stefan, and he was sorry he had not been able to better protect his friend. But more so, he was angry and frustrated by his lack of progress. Slowly, his eyes closed and he fell asleep.

The men slept in, both for different reasons. Joe had a fitful night and his neck ached from his positioning, having stayed in the chair all night. Stefan, well drugged, hadn't moved since he had fallen asleep. He was surprisingly in very good spirits.

"I'm starving. We didn't get to eat our dinner last night, did we? How about you, Joe? Hungry?"

They made their way to the breakfast room, where a smiling girl promptly brought them two cups of hot coffee.

"Are you in pain?" asked Joe.

"Surprisingly not," Stefan answered. Then he added with a smile, "Nothing else hurts quite as much as an angry look from Sally."

Following a hasty breakfast, they made their way out to the car park at the rear of the hotel. Stefan saw a red car parked down the street but could not be sure if it was the same one, as it was pointing in the opposite direction. He just wanted to get out of there.

Joe pulled onto the motorway, even more angered

that their attempts to locate Hero had been laughably unsuccessful. And he was worried at the prospect of losing his only connection to any news of Hanna. They were halfway home when Joe's cell phone rang.

Chapter 34

Regardless of Joe's failed efforts at what he had set out to accomplish, he was no doubt relieved and extremely thankful to hear Sally's news.

"Joe, it's me, Sally. Where are you? It's about Hanna, Joe. She is safe. And she's coming home. She just called me from the train."

A flummoxed Joe handed his phone to Stefan. "Put this on speaker, will you?" he asked.

Sally's voice was heightened. "She wasn't ready to speak with her parents, so she called me. She asked if I can please come and get her at the station."

"Did she say where she had been? Did she offer any explanation?"

"We didn't speak for long. She said something about Carl and Hero and a closet. I'll meet her and take her home to our place."

Joe answered emphatically, "I want to be absolutely clear when I say don't go there; it might not be safe. The wrong people might now know where you live. If Hero could find you, who knows who else could. Or someone could be following her. Be careful, Sally."

"Then where should we go? She'll be here in just over

an hour."

Joe checked his watch. "I will try to meet you at the train station. I should have enough time to get there. But if I'm not there, and you don't feel safe waiting for me, go to my office. I'll be there as soon as I can. Call me when you have her and I'll let them know you are coming. Please just do it."

"Okay, I'll let you know."

Joe forcefully stepped on the accelerator. Stefan hung on as their speed increased. Joe had accomplished the mission, albeit inadvertently, which left him less than pleased. He suspected Hero had been influential in the outcome, for which he was grateful. He was eager to call Ray Lawson and let him know his daughter had come home. There was a hint of a smile on his face, although he still had a great deal of questions.

They quickly passed through Glossop and were soon nearing the city, driving past the Royal Hallamshire Hospital and turning onto Hanover Way. Joe pulled up at the train station just as he saw Sally disappearing into the building.

"Stefan, I'm sorry but you need to stay in the car. You are injured, and if Hanna has been followed, I don't want to subject you to any more violence." Stefan agreed, and Joe ran inside the station.

Spotting Sally ahead of him, he called her name, loudly. Seeing Joe, Sally ran back to him and hugged him just as the train pulled in. They stood anxiously watching the passengers disembark, looking around frantically for a glimpse of Hanna. Then Sally heard a meek voice from behind calling her name. They turned around, and there she stood, dirty and crying. Sally barely recognized her ashen and shivering friend. Not only had she lost weight, but there was an almost crippled look in her eyes. Her once enviable honey-coloured tresses were haphazardly shorn, nearly to the scalp in places, and dyed black. She stood there meekly, not moving. Sally took a step forward and fiercely hugged her dearest, Goth-looking friend. Hanna started crying.

Turning to Joe, she introduced him to Hanna while Joe was trying to turn them both towards the exit. "This is my friend Joe. He's been looking everywhere for you. Him and Stefan."

"Not now, Sal. We need to get out of here."

Once outside in the fresh air, Joe herded the two frightened girls to the waiting car. He opened the back door and ushered the girls inside before himself getting back behind the wheel. He scanned the area outside the station before turning to Hanna.

"Hi, Hanna, I'm PI Joe Parrott. This is Stefan Nowak, my partner. We've been desperately looking for you. Hero told us what happened. We know none of it was your fault."

"I've heard Hero talk about you two. Thank you both so much. I was so afraid. I thought I murdered that man. It's so fuzzy, and actually, I don't even know anymore what happened. I wanted to come home, but then Ian died, and Hero kept telling me it wasn't safe. Thank you so much for coming to find me. I think Hero helped me because of you."

"But why do you look like this?" Sally asked.

"It was Hero's idea. He didn't want anyone to recognize me. It was why I couldn't leave. He said Carl and his boys would be everywhere, watching and waiting."

Sally persisted. "Who is Carl? Where have you been? Why didn't you call sooner?"

Joe interrupted, "Why don't we continue this conversation at my office, Sally. Let her breathe."

Once safely on their way, both girls seemed to have settled in the back of the car, Sally and Hanna squeezing each other's hands tightly. Hanna nervously began speaking.

"Carl had me, in his flat. He locked me in a closet. Then Hero came. We hurt Carl, then ran away, and now I'm scared. Hero says I was meant for Monty, and I can't imagine what Monty will do when he finds out I've gone. Hero will be in danger, and I'm worried for him. I should have brought him with me."

"What happened?" asked Joe.

"He stabbed Carl, and then I hit him with a lamp. Then Hero took his keys and helped me get away. Carl won't let him get away with this. You should have seen him—his bleeding eyes were on fire. No matter what he felt he owed Hero, he'll not let this go. Ian is no longer here to protect him, and I don't know if Hero realizes that." Through tears, she continued, "Someone has to save Hero. I should have made him come with me. I really don't know what I was thinking. He can't go home, and he can't go to work. And I know he won't go to the police. Someone's got to stop Carl or find Hero before

Carl's boys do. Carl will want to find him before Monty, because Monty might want to kill them both." Then, through eyes rubbed raw, she pleaded, "I'm so sorry, but I need to tell you, you need to find him before the police do."

"Why before the police? Won't he go to them?"

"There's some police that like to hurt him. They always do because they think he does stuff, but it was always Ian. They hurt him to keep him quiet, or so they say. If you bring him in, he'll be safe. But on the other hand, if Carl or Monty think he will talk to police, they will kill him without hesitation."

Joe knew that what she was saying was true because he had heard as much from the bald-arsed copper named Thom.

"Where might he be, Hanna?"

"Could be he went back to the marina. He said it was safe there."

"Do you know which marina, Hanna?" Joe was watching her through the rear-view mirror. She really did look a mess.

"I know it was near the River Wye. It was a big old boat."

"I don't suppose you remember which boat? A model? Name on the front?

"I don't know! I can't remember!" She was punching the sides of her forehead as if hoping it would help to conjure up the answer. "I remember it had plastic covering the back half. We had to walk into an opening at the back."

Sally sat staring at Hanna in disbelief. The change in her friend was astounding. There was wildness in her eyes, and even the way she held herself and gestured was profoundly different. It suddenly seemed like she hadn't seen this person in years—if ever. Hanna had settled down slightly, and even though she held Sally's hand firmly, she had not made eye contact with her friend since getting into the car.

Once they arrived at ARD Investigations, Stefan took Hanna and Sally inside while Joe parked the car. He again stood outside for a few minutes, looking around in all directions to see if they had been followed. Once inside, he patted Hanna on the shoulder to check that she was doing okay. Hanna looked up at him and smiled. Joe then called Aisha. He asked if she could please come and take Hanna to her clinic.

"She appears traumatized. She needs to sleep and clean up. And I need to keep her some place safe. Yes, okay, thanks. We will all be here waiting for you. Please hurry." Joe hung up the phone and again walked over to Hanna. Kneeling before her, he touched her arm gently. "Hanna, we can talk tomorrow. I have a friend that will come and take you some place safe, okay?"

Her words were slow and mechanical. "I don't want to talk tomorrow; I want someone to help Hero." By this point, Hanna's eyes seemed to be losing focus. She was shivering and nearly catatonic. Sally sat holding her hand. The four of them sat and waited, not doing much more than staring at Hanna while trying not to. Joe brought Hanna a glass of water, of which she took only a few sips. Stefan was fidgeting, his wound causing him some discomfort.

What seemed like hours later, they heard the front door open and close, and Aisha came into the room carrying a blanket. Seeing Hanna sitting there, she looked at Joe with a concerned look on her face.

"This girl does need food and water," she whispered to him. She wrapped the blanket snugly around Hanna. Kneeling, she spoke calmly. "Hi, Hanna. My name is Aisha. I'm a friend of Joe's." She sat down in the chair beside her, waiting for a sign of responsiveness.

At this point Sally stood up and, without a word, rushed out the door. Stefan hurried after her.

"Sally?" He walked up behind her as she slowly sat on the top step. She was a wee thing, but now looked even smaller, framed by the immense archway.

"I can't do this anymore," she said as she rubbed her face with open palms.

"Do what?"

"This! It's not what I signed up for. She's different, Stefan. Have you seen her? She will need things that I can't give her—things I'm not capable of."

Stefan asked, "Can I sit beside you, Sally?" She nodded, and so he sat very close, their arms touching. "But she might be okay. Aisha will help her. She's really good at that."

"But you see, I didn't want my life to change. I'm tired, Stefan. Look at me! Look at what the past couple of weeks have done to me. When Hanna got on that train, she changed MY life too. And now it can't be unchanged."

"Give it time, Sally. Like you said, you're tired. Maybe you just need a few good nights' sleep."

"But I don't feel safe anymore. They know where I live."

Stefan was quiet. At that, he really didn't know how to respond. She may well be right.

"But it's more than that. It's also about you. Now that the case is closed, you won't need to see me anymore. I know that sounds selfish . . . to care about you now and not Hanna . . ."

Stefan took her hand and squeezed it tightly. "You'll never lose me, Sally. Not anymore. Not ever."

Sally's hand squeezed his tightly as she smiled, but she didn't look at him.

"It's perfectly fine to care about Hanna and care about me. Joe and I will do our best to close this thing. We will go and find Hero, Sally, and bring him back. He can tell his story and hopefully put those bad guys away. Then you will be safe. Let's take this a day at a time. And besides, they don't know where I live."

Now Sally looked at him with curiosity. He wanted to say more but held back. His pain was causing him to fidget. He felt he may say too much, as this was also not the best time to explain the wound beneath his shirt.

Joe appeared on the doorstep. "Are you two okay? Can you come back inside, please? We need to talk."

Hanna was much calmer. She appeared lucid as she was listening to the conversations around her. She looked at Sally and smiled as she came back into the room. Aisha knelt before her and said to her calmly yet firmly, "Hanna,

I'm going to take you somewhere safe. Please, you need to come with me now."

Hanna hesitated, holding her breath, but Sally nodded, convincing her that she needed to go. Hanna's eyes looked up at Aisha as she asked in a whisper, "Can Sally come too?" Aisha nodded to both girls. "Yes, she can come for a spell, but she can't stay. I also need to call your parents and have them come."

"They can't see me like this."

"You can shower and change first, but I really don't think they will care. They are both beside themselves with worry. Okay then, let's go."

Brushing Joe's cheek, she put her arm around Hanna and herded her out the door. Sally looked at Stefan, who said only, "I'll see you soon."

Aisha drove the girls to her shelter, where a bed was being prepared. It was a short drive for which Sally was grateful, as she was concerned that Hanna's behaviour may again change. Once they arrived at the shelter, the charge nurse gave her some privacy so she could shower and put on a clean nightshirt. Then after a sandwich and a glass of juice, Aisha gave her something to help calm her nerves. Sally hugged her friend, promising to come back in the morning, and then she and Aisha left. Before closing the door, she looked back and saw that Hanna was already close to sleep.

While Aisha was driving Sally to her flat, the car was quiet. Sally at last spoke. "I hope she will be okay. It's funny, you know, Hanna used to put my life on a pedestal, as if it was so great. It was different than hers, I agree, but whose to say it was better? I hope now she can realize that her life was pretty good, so she doesn't need to go off like this again."

Aisha put her hand on Sally's knee. "I don't think you have to worry about that anymore, Sally. I have a feeling you will be seeing a new and improved Hanna."

Unconvinced, Sally stayed quiet.

The next morning when Joe woke up, Aisha had already left. A little while later he received a call from a woman at the shelter, saying that Hanna was awake and fed, and had said she was ready to help. Joe quickly finished his coffee and headed over to pick her up. Aisha was waiting for him when he walked in the door.

"I spoke with her, Joe. She told me the story. And I'm sorry, but I think you do need to go and look for Hero. Tell me what you think, after you have heard what she has to say."

Joe nodded, kissed Aisha on the cheek, and took Hanna gently by the arm and out to the car. While driving straight over to see DI Wilkes, Hanna was again crying uncontrollably, saying that Joe needed to go find Hero. Joe asked that she please talk to DI Wilkes as well. He might be able to help. "Just wait a few moments until we get there. You need to tell the story to both of us. We will help, I promise."

A room had been prepared at the station, and DI Wilkes greeted them warmly. Sitting with Joe and DI Wilkes, she began telling her story with ease. And Joe noted that she retold this same story almost exactly as Hero had told it. He wasn't sure this was a good thing. Could two people recall events in exactly the same way? Was it rehearsed? He pushed the thought from his mind and listened.

Hanna said the trouble had started at the zoo. "Some blokes from the stag do were drunk and aggressive and were yelling at Ian about 'free the animals' and all that stuff. Then there was a lot of pushing. Ian, he really had a temper. Me and Hero, we tried to stop him, but he told us to shut up. Ian pulled out his knife, which I didn't even know he had, and cut one of them. The blokes were ready to jump on Ian, but then security came. Ian had his badge on and started to act all innocent and said they started it. They were detained, and we were told to walk back to the security office to sort it out. But Ian didn't want to, so then we ran—me, Ian, and Hero. Hero was mad at him; says he was an idiot.

"Hero later told me that it wasn't about the zoo animals at all, but about a girl that Ian tried to take away from her boyfriend, who happened to be a bloke named

Liam. He said something about trying to introduce the girl to Monty. At the time, I didn't know what that meant.

"That same night, we went to the pub to eat. It was a mad scene in town. There were lots of parties on the beach that night. Wedding parties or something. Like hen dos. Everybody there was all, like, trying to pick each other up. It's just for one night, so who cares, right? It's like that saying, what happens there stays there. But that night was exceptionally bad. The guys at the stag events were all riled up. And the girls were all in a partying mood. Like I said, I think everyone was hoping to get lucky that night. It was also a good distraction for the locals to act out.

"Then we saw the same guys again . . . the ones from the zoo. Only this time they brought Liam with them. They came into the pub. I wanted to leave. When we went outside, Ian took off running down the street. Liam yelled for his two friends to follow him. I looked around and couldn't see Hero, so I started walking fast, towards the water. Liam was following me.

"I thought, 'what is he doing?' I looked back at him, like where was he going? But then I kept running. Someone needed to protect me. By the time Liam caught up with me, I had run up to the top of some stairs by the beach. Then Hero was there—he doesn't walk so fast, don't know where he came from. There was a big struggle, and I screamed. Liam tumbled down the stairs, and I think he fell on his own knife." She paused and looked at Joe. "Or Hero might have helped it to get there."

Hanna had calmed down by this time, relieved to be

finally talking to someone she could trust. "We hurried back to Hero's flat before anyone saw us. What happened on the stairs, it was accidental. But it wasn't really Hero, you see. It was because of me. But please, Mr. Joe, you have to find him. I'd be dead if it weren't for him. He's had enough misery in his life. He saved me."

She looked up at Joe as she continued speaking. "But when Ian came, he was angry. He said that everybody would think he killed Liam. He's the one who had reason to want to kill him. He said that Monty would be really mad. I started to see him differently once I realized the stuff he was up to. And he kept mentioning this police-man, Thom, who would be looking for him as well, as Thom and Monty are pretty close."

DI Wilkes leaned forward and gently spoke to Hanna. "Will you be okay to give a statement to one of my offi-cers? It would be best if we did it straight away."

Hanna looked more relaxed. Blowing her nose, she nodded in agreement.

"We will leave you to it then," said Joe as he stood. "Don't worry, Hanna, we will do what we can to find Hero."

"You need to understand, Joe, he is the only one who can stop these people. Nobody will believe me by myself. He's your proof—your first-hand witness. None of us will be safe until they are stopped. They know where I live!"

"I need to call police in Blackpool, for their help as well," DI Wilkes announced.

"No, please don't do that until Joe looks first. Hero said not all of 'em can be trusted, and you don't know which ones can."

Joe looked at his old friend Wilkes. "Can you give me twelve hours?"

"I'm not liking this, Joe. I will give you eight. But you need to tell someone there. Someone needs to have your back."

"There is one man. It's Hall. I will call him."

Wilkes agreed, albeit reluctantly, and Hanna smiled. "Will you look at the boat as well? He could have gone back to the boat. Maybe he is safe there."

Joe walked down the corridor, where a determined Stefan was waiting. "Joe, I'll go back. These gangs will want to stop Hero from speaking with the police. He seems to be the only real witness to a great deal of goings on. He might have to talk to save himself, and we don't know what the police will do to him to make him talk. So he really won't be safe anywhere."

Joe agreed. "This much I will do. He found Hanna for me, now I will try to find him for Hanna. Let's go. You drive—I need to make a call."

Chapter 35

Hero lay very still. He knew moving would not be good. He thought about Hanna, the way she had looked at him through the window as she left the tram. She was smiling, and she blew him a kiss before leaving. He was watching, and he saw her turning and disappearing into the station. He hoped she was safe.

Hero was thinking of his family—his mum most of all. He was remembering the story of how she had hugged him that day of the fire, when he had cried and saved their lives. She told him she had almost suffocated him with her bosom, all the while he was crying. His mum would take him to the cobbler for his special shoes. The cobbler would tease him, saying that his feet grew too fast. He said all heroes had big feet, and he should feel proud. He said Hero should get bigger shoes and stuff the toes until he grew into them.

Hero remembered his dog, Ginger, laying by his feet during his piano lessons. Whenever he played Chopin's Prelude No. 7 in A Major, it induced Ginger to kick his hind leg and softly whine. His dad would laugh and take the dog for a walk until the lesson was over. Ginger would come home again, wagging his tail so hard he would fall over sideways. Hero again wondered what had happened to his dog. It had been taken away when he went to live with his uncle.

Then, unexpectedly he remembered his little wooden clock hanging on his bedroom wall—the one with the Bambi head on it. The eye would move back and forth with each swing of the pendulum. Tick. Tick. His parents had bought it for him on his ninth birthday. He would lie in bed watching the movement of the little eye and fall asleep to the gentle sound of the ticking. His room came to mind, and he could see the wall where the clock had hung. He was visualizing the walls, which had been a soft blue colour. His bedcovers were also blue but darker.

Hero remembered he had a dark blue jacket and a set of racing cars. Where was all that stuff? And under his bed was a basket full of magazines—*How It Works* and *Dr. Who Adventures*, but mainly his football books. Where did they all go?

Hero lay still and smiled as he remembered how he loved the taste of water through a rubber hose on a hot summer's day. He loved how the bubbles stayed in the tub long after his bath. He loved his yard and the local football pitch, where he spent many hours kicking the ball around with his dad and Davy. He would watch out his bedroom window for his dad to come home on the nights that he was late. His dear, gentle, careful dad—a man with deep-rooted beliefs that everyone carries self-respect and that nobody should be hurt by word, fist, or even silence. He shielded his family from harm as best he could.

"The Promenade is for special occasions only," his father had told him, "and not a place to frequent, particularly not for young lads like you and Davy."

Where was his best friend Davy? When Hero had returned to Blackpool years later, Davy had already gone. Where to, he didn't know. But Hero had been gone a long time, so he didn't bother looking for his friend. He wouldn't go into his old neighbourhood to see his old house with other people living in it.

But right now, he had to not move.

He cried as he remembered life at his uncle's, a place just outside of Standish, near Wigan. He didn't have his own room there; he had slept in a small cubby off the pantry. His sheets smelled of vinegar. It was dark, and he had no night-light like the one back home in his own room. It was a small blue light that had made him feel safe. They told him that what had happened to his parents had been his fault. They told him he needed to be punished for it and didn't deserve to feel safe. They told him he was no Hero at all, and they laughed.

Forgetting his tears, Hero smiled. Hanna was safe. She had pressed her fingers against her lips, smiling as she blew him a kiss.

Then he grew angry as he thought of Ian. He should have been the one that killed him, and he should have done it a long time ago. He wasn't sorry for what he had done to Carl. He wondered how he was and how badly his leg had been cut. But he didn't care. He hoped the leg fell off. He smiled when he thought of Carl's leg falling off.

He didn't know how long he had been lying there,

but he knew he needed to keep very still. He should have stayed under the pier. He should have stayed there longer. Hero felt afraid. He closed his eyes and silently wept.

Chapter 36

As soon as Joe had Chief Inspector Hall on the line, he filled him in on the news while Stefan drove the car. "Hanna is giving her statement as we speak. I know I'm asking a lot, but can you please keep this under your hat for the time being? I need twelve hours. I honestly don't know whom to trust, but I feel certain there are some who may be involved. I know you might not take kindly to the accusation, but until I find Hero, we may never know. Once I've had a chance, then your men can step in to find Carl. It's kidnapping, Andrew. At least we can get him for that. You'll need to keep an eye out for Monty and his crew as well. Hero stabbed Carl and took the girl. Apparently she was meant for Monty as some kind of peace offering. There will be a reckoning. Both Monty's and Carl's boys will retaliate. We need to protect Hero and bring him in safely."

He would tell the inspector later about the possibility that Hero may have killed Liam. Certainly, an investigation would need to take place before any more speculation was thrown around. After all, the first set of fingerprints could have been wiped from the knife. It could have been handled many times, by anyone.

Once Joe had disconnected the call, he felt uneasy. There was something about the inspector's tone that didn't fit. He wondered if the man would send out his officers regardless of Joe's plea not to. Could it be possible that the police stayed out of the way of these gangs? What was it again? "*Anything for a peaceful life. They don't hurt us—we don't hurt them. Every one of 'em we can get rid of is good news.*" It occurred to Joe that maybe the police preferred to sit back and let the gangs kill each other and not get in the way. And Sergeant Thom had already made it clear that they weren't fond of Hero. Perhaps saving him was not a priority—perhaps even inconsequential. Call it "of the utmost unimportance." Maybe it was important to get rid of Hero so that he wouldn't talk?

They had a long drive ahead of them, and Stefan was speeding along the M6 knowing he'd be in serious trouble if he were pulled over. Joe's foot was pressed into the floorboards as though he was helping the vehicle to accelerate.

While Stefan drove, he thought of Sally. She had looked at him with pleading eyes. "But Hanna says you've got to go back; they're after Hero." She then had looked at Joe. "Hanna told me where we might be able to find him. You have to find him before police do. He'll be scared. He has no one to protect him now." She had looked back and forth from Joe to Stefan, wringing her hands. She looked so small, so vulnerable and innocent, and he was amazed at how his feelings for her had become so profoundly intense.

"What did the chief inspector say? Is he on board?"

Joe rubbed his face hard, thinking of how to answer. "I'm not sure what to think. Maybe he wants to let this thing play out, then go in afterwards and clean up whatever mess they leave. He said he would poke around, and if he hears anything useful he'll call. So what does that mean? Does good mean before the battle or after? Is he at all bothered about finding Hero? He's new to the job, we should remember. Perhaps he doesn't want to ruffle any feathers, doesn't want anything revealed about any of his men."

"I think Hanna was right when she said we need to find him first. I can't believe the apathy towards him." The exasperation came through in Stefan's words.

The drive seemed long, but thankfully Hanna's directions were good. The car was just pulling up to the quiet marina. There were very few vehicles in the lot, and not a person in sight. Joe stood outside the car and looked around, trying to visualize the location that Hanna spoke of. He motioned Stefan to follow as he spotted the pier she had spoken of. He was again grateful for her accurate recollection. Walking along the swaying pier, he soon spotted the boat. Looking at Stefan, he held his finger to his lips and knocked on the side.

"Hero," he whispered. "It's Joe. I've come to help." No answer.

Stefan stepped forward. "I'm going on board. You need to be sure he's not in there. Or if he is in fact hiding in there, I want to be sure he's not hurt. Or dead."

The boat creaked to life as Stefan moved the tarp at the rear and disappeared inside. The damp smell made his nostrils flare. He covered his nose with his arm and slowly walked through to the front. There was no sign of anyone. Strewn across the floor, he saw what was likely Hanna's golden hair, scattered in clumps. By the sink, he saw the remnants of the hair dye—used plastic gloves stained black, empty bottles of solution, and the box— lying on the counter. He quickly headed back outside into the fresh air.

"This is definitely the boat. But there's nobody there, and no sign of a scuffle, or blood or anything like that." His pronounced sigh indicated relief.

"Okay, we've no time to waste. Off to his house," exclaimed Joe as he turned towards the exit.

When they reached Hero's flat, Stefan dropped Joe off just around the corner and parked a block away to keep an eye on the street. Joe walked to the door slowly, looking every way for signs of anyone who may be watching. He made sure he wasn't followed. When he leaned on the door and gave it a swift kick with his boot, the door gave way without resistance. Walking slowly up the stairway, he realized that stealth was out of the question, as the old stairs creaked and groaned under the weight of each step. Entering Hero's room, Joe was aghast at his living conditions. The tiny room was covered in years of filth, yet a small drying rack by the sink held clean dishes. On the small table stood a half-cup of tea and a spoon. Joe turned quickly and left, his heart full of compassion for this sad, unfortunately neglected soul.

They had no better luck at Pleasure Beach, where they were told Hero hadn't been seen for about three or four days. Asking as many employees as they could find, it seemed nobody had any idea where he was. "It's not like him to stay away from his work" seemed to be the collective response.

"I need to call Hanna." The edginess in Joe's voice was ripe as they walked along the Promenade.

"I know of a place where he once took me. It was near a pier, actually below the pier, at the far end, under the pilings, where we hid right after the stabbing. It's Hero's place; he goes there sometimes when the tide is out. And I'm sorry, but I don't remember which pier it is. Maybe the one nearest to the amusement park?"

Joe thanked Hanna and nodded to Stefan.

"We will start with that one since it's the closest. It may mean we have to hit all three piers."

Joe swore aloud. It wasn't an easy task, getting quickly from one pier to the next. "Nothing quite like trudging along the sand in the wind, crawling under pilings. What a great way to pass the time," he mumbled sarcastically. The sunshine began to disappear behind a blanket of ominous-looking cloud, just as the wind began to pick up. Another blustery summer afternoon on the Fylde Coast. A high tide was on its way in, bringing with it high winds—and today, rain.

It was pouring now; the incessantly howling winds were coming from the west. The crash of the waves reverberated in their chests. They both glimpsed a shadowy figure ahead as it disappeared down the road. Joe called out as Stefan tried to pursue. but stopped when he saw that Stefan almost immediately had abandoned the chase. He didn't want to risk another attack by a knife-wielding wanker. They needed to stay focused on finding Hero. Continuing their search where the shoreline met the pier, they made their way to an area that appeared exactly as Hanna had described it.

Stefan paused. "This is the place, Joe. I'm sure of it." He headed towards the edge of the pier and proceeded down the side.

Joe held his finger up and asked Stefan to stop. He had indistinctly heard a sound coming from under the pier that sounded like a cry. Stefan and Joe quickly slid down the wet, grassy embankment. It was raining steadily, and the cry beneath the pier had quieted.

Joe reached the body first, which was lying still on its side. His heart sank as he gently turned the figure over onto his back. He already knew it was Hero. He took out his phone and dialled 999.

Hero moaned gently, "I'm not to move. I need to lie very still."

Stefan's heart was thumping as he came up beside Hero. He fell to the ground, walking forward on his knees, grabbing Hero's hand gently and muttering, "No, no. Please no."

Hero looked up at him, smiling. "It were a good football match. David Beckham would have been proud."

"What happened?"

"I had to go to Carl's; he had the ball and I had to force him to give it over. But she's safe now, right? Just tell me that Hanna's safe."

Stefan was distraught at seeing Hero like this. It was

the first time he had seen a man in this state. "Yes, she's safe. You did it, Hero. You saved her."

Hero saw the expression on Stefan's face and said, "It's okay, mate. What's a bloke like me going to do anyway? Take my phone. It's in my back pocket. It's got the pics and some messages that you need. There's some things there that might help."

Hero closed his eyes for a minute. Stefan stood up and looked for the police or ambulance. No one had arrived yet.

Opening his eyes again, Hero said, "Can you hear that? The piano?"

Joe and Stefan's eyes met, but neither spoke.

"That's it! That's the song my mum would play for me all the time. She were teaching it to me just before she died. Can you hear it? It's beautiful. And now it's so loud. You can hear it, can't you, Joe?" His eyes were wide and beseeching.

Joe looked at Hero's face, nodding. "Yes, I can hear it."

Stefan looked at Joe, his eyes questioning. He didn't understand how anything could be heard over the howling wind and the surf smashing on the rocks all around them. Joe simply shook his head and brought his finger to his lips in a hushing gesture. Hero was smiling and humming along to the tune, his eyes closed.

As Joe bent over Hero, a small gust of wind pushed its way between them with a sense of urgency, and it passed through, taking with it Hero's last breath.

Hero's grip on Stefan's hand slowly began to lessen. Then there was no grip left. Stefan let go of Hero's hand and looked up into the rain, allowing it to wash his sorrow away.

Chapter 37

The rain had once again turned to drizzle. Joe was tired and not looking forward to the drive back to Sheffield. Stefan sat in the passenger seat, crumpled over, forehead resting on the side window. The only sound was the intermittent thumping of the windshield wipers. Neither man spoke, and for a while, Joe wasn't certain whether Stefan was asleep or awake.

Once the police had arrived, there wasn't much left for the two of them to do. The chief inspector had rung Joe to tell him to go home and get some sleep. He would call him in the morning. They had waited for the coroner and had watched as Hero's body was quickly removed before he was dragged out to sea by the tide. And there it was—crime scene washed away.

The expression on Stefan's face was having an impact on Joe. The guilt he was feeling stemmed from involving young Stefan in this case. He had met this young, optimistic, seemingly unflappable person who had pulled himself from adversity and misfortune and created a safe, happy environment for himself—only to be dragged down by the week's turn of events. The spirited young lad, who a few years ago had told Joe he ought to learn how to colour his grey, now seemed coated in a blanket of it.

The drive seemed to take days. By the time they arrived at Stefan's flat, he was sitting up straight and staring out the window. He at last spoke to Joe, just as the car turned onto Greystone's Close. "So, that's it?"

"Hero saved Hanna, Stefan. That was our goal, wasn't it? Finding Hanna. I told you this job wasn't always easy."

"But what about Hero, then?"

"That's now for the police to deal with. CI Hall will take care of it. It's not our job. We're not cops; we just do what we are hired to do."

Stefan was frowning. "It just seems like we didn't finish. It's not over."

"It's over for us, Stefan. We've handed all evidence to the guys in Blackpool. They have Hanna's statement. The rest is up to them. Hopefully the bad guys won't get away with it, but it's not for us to investigate. We are Sheffield, not Blackpool. We are private investigators, not cops."

"It just feels so unfinished, Joe."

"Now listen, this was a good chance for you to see what I do. Truth be told, it's not always this bad and can often be quite tame, following scammers and cheaters around and routine things like that. You've not signed any lease yet. So you still have time to change your mind. You sound like you might be happier doing something else, Stefan. Your goal seems different than mine. I think you could be more interested in helping people. Perhaps you should think about going to work with Aisha, at the shelter. Might be good for her to have a bloke around, to help deal with any young men who might also need help. A male perspective."

Stefan sat still, his hand on the door latch. He took a deep breath and let it out slowly. "Maybe you are right. Sally says we don't get to choose. It's our hearts that do."

"Sally's right there, mate." Joe continued, "Why don't you go inside and think about it for a while? You don't have to decide tomorrow; you have lots of time to sort things out. You are a prolific thinker, Stefan—the answers will come to you. Take some time, my friend. Perhaps you could do with a visit to Cottingham to spend some time with your nephew."

Stefan looked at Joe and nodded his head. "Yes. Aidan. I'd like that." Then, punching Joe lightly on the arm, he got out of the car. Joe watched him laboriously climb the steps to his door with what seemed like a great deal of effort. He watched the door close behind Stefan before pulling out of the parking spot and driving away.

Joe arrived home well after midnight. He entered the house quietly, took off his still-wet clothes in the kitchen, and threw them over a chair before tiptoeing to the bedroom and crawling under the covers.

He was still awake two hours later. In the moonlight, he could see the outline of Aisha's face, sleeping peacefully beside him. He listened to her soft, steady breathing. He watched her chest rise and fall with each life-filled breath.

Joe thought about Aisha and the trauma that befell her. How well she had handled it, he would never know. He thought about his daughter, Susan, and her young child, and hoped they would never have to deal with anything like that. Joe thought about Stefan and Sally and even Hanna. How their lives seemed to be, as Susan had called it, blissful and rosy when compared to Hero's life. The life he had no control over.

Who knows what makes a person strong. It's not something that can be taught in school. It's an individual's constitution, their essence that makes the struggles not so bad. There were those who were able to pull themselves out of the misery, and others who were left floundering. Could things have been different for Hero? Perhaps. If he thought he had someone to turn to. But maybe none of that would have helped. Nobody really knew.

As Joe lay there, he imagined the spot under the pier that by now was filled with water, the tide washing away all signs of the tragedy that had just happened there. And somewhere over the crashing waves rode the gentle sound of the piano music, loud and clear. At last, Joe closed his eyes and found sleep.

On the other side of town, Hanna lay wide-awake in her own bed. She was clean and she was comfortable. She thought about the past week - how she had feared she would never get back here again. All was peacefully quiet. She smiled, knowing she was safe. She was comforted by the thought that Joe would be bringing Hero back safely. Because, after all, she knew he would never tell what really happened.

We don't lie to protect the other person. We lie to
protect ourselves from the consequences. We lie because
we don't want to deal with our own feelings. We lie
because we don't want things to change.
Not by our hand.
So a wall starts to build . . .

Elisa Marie Hopkins

Acknowledgements:

To Frank Giampa, my friend, my motivator, who taught me to believe in myself.

To my late brother-in-law Dr. Terrence Nimmon, who said he knew I had it in me.

And to my family, for their ongoing encouragement and support.

I would also like to acknowledge beautiful Blackpool, and all the lovely people I met there.

Although *Hero of Blackpool* takes place in 2017, little has changed since then. While there have been millions of pounds spent on local improvements, Blackpool remains troubled. Crime, poverty, and inadequate housing conditions rank amongst the biggest issues. I remain hopeful that one day things will improve, as I found the seaside resort magical. The town was clean, buildings were colourfully painted and well maintained, the restaurants were fabulous and eclectic, and the people warm and friendly. At no time, day or night, did I feel unsafe. But then again, like Stefan, I was a tourist.

Disclaimer

This is purely a work of fiction. All the names, characters, businesses and incidents are either the product of the author's imagination or are being used in a fictitious manner. While some events, places and incidents may be real they are used in a purely fictitious manner. Any resemblance to actual persons, living or dead, is purely coincidental.

Note:

The Dictionary of Obscure Sorrows is a compendium of invented words, written by John Koenig.

I first heard of the existence of this book through my friend, Juan, from Panama.

About the Author

This is Alyssa Hall's fourth novel. Alyssa writes from the heart and has keen insight into the things that influence and motivate people, and about the human spirit. Her love of England inspired her to write this story, and she had already envisioned her fourth novel, Hero of Blackpool, before ever visiting the seaside town. Her eventual journey to the area helped her to finish the story with credibility and accuracy. Her other books include Wanting Aidan (2021), Trusting Claire (2020), and Romero Pools (2022). Alyssa lives in Langley, British Columbia, with her husband, David. Along with writing, Alyssa enjoys travelling and spending winters with her husband in Tucson Arizona, where she can get lost in her thoughts hiking in the desert. Find out more about Alyssa and her books at her website:
http://www.alyhallwriter.com/